Shawn Reed woke ⟨...⟩ like paradise. Perh⟨...⟩

But he didn't r⟨...⟩ remember much at all. And what sort of paradise was full of talking statues, and some really weird laws? And why did everyone there seem to be from his half-remembered past?

Perhaps he was in Hell ...

And then he started to have some very bizarre dreams, none of which he would have chosen himself.

If Freedom Beach wasn't Heaven or Hell, what was it?

Who had imprisoned him there, and why?

He was determined to find out.

FREEDOM BEACH

JAMES PATRICK KELLY & JOHN KESSEL

UNWIN PAPERBACKS
London   Sydney

First published in Great Britain by Unwin ® Paperbacks,
an imprint of Unwin Hyman Limited 1987

© James Patrick Kelly and John Kessel, 1985
This edition published by arrangement with Bluejay Books and
St Martin's Press

"Freedom Beach" appeared in different form in *The Magazine of Fantasy and Scientic Fiction*, copyright © 1984, Mercury Press.
"The Big Dream" and "The Empty World" appeared in different form in *Isaac Asimov's Science Fiction Magazine*, copyright © 1984, Davis Publications, Inc.
The poem "Sea Change" originally appeared in *Amazing Science Fiction Stories*, copyright © 1982, TSR Hobbies, Inc.

All rights reserved. No part of this publication may be reproduced, stored in a retrieval system or transmitted in any form or by any means, electronic, mechanical, photocopying, recording or otherwise, without prior permission of Unwin Hyman Limited.

UNWIN HYMAN LIMITED
Denmark House
37–39 Queen Elizabeth Street
LONDON SE1 2QB
and
40 Museum Street, London WC1A 1LU

Allen & Unwin Australia Pty Ltd
8 Napier Street, North Sydney, NSW 2060, Australia

Unwin Paperbacks with Port Nicholson Press
60 Cambridge Terrace, Wellington, New Zealand

CONDITION OF SALE: This book is sold subject to the condition that it shall not, by way of trade or otherwise, be lent, re-sold, hired out or otherwise circulated, without the publisher's prior consent in any form of binding or cover other than that in which it is published and without a similar condition including this condition being imposed on the purchaser.

British Library Cataloguing in Publication Data

Kelly, James Patrick
   Freedom Beach.
I. Title   II. Kessel, John
813'.54[F]   PS3561.E3942
ISBN 0-04-823385-4

Printed in Great Britain by
Cox & Wyman Ltd, Reading

For our parents

"Freedom is nothing else but a chance to be better, whereas enslavement is a certainty of the worse."

—Albert Camus

"Life is short; live it up."

—Nikita Khrushchev

Freedom Beach

"Are you going to stay in bed all morning?" She entered the bedroom, carrying a glass of orange juice. "Volleyball, today. Down on the beach." Her long red hair brushed his ear as she bent to kiss his forehead. She wore shorts and a halter over a tan that was a work of art. "I brought you some juice." There was a spray of freckles across her cheeks and the hint of a smile on her lips. Her eyes were green. As far as Shaun Reed knew, he had never seen the woman before in his life.

He thought it must be a dream. He was sitting up on the left side of a king-sized waterbed. He suspected that he had not slept alone. The room was large, functional and unrelentingly bland. There was a closet with folding mirror doors. One wall was concealed by blue drapes.

"Who are you?" said Shaun. "Where am I?"

"What do you mean, who am I?" Suddenly her voice was hard and flat. "You've been here for two days already. We spent last night . . ." She spun away from him and tore the drapes open. He glimpsed a sunlit atrium through a wall of glass; the brightness made him blink in pain. "You can't keep doing this to me!" The woman opened the sliding glass door and stepped through. "Damn it, five minutes ago he was fine."

Shaun could not remember last night, last week, the last ten years. He could not remember his father's name. Trying only made his head ache. He pulled back the sheets; he was naked.

Behind the closet doors was the menswear department of a small sporting goods store. Sky blue sweat suits, jerseys, trunks, jocks, headbands, wristbands, knee braces, running shoes and sneakers. Thirty pairs of white socks. He pulled on trunks and followed the woman.

In the center of the sun-splashed atrium was a fountain with a bronze Poseidon astride it; jets of water spurted from his trident. Around the atrium were walls of dark windows shaded by a terra-cotta roof. Shaun saw himself in the glass: a man in a strange place wearing nothing but gym trunks and a bewildered expression.

"Welcome to Freedom Beach," said Poseidon.

"Somebody screwed up." The woman shook her head wearily. "Now we'll have to start all over."

Shaun could remember the words to "The Star-Spangled Banner." He understood the difference between principle and principal and could describe the rules of tennis. He had never heard of Freedom Beach.

"You'll be sharing this villa with three other guests," said Poseidon. "Yours is the blue suite to the north. Perhaps you'd like to take a few minutes now to inspect your rooms and see if everything is satisfactory?"

"I don't believe this." Shaun looked to the woman for an explanation.

"I'm sorry, but I don't feel much like talking right now." She went to the sliding door on the opposite side of the atrium and opened it.

"Wait!" He started after her. "You can't just go. What the hell is going on here?"

"Don't you give me orders!" She turned on him, seething. "Just leave me alone, understand?" He recoiled from her anger. They stared at each other in the hot sun and then she shrugged. "It's still a shock when this happens. Give me a few minutes by myself and I'll be all right. See you at the beach, okay? In the meantime, try your questions on the statue." She closed the door behind her.

"On behalf of the dreamers, let me welcome you to Freedom Beach." Poseidon's voice was deep, masculine and on the verge of laughter.

He waded into the pool. The statue was muscle-bound and larger than life-sized; its dark patina was streaked with jade-colored veins. Its eyes were faceted sensors; a microphone was wedged into its sneer. "Dreamers?"

"I welcome you on their behalf."

"Who are they? Who are you?"

"Yours is the blue suite to the north."

Shaun scooped several handfuls of water at the statue's face. If there were a short, maybe someone would come to fix it.

"Your other neighbors will be on the beach," said Poseidon. "Perhaps you would care to join them?"

History, thought Shaun in a flash of inspiration. Washington, Adams, Jefferson, Madison . . . Reagan. He knew that the dotty old actor had crushed Mondale to win a second term. He had no idea which one he had voted for or whether he had voted at all.

He splashed out of the pool and crossed the atrium to the blue suite. Off the bedroom was a bathroom with a shower—no tub. The living room had a blue modular couch, a chrome-and-glass coffee table and a small built-in refrigerator filled with fruit and juice. The front door opened onto a sunny, cobbled and deserted street. He returned to the bedroom for shoes and a shirt.

Most of the buildings of Freedom Beach clung to the flanks of a landscaped hill. The beach below was as white as spindrift. Shaun thought he saw a blue smudge of land on the horizon. There were people on the beach, and he started down toward them. On the way he counted nine pastel stucco villas like his own nestled amid the palms and tree ferns and broad-leafed evergreens. He stopped counting statues; every corner had its Buddah, saint, king or hero. All had insect eyes and the glint of metal between pursed lips.

On the flat above the beach was a boggling array of playing fields and courts. A larger version of the villas was surrounded by patio furniture. Beyond were the people he had seen from above: eight of them, playing volleyball on the sand, laughing, shouting, naked. Shaun paused, hiding behind a sleek monument of black marble. He was afraid of what these people might tell him of himself. He closed his eyes, pressed against the cold marble and tried one last time to punch through the pain to his lost memory.

"Look! Who's that?"

The game stopped; the players stared at him.

"It's the new boy. Hey, Shaun! Come on; we're short."

He stepped from behind the monument and for the first time saw the words engraved on its seaward face.

YOU CAME TO FREEDOM BEACH VOLUNTARILY.
PRIOR TO MEMORY EDITING YOU UNDERSTOOD
AND AGREED TO THE CONDITIONS OF YOUR
THERAPY. THERE ARE TWO RULES. PLEASE
OBEY THEM.
   YOU MAY NOT HARM ANOTHER GUEST.
   YOU ARE FORBIDDEN TO WRITE.

"But how did I get here? I don't remember anything."

"Nobody does. And tomorrow you may not remember today." The woman's name was Myrna. She had caught up with him as he hesitated by the monument and had led him down to the volleyball game. "Nice save, Jihan. Beautiful."

The others had given up trying to coax him to join the game and had resumed play. Myrna and Shaun sat in beach chairs beside a table on the esplanade; she refused to let him bother the players. She poured herself a drink from what looked like a pitcher of margaritas. His questions fell like stones into a bottomless well.

"Who are these dreamers? Where are they?"

"No one here has ever seen them."

"You mean there's no one here in charge?"

"Not unless you want to be."

"You say I've been here two days?"

"That's the way I remember it. Of course, that doesn't count for much here."

"What was I like when I arrived?"

She smiled. "About the same."

"How long have you been here?"

"Lost track."

"You don't even care anymore, do you?"

She shook her head.

There was sand in his sneakers. "I could use a drink."

"So could I," said Myrna, "but all we have is limeade."

Eventually he entered the game just to escape her. He stared as Myrna stripped off her shorts and halter; she said it was "to keep them from getting sweaty." Watching her undress made Shaun feel like putting on more clothes. They went to opposite sides of the net. Shaun's teammates introduced themselves and placed him in the center back position. "Stay low when Vic's serving," said Akira, who had curly gray hair and the lean body of a miler.

The brown-haired server on Myrna's team palmed the ball, threw it high and hit it with his arm fully extended. It spun over the net toward Shaun. He dropped to his knees and managed to get his wrists under it, but the ball skewed out of play.

"Ten-seven," called Vic.

The next serve shot straight at Shaun. This time his return stayed in play but was too hard. It sailed over the net and deep to Myrna who set it up for her front line to spike.

"See what she did?" said Akira. "That's what you want to do."

"Yeah, yeah, I know." Shaun pulled his sneakers and socks off and slithered out of his shirt.

The ball, unmarred by writing, seemed whiter and harder than any Shaun had ever seen before. Whatever else these people were, they were superb athletes. They concentrated on the game, joked between points and offered advice and encouragement in the manner of old friends. Near the end of the third game of what seemed an unending series Shaun tried to sneak in a few questions.

"You're all pretty good at this. Play every day?"

"Jihan's good," said Akira, nodding at the woman who had rotated into position next to him. "I'm an old man."

"You weren't an old man last night," said Jihan.

"I'm the one playing like an old man," Shaun said. "I'm not used to this. How long have you folks been here?"

"Since breakfast." Akira crouched to receive serve, but it tipped the net.

"Net serve," said Jihan. "He means at Freedom Beach. Look, Shaun, I know it must seem important to you now, but after you've been here a few days the only time that counts is mealtime. Now move so I can serve."

She promptly served out the game and they decided to play again. "What I don't get," said Shaun, "is this therapy business. What kind of therapy is this?"

A dark woman smiled at him. "Some say sex therapy."

Shaun tried to ignore her. "But what does that have to do with writing?"

Akira glared at him as if he were a stubborn child. "You have a novel, right? Just bursting inside you?"

Shaun hated being patronized. He felt as if the beach were turning to quicksand beneath him. "You don't even care, do you? I don't understand it. Maybe you've been out in the sun too long."

No one would answer him.

Although he stood just under six-three, Shaun had never been much of a leaper. His growing anger at the absurdity of his situation transformed him. On the next point he managed to get two hands over the net to block one of Vic's spikes.

"Nice play, nature boy," said Akira, patting him on the rump.

But when Shaun tried the same strategy a point later, Vic

was ready. He smashed the ball between Shaun's arms; it bounced off the bridge of his nose and sent him sprawling.

"You all right, sport?" Vic ducked under the net to help him up.

"Now he's got something to remember," said Myrna. Everyone laughed.

At lunchtime the trashcans came out of the woodwork. As the volleyball players entered the commons the oak wainscotting folded away from the walls, revealing a dozen cartridge-shaped servomechanisms. Made of burnished metal, standing four feet tall, they tracked through the room on rubber padded belts, silently taking orders and disgorging food through hatches near the tips of their shiny heads. Except for alcohol the trashcans would deliver anything a guest ordered; however, the portly bronze Balzac by Rodin that dominated the commons informed Shaun that he would be limited to twenty-nine hundred calories a day.

Shaun chose to eat by himself next to the statue. He tested the kitchen by ordering spinach quiche, a cup of cold borscht and a cherry cola. The trashcan scuttled off to its berth and returned minutes later. The food was excellent. As he ate, Shaun interrogated Balzac. The statue responded politely to all questions but those which most interested Shaun. It would say nothing about the origins of Freedom Beach or about the dreamers, nothing about the personal histories of Shaun and the thirty-one other guests or about their supposed therapy.

On their way out after lunch, Vic and Myrna invited him to come for a swim. The pool was a marvel, fifty meters long, filled with salt water and lined with thousands of brightly colored tiles. At one end, set off from the rest of the pool by a transparent wall, an enormous golden statue jutted from the water. Surrounded by monsters and tritons, Apollo stood on a chariot harnessed to four magnificent horses. The piece seemed to be emerging from the water, headed west.

"Is that solid gold?"

"Gilt," said Myrna. "Like the one at Versailles."

"How do you know that?" Shaun was certain that she had made a slip.

"We're not quite as shallow as you think, sport," said Vic. He sat on a beach chair and untied his sneakers. "Everybody has their own little specialty. Myrna likes statues."

"What's yours?"

Vic pulled off his shirt. "The boundaries."

"What boundaries?"

He sighed. "This isn't the time, but—" He stripped off his shorts, crouched by the side of the pool and splashed water on himself. "For example, the only swimming you want to do is right here. There are sharks in the ocean and big men-of-war. A coral reef farther out that could cut you to bloody rags. And then there's the current."

"How do you know?"

Vic dove into the water.

"He found out for himself." Myrna gazed at the islands on the horizon.

Now that his headache had subsided, Shaun found it difficult to stay angry with these people. They were carefree, infectiously cheerful and bursting with life. They were not trying to shun him, only waiting for him to learn and observe their rules. When he participated in their impromptu swim meet, they cheered as loudly for him as for anyone. The monolith said that he had come voluntarily to Freedom Beach. Without knowing his reasons, he could understand why.

After dinner the trashcans passed among the assembled guests distributing the daily dose of communion. Each received a single white wafer the size of a quarter. Shaun hesitated before eating his. Jihan, Murray, Akira and Myrna, his tablemates, eyed it greedily.

"I'll have it if you don't want it," said Murray with forced indifference.

"We'll split it four ways," Myrna said firmly.

Shaun did not want to cause trouble. He popped it into his mouth; it tasted of honey. There followed several minutes of silence. Shaun waited in vain for the drug to take effect.

Supper was a pleasant weight in his stomach. He could appreciate the sensuous hiss of the surf and the coolness of the salt-laden breeze. A trashcan was setting up oil torches on the plaza outside the commons. The flames writhed and glittered. When he shut his eyes the colors still danced on the inside of his lids. Muscles he had never known before relaxed; he felt as if he were melting into the chair. Not rapture—a vast and impenetrable contentment. No more questions need be answered, no motives deduced, no more becoming, nothing better to do but float through the warm oceanic now . . .

Someone on another planet said, "Wake up the new boy."

"Shaun." Myrna shook him, laughing. "Shaun!"

He opened his eyes, and this time fell in love with the red hair tumbling across her face, the spray of freckles on her cheeks. His sudden affection was so unsurprising, so natural, that he wondered if he might have known her before. Though she was wearing a sweat suit he could still see her at the pool, naked. She was not voluptuous, but rather compact, hard, solid. The sturdy intelligence written on her features made her laugh irresistible. He smiled at her and pulled her into the chair next to him, holding her hand. When she made no effort to withdraw it, Vic wandered over to their table.

"Shaun thinks we need a leader, Vic." Myrna feigned concern. "He wants to take command."

"I thought that was your specialty, Vic," said Murray, a short man with a mustache and black hair.

"I lead," said Vic, "but no one follows."

"Tell me more about your specialists," Shaun said. "What can I do?"

"Specialists," Vic said. "Jihan, for example, is our historian: fourteen-ninety-two, Columbus sailed the ocean blue and all that. Akira sings. When he wraps his tenor around an Irish ballad, even the statues get a little misty. Let's see, we have storytellers, masseurs, botanists, menu mavens—and of course, champions in every sport.

"And then there's Murray. His specialty is—what would you call it, sport? Worrying about why we're here?"

"I'm an inductive theoretician." Murray was deadpan.

"Which means I still think about matters of greater import than what kind of cheese to eat with melon."

"Glad to hear it." Despite his communion-induced calm, Shaun suspected that he was being set up. "So tell me, why can't we write?"

Murray held up his index finger. "Simple. We're part of an experiment. If we were to write it would spoil the results. You need a control to do an experiment, yes?"

"A control?"

Jihan pushed out of her chair and moved to Akira's lap. She looked bored.

"You know, a test group where nothing happens. Somewhere there's another Freedom Beach full of typewriters. The dreamers want to see what the other group will come up with when they can't remember anything. No writing for us; we're the control."

A wave formed on Shaun's glassy sea of contentment. "Who are the dreamers?"

"Aliens." Murray had large and tricky brown eyes. "They wiped our memories with their superscience and brought us to this place. They monitor everything we do. Right now, Shaun, every word we say, they hear."

Shaun was not sure whether the derision he noticed around the table was directed at him or Murray. There was something of the put-on artist, the smart aleck, in the man's delivery. Shaun thought he detected the flaw in Murray's reasoning. "Wait a minute," he said. "If you know that we're part of an experiment, and the dreamers are listening and know you know, then another variable has been introduced into the control group and the experiment is wrecked. But they haven't called it off. Therefore, you must be wrong."

Murray frowned while everyone else laughed. "You forget," he said, "that if they call off the experiment they would be admitting to me that it is an experiment, so the only way they can keep the experiment going is not to call it off in the hope that I'll think it must not be an experiment after all."

Akira removed his hands from beneath Jihan's sweatshirt

and clapped. "Bravo, Socrates, bravo! Thus do we see how the weaker argument defeats the stronger."

"Besides, what about the therapy?" Jihan murmured, not lifting her head from Akira's shoulder.

"Sorry, Virginia, but there is no sanity clause." Murray waited for a laugh that did not come. "Do you really think you're getting better?"

"If she got any better, I'd have a stroke," said Akira.

Jihan chuckled. "You could do worse than die in bed."

Murray ignored them. "I'm telling you it's the classic red herring. The therapy is just a cover story to protect the experiment."

Myrna looked annoyed. "You all just don't get it, do you?" She freed her hand from Shaun's sweaty grasp. "This place is too pointless to be an experiment."

Jihan nuzzled Akira and said in a throaty whisper. "Maybe we all died and went to heaven."

"Right," said Myrna. "Only heaven could be this mindless. Did you ever hear any description of heaven that made it sound like an interesting place?" Myrna pulled her hair back from her face. "We have all the free time anyone could want, nobody gets sick, unless they get sick of Murray's nattering, the food is great, the weather perfect, there are plenty of games to keep us busy. Even the sex is pretty good."

Shaun raised an eyebrow. "Sex in heaven?"

"Sex is heaven," said Akira, dumping Jihan from his lap. She slid to the ground with an outraged squawk; they both laughed. "And on that note, we bid you adieu. Coming, my sweet?" He helped Jihan up and they went off arm in arm.

"So you think we're dead?" Shaun snaked his arm around Myrna's waist. "The corpse is still warm."

"Not dead, no! We would know—*I* would—if I had died." She was no longer bantering; her quiet sincerity lanced through the chemical fog in his brain. "That's the lie they've spread about heaven: in order to get there you have to die, give up life and everything that made it worth living. But you have to be alive to enjoy heaven, let it fill your senses. Not the end of life, an intensification of it. The amnesia we've got is the dreamers' way of purifying us so that we're ready to accept heaven. Otherwise we'd have to fight the lies we've been told before we could enjoy this place and that would screw everything up."

Murray caught Shaun's attention and rolled his eyes.

"When did you decide all this, Myrna?" Vic seemed puzzled. "You've called this place a lot of things—never heaven."

"I don't know—today, yesterday, maybe just now." Shaun felt her shiver. "I was fooled before because there were no angels, no Saint Peter at the gates to keep the assholes out."

"What about the dreamers? The guys in charge?" Shaun grinned. "If this is heaven, where's God?"

"You know, the guy is *never* around when you need him," said Murray.

"My dear Murray," replied Myrna, "go fuck yourself." She twisted free of Shaun and stalked out of the commons.

Murray watched her go. "Excuse me," he said. "My soul is double parked." He strolled off in the opposite direction whistling "Beautiful Dreamer."

Shaun thought he might still catch up with Myrna until Vic sat next to him.

"Stay a minute, sport. You were teasing."

"Why not? It was a silly idea."

"Maybe," said Vic. "But that's not the point. The point is that we're all trying to come to an understanding of this place. Some belief—even if it's a lie—that helps keep us going. You don't mess with that, sport. Not ever. Murray was just playing, but Myrna was serious. That's why we don't discuss these things."

"How existential of you." Shaun was trying to conceal his embarrassment.

"Don't be an asshole," Vic said. "You can think whatever you want of us. You can think we're a bunch of fools, and you wouldn't be the first who thought that. But don't think that anyone here will respect you for being independent. That's just another delusion, sport. Because whatever else it is, Freedom Beach is a prison."

Shaun stood. He did not want to antagonize Vic, but the man's smugness irritated him, and Shaun was damned if he would apologize for a natural mistake. But he could not avoid the fact that he had wounded Myrna.

"You win the prize tonight." Vic clapped him on the shoulder, as if in congratulations. "She's your neighbor, you know. Green suite. 'Night."

Instead of going back up the hill, Shaun walked along the beach, listening to the surf, thinking. Nothing became any clearer. Eventually he gave up, went back to his rooms, had two glasses of grapefruit juice and dropped his clothes in a pile on the floor. The warm waterbed shivered like Jell-O as he climbed into it. The events of the day spun through his mind, more and more slowly, like a merry-go-round coming to a stop.

Someone screamed. At first he was not sure whether or not he had imagined it. The second time it was louder.

He pulled on his shorts and bolted through the door into the atrium. The fountain splashed. The screaming started again and did not stop.

He ran into Myrna's suite. She was on the floor, naked, writhing. The pale green sheets trailed off her waterbed. He knelt by her side, comforting her and at the same time restraining her. Finally she subsided into tears.

"Are you all right?"

She swallowed. "Nightmare." She brushed her wet face against his chest, and he rocked her in silence for a time.

She breathed deeply and let out a strangled little laugh. "Did you ever think . . . ?" She took another breath. "What kind of dying frightens you the most?"

Shaun did not want to take the question seriously but he dared not make a joke. He tried to pretend she was wearing clothes.

"I don't know," he said. Suddenly a memory dropped into his mind as if it had fallen from the sky, so vivid that he shivered. "When I was a boy I stepped into a bees' nest. I remember running, but they had flown inside my clothes. I was in the hospital for a month. If it ever happened again I'd go crazy long before they could sting me to death."

A strand of hair had stuck to the tears drying on her face. "I was sailing with my brother." Her voice trembled. "The boat tipped, he drowned. I should have, too. Then I wouldn't have these nightmares."

Neither spoke. Just when Shaun was beginning to feel self-conscious, she pulled herself up to the edge of the bed. "Thanks for coming." She wiped at the corners of her eyes and smiled.

He kissed her tentatively, then with purpose.

"This is serious," she said.

"Yes."

They fell into bed, and Myrna took him with a kind of desperate earnestness. She knew what she wanted and when she had it she laughed. "Now you've done everything there is to do here."

She fell asleep first, draped over him as if they had been murdered together. Shaun drifted to the edge of consciousness. Someone far away was laughing, and it came to him that his father's name was Harry.

Shaun decided that for the present he would accept Freedom Beach as he found it. He saw no purpose in making enemies of the others, so he gathered with them each morning on the lawn by Discobolus's shed. There the marble statue would tell them what to play that day. Discobolus's word was not law; one day when he offered nothing but hickory crosses and hard rubber lacrosse balls most guests spent the day at tag and hide-and-go-seek. Those who felt ridiculous kept it to themselves.

He kept waiting for something to happen, for the reason for his being there to come clear. He tried to keep track of time. He stole a knife from the commons and each day carved a notch on the inside of the closet door molding. He got up to sixteen before they disappeared. Then he collected pebbles in a sock he hid beneath the skirt of a petticoat palm. When he returned one day the entire plant had been replaced by a cigar-store Indian.

"Why bother?" it said.

There were no monogamous relationships at Freedom Beach. Shaun sampled bodies and offered his own freely, but his preference was for Myrna. Their lovemaking was never spectacular; it was the before and after that attracted Shaun to her. Occasionally he was able to bore through the defensive taunts, the cynicism and the anger, to the core of her tortured honesty. Late at night amid the scattered sheets as the sweat dried on them and carried with it the false euphoria of communion, they shared their fears of the awful silliness of their lives. It was on one such night, weeks after he had arrived, that he got her to answer the question that no one else would.

"Do we ever get to leave?"

"Leave heaven? What for?" She rolled to the edge of the bed and sat with her back to him. "Ask someone else. Vic would tell you, if you'd stop spitting in his face first."

"I'm not asking Vic for a goddamned thing. Someday he's going to have to come to me." He skimmed his forefinger down her vertebrae. "I'm asking you because you're the only one I can ask."

She was silent for a time. "A few have tried to escape. Some made it back—Vic did." She stooped to gather her clothes. "Then there are the rule breakers. The benevolent dreamers withhold communion as a punishment. You're addicted, you know." She chuckled bitterly at his shock. "If it's only a day or two you recover. But after a week . . . Some take the long swim. Others disappear into the boundaries."

"They die?"

She slipped into her T-shirt. "Maybe. Probably. But the beauty of it is that we've never found a single body. Only . . ." She pulled on her shorts and stepped into her sandals. "Have you seen the sphinx yet? The alumni?"

"No. Where?"

"You're overdue, then. Walk west along the beach—look for the stairs. Oh, and by the way—" She opened the door to the atrium. "I'm not sleeping with you anymore. You ask too damn many questions."

The tide narrowed the beach until Shaun was skirting the verge of a precipitous jungle and clambering over fallen trees awash in the surf. He was beginning to suspect that Myrna had tricked him when he came upon a stone stairway cut into the side of the hill. It climbed steeply and then descended to a wide prospect on which crouched the Great Sphinx of Giza.

It was some sixty feet tall and two hundred long and was covered with brightly painted plaster. Sensors the size of roadgrader wheels stared at the hazy islands on the horizon; the face was unmarked by time or Turkish bullets. The sphinx loomed between Shaun and a statue garden at the far side of its park.

"Good afternoon, Shaun." It spoke with the voice of Niagara Falls.

He staggered. "Lower. Please."

"How's this?" it boomed.

"Better. Will you answer questions?"

"Ask."

Shaun sat cross-legged on the bottom step. "What is it that goes on four legs in the morning, two legs in the afternoon and three legs in the evening?"

"A man."

"Tell me how you knew the answer."

"You are not the first to ask."

"Did you read about it?"

"I do not read. I know."

"Does that mean you can't read?"

"A meaningless question. Since there is nothing for me to read, the occasion does not arise."

"Suppose I were to write a note and hold it up to your sensors?"

"You have nothing with which to write."

"I could slash my wrists and write in blood on the stones."

"Why bother? Talking is less painful."

Shaun strolled between the massive paws as he marshaled his thoughts. "Some things can only be expressed in writing."

"I find that hard to believe."

"Poetry."

"Comes from an oral tradition."

"Some things hurt too much . . ." Shaun was getting hungry; he was already hot. "I would find it hard to say that I was ashamed of myself, for instance."

"Why?"

He knew he was losing the advantage again. Yet the question demanded an answer. "If I wrote it, I wouldn't have to face the person I was telling it to."

"How passive," said the sphinx. "Besides, it is my observation that people are generally not interested in the problems of others."

"You're wrong! Maybe not here; you've seen to that with your drugs and your pointless games. But there are other places."

"Things were different where you came from?"

Shaun realized that he had scored a point. This was the first acknowledgment he had had from the statues that other places existed. But a small triumph could not satisfy him; it only made him angry. "I don't remember! You took that away from me!"

"Nothing has been taken from you that you did not surrender voluntarily."

"How do I know?"

"Why would I lie?"

"Fuck you." He picked up a stone and hurled it at one of the sensors. It bounced away harmlessly.

"That is not an option of which I am capable."

"Fuck you anyway."

"There is no content in your response."

Shaun restrained himself from throwing another rock. "Your round." He circled behind the sphinx toward the group of statues Myrna had called the alumni. "Who are the dreamers?"

"It is not for me to say."

Shaun nodded grimly. "The monument says we're here for therapy. What kind of therapy is this?"

"Dream therapy."

"Dreams? But I don't remember having any."

"One does not always remember one's dreams."

Shaun filed that for future reference. "What's so wrong with us that we need therapy?"

"That is for you to determine. You are not ready yet to accept my opinions."

It was right about that, anyway. Shaun wiped his arm across his brow. "I want to leave this place."

"Where do you want to go?"

"Send me back to where I was before I came here."

"Where was that?"

He smiled humorlessly. "All right. I'll settle for those islands over there."

"There are no islands."

Shaun paused and squinted at the islands. From this vantage he could count four. They were all mountainous; the largest was mottled with eggshell patches as if there were dunes or chalk cliffs along its coast.

"No islands! Straight ahead—you're looking at them!"

"You mean the mirage."

"The what?"

"The optical illusion resulting when light from a distant object is bent as it passes through the interface of air layers of varying density."

"I don't believe you."

Silence.

"The jungle then," said Shaun. "What's on the other side of the jungle?"

"There is no other side. The jungle is endless."

By this time Shaun was close enough to count the twelve pieces in the statue garden. He drew closer. None had the usual sensors and microphones. All were captured in their death throes. Aghast, Shaun stumbled from agony to agony. He had once seen the castings made by pouring plaster into the hollows left by Pompeiian corpses buried beneath the hot ash of Vesuvius. These were far more terrible in their detail: silent screams, madness and despair on grotesque faces.

"Who . . . ?"

The sphinx said, "They tried to leave before their time."

Shaun stopped going to morning assembly; he did not participate in the games. He saw the other guests at meals. He was not unfriendly, but their chatter of strikes and backhands and caroms and grips soon bored him. He wanted to talk to Myrna about the sphinx and the alumni but she would not listen. Perhaps he had given her more credit than she deserved. Perhaps she was as afraid as the rest of them. During the day Shaun would stay in bed or sit alone on the beach. At night he would savor communion, take a lover or not, think his thoughts.

YOU MAY NOT HARM ANOTHER GUEST. Yes, of course. A simple law which humans had always found complicated reasons for breaking. Food, shelter and the Golden Rule; these should have been the ingredients for paradise. And yet, YOU ARE FORBIDDEN TO WRITE. Writing was a kind of memory and Freedom Beach was founded on amnesia. Writing was the key to change and Freedom Beach was petrified.

Murray was growing a beard. It must have been very hot, but he was the only guest with one. A poor athlete, he lusted after distinction. On an occasional afternoon he, too, would leave the games and visit Shaun. Together they would puzzle over their fate. Murray had finally come around to the theory that all the guests were writers and Freedom Beach was some exotic kind of cure.

"And the statues are actually psychiatrists." He snuggled his toes into the hot sand of the beach.

"But the sphinx claims what we're getting is dream therapy."

"Yeah, sure. Talked to any burning bushes lately?"

"It's strange." Shaun shook his head. "I can't remember my dreams. That has to mean something." He picked up a broken shell. "What about the dreamers?"

"The visionaries who built the joint. Dreamers as in idealists."

"I like it." Shaun mused. "But then this place must really cost."

"Couple of hundred an hour, minimum. And that's just the labor."

Shaun watched some of the guests playing tag football at the edge of the surf. He was still deciding about Murray. His ideas were interesting, his jokes occasionally on the mark, but his personality was insufferable. "How do you figure the alumni? Dead clients might put a damper on business."

"They're not dead, they're cured. They had such a burning need to write that they risked death to do it. The dreamers let them go."

"But what are we supposed to be cured of?"

"Unhappiness." An errant pass bounced nearby and rolled toward them. Murray retrieved it and threw a wobbling ball to the nearest player. "Everyone thinks that writers live the good life; it's a myth. We were all rich and famous, see, and busy drinking ourselves to death, doing heavy drugs, sticking pistols into our mouths for fun. We got so desperate that we signed on here. You see, some of us were meant to be writers and some of us just drifted into it. Now the real writers go back to the real world and the rest of us work on our tans."

"And did we know each other before we came here?"

"Possible. Sure, maybe we bumped into each other on talk shows. Vic did sex manuals. Akira wrote sensitive stories about drunken Irishmen. Myrna was into self-help. Happy hours in the Village. Writers' workshops in Vermont. Cocaine weekends at Cancun."

Shaun considered for a moment and then for the first time broke one of the rules. BULLSHIT, he wrote in the sand. He looked at Murray.

"What the hell are you doing?" Murray glanced nervously at the players and then up at the sky. "I've got to go. Okay?"

The gazebo was under siege from the jungle behind it. Vines snaked up its corner posts and overran the roof. Inside was a water bubbler and a bronze that Myrna had identified as Picasso's *Baboon and Young*. The head of the parent was a toy car with windshield eyes and a bumper mouth.

"I'm going into the jungle." Shaun stooped over the bubbler and drank. "What will I find there?"

"You will find that you are lost soon enough."

He patted the baboon on the hood. "Well, if anyone asks, you know where to find me."

The bravado lasted fifty yards. To be sure that he was not going in circles, he tried the old Boy Scout trick of walking to landmarks and then sighting back to the previous mark. But marks were hard to spot as he picked his way through the dense underbrush. He was ill-prepared for a long trek; he should have squirreled away some provisions, perhaps stolen a fencing foil from Discobolus to hack at the jungle. But he was resolved to explore the boundaries of Freedom Beach, if not to cross them.

Shaun rested against the bole of a tree and swiped at the cloud of flies around his face. He had no idea what time of the day it was; the treetops hid the sun. He had been walking long enough to be thirsty. Maybe he should climb a tree. He licked his lips. Check his progress. He tried to shinny up several of the branchless trunks. The farthest he got was thirty feet off the ground, a third of the way to the canopy. He stopped climbing and clung, wrenched by acrophobia. He was slipping. The rough bark tore his hands. He fell the last few yards, struggled up completely lost and stepped into a bees' nest. When he flailed at the swarm the jungle slapped back. He ran.

Shaun burst through one last wall of green and saw the roofs of Freedom Beach. Flying down the cobbled street he realized that he had outrun the bees, had not even been stung. He did not slow down. At the edge of the pool he dived and stayed under as long as he could. He surfaced in front of three impatient swimmers waiting on the starting blocks.

"You about done, sport?" Vic stooped and offered a helping hand.

"Yeah, get him out of there."

Shaun glared at them. "I went . . ." He breathed deeply. "I went for a walk. In the jungle."

They laughed at him.

"You can't get out that way." Vic boosted him onto the side of the pool. "The jungle is full of boogey men. You should have asked me."

"Time to stop acting like a rookie." Akira offered him a dry towel. "We've got a new arrival."

"Where?" Shaun asked, still slightly dazed.

"He wandered into the commons a while ago, asking the usual questions."

"Where is he now?"

The swimmers were silent for a moment.

"I think someone took him up to the clubhouse," said Akira. "He'll be out soon enough."

"They're in the hot tub," Jihan said. "Akira, don't tell me you're turning into a prude."

Akira touched Shaun's arm. "Let's eat something. I wanted to change into some dry clothes anyway."

"I'm not hungry."

"Forget it, Akira," Vic said. "Shaun, if you weren't so damned stupid, you'd let someone do you a favor."

"Myrna's introducing him," Akira said quietly.

"He didn't seem to need much introducing," Jihan said. Everyone laughed.

"I just had some questions." Shaun was angry at himself for being embarrassed. "They can wait."

"Myrna couldn't." They laughed again.

When Myrna and the newcomer—Rick—showed up later, Shaun did not have any questions. Myrna looked haggard. She would not meet his gaze.

Shaun had decided. After breakfast each morning he went straight to the pool and swam laps. He made his tuck turns without touching the sides. After lunch he napped, then back to the pool.

Soon he was logging as much as six kilometers at a stretch. He swam like a machine. Once he had established his rhythm his thoughts slowed to the ticking off of laps. Balzac told him that his caloric maximum was being raised to four thousand, then to forty-five hundred.

In addition, Shaun steadily—and surreptitiously—cut down on his intake of communion. Each night he nipped the wafer with his fingernail and discarded as much as he dared. The first time proved a disaster when he stashed the leftover in the pocket of his tennis shorts. When he realized that the lesser dose would leave him far, far short of his accustomed euphoria, he retreated to the bathroom, turned the pocket inside out and ate the dregs, lint, crumbs and all. The next time he flushed the shard before the drug could wear down his resolve.

Each night he ate less until he was throwing away half, occasionally more. Over the long term detoxification was easier than he had expected. He ached from the workouts anyway, and he was so tired that insomnia never became a problem. He managed to keep his withdrawal a secret from the others.

Confidence swelling, he switched the afternoon workout to the ocean. His first attempt was almost his last. The waves disrupted his breathing and he swallowed enough water to fill an aquarium. Without lane markers to guide him he had to lift his head high above the waves. The salt water corroded his vision until he saw everything through a tunnel of haze. When he collected his first jellyfish sting, an ugly five-inch welt on his calf, he limped to shore and collapsed.

But he came back the next afternoon and the afternoon after that, and soon he had adjusted to the rigors of open-water swimming. Eventually he tried to swim while wearing his lightest pair of jogging shoes. His final victory was reaching the coral reef that Vic had mentioned. With his feet protected he was able to walk across it safely. He stood in water up to his chest and gazed at the islands. They looked closer—and more real—than he would have imagined from the beach. He guessed that he was now about a quarter of the way to escape.

Then he saw the fin slicing through the water. He had a glimpse of the sleek, dark body. Shaun stood dead still, mouth open, gulping air to quench his fear. He told himself that it was probably only a hallucination like the bees, part of the psychic fence that locked the guests in. But the jellyfish welt, burning on his leg from the salt water, was real. He reminded himself that there were only a few species of shark that could kill a man. Yet in Shaun's imagination the dark shape out there was deliberately stalking him. It circled and then disappeared beneath the waves. Shaun was shivering so badly that he could hardly keep his balance. Nothing happened. He started counting. One-one thousand, two-one thousand, three . . .

In time he realized that he had been reprieved. It was a bitter comfort, for he knew now that he would never be desperate enough to reach for the islands. Suicide was one game he would never play. He walked back across the reef and struck out for shore.

He wanted to tell Myrna that he had surrendered to Freedom Beach; of all the guests, she was the only one he thought might be disappointed. But she skipped supper that night and made only the briefest of appearances during communion. She had lost weight, and she shuffled through the commons listlessly.

"What's with her?" he asked Akira.

"Don't you know?" Akira shrugged. "We haven't seen much of Myrna recently. We thought you two might be hermiting together."

"I thought she was spending her time with the new guy."

Akira seemed surprised at his ignorance. "That didn't last past the introduction."

"She looks awful."

He returned to his rooms. On his bed he found a rolled-up white towel. He shook it open. Someone had written on it in what looked like grape juice. The letters were twisted and barely legible.

> I feel light as a handful of air,
> My moonbeam bones frame sea mist,
> I am nothing but glitter and the tang of salt.
> Tie me down! Chain me to these slippery stones.

> The cry of a passing gull could carry me off,
> Scatter me like rain across the water.
> The waves sigh as they lap at the beach.
> They say there is no place but this.
>
> I will breathe deeply of night and the stars,
> Break this leash of reason,
> Shed this harness of appetite
> And yield, unbodied, to the tide.

Shaun was stunned with delight. He laughed and danced around the bed, never once taking his eyes from the words. There was someone else! Thinking he knew who it was, he ran to the door of the green suite. He knocked, then pounded; he called her name. No response.

It did not matter whether he saw Myrna then or later. Or whether she had written the poem at all. Whoever it was, yes, even if it were Murray, that person had earned his love. He spent the evening in his room with the door locked, memorizing the words, speaking them aloud. Writing was not the only freedom that the dreamers had revoked: he wondered if reading might not be the greater loss. It took a long time for Shaun to bring himself to destroy the towel to protect his unknown friend.

The next morning, after searching unsuccessfully for Myrna, Shaun went back to the pool. Instead of swimming laps he floated on his back beneath the golden statue, watching the clouds. All that day he waited for some sign from the poet. At times he felt as if he would burst with his secret, yet no knowing eyes met his.

He finally found Myrna picking at her supper. Throughout the meal he tried to attract her attention. She ignored him sullenly. He had begun to think he was wrong about her when the trashcans distributing communion quietly passed her by.

"Give it to me!" she cried. "You tin bastard!" She picked up a glass and hurled it at the offending trashcan. "Give it!"

The assembled guests seethed with whispers. All but Shaun

gobbled their communion wafers as soon as they received them.

"What did I do?" Myrna staggered from table to table in search of help. Her friends shrank from her. "It's a mistake." Fear disfigured her face. "No. Do you hear? No! Listen to me!" She spied Murray receiving one of the last wafers and lurched toward him. "Give it to me, Murray. It's mine. Come on, Murray, they'll give you another. Murray!" As he stuffed it into his mouth she lunged. He pushed out of his chair and blocked her with his forearm. She grunted and sprawled across the table, which tipped her onto the floor. She lay amid the cutlery and broken dishes and beads of her own blood. "A mistake. A mistake."

Vic and Shaun ran to her from opposite sides of the commons. Vic arrived first and crouched by her. "All right, Myrna. It's all right." He slipped an arm around her shoulder and sat her up. "We'll go home and clean you up. There's nothing we can do here."

"Get away from her!" Shaun knocked him backward. Vic vaulted to his feet, ready to fight.

"What were you going to do, big man?" said Shaun. "Lead her away so the rest of us wouldn't have to watch her suffer?" He held up his communion for all to see.

Vic's fists dropped to his sides. Myrna fixed the wafer with a glistening stare and coiled herself like a snake about to strike. Shaun broke it and was about to offer her half when she sprang. Surprise sent him reeling. He dropped Myrna's piece and she pounced on it.

"It's not enough, Shaun." Vic waved off the other guests. "For either of you."

Shaun hauled Myrna to her feet roughly. "Go," he said, pushing her toward the door.

"I'm sorry." She made it sound like a confession obtained under torture. Shaun cleaned the cuts on her knees in silence. He tossed the bloody washcloth into the sink and sat at the edge of her bed.

"Vic is right, you know." She seemed to be looking right through the ceiling.

"I liked your poem."

She laughed. Nothing moved but her mouth.

"I wanted to see you the other night. I knocked, you didn't answer." He touched her motionless hand. "They say you've become a recluse."

"I've been purifying the flesh. You know, clear the mind, dull the senses."

"You're starving yourself to death."

"That's one theory."

He grabbed her by the shoulders and shook her. "You listen! From now on we share communion. You're going to eat if I have to force it down your throat. And you're going to train with me until you're ready to swim to the islands." She looked at him blankly. "Listen! You can't let the dreamers get to you like this. If you kill yourself, they win. You and I will fight them."

"You don't understand." For the first time she seemed to be in the same room with him. "The dreamers don't matter anymore. I'm not doing this because of them."

"The hell you aren't. Suicide is the coward's way out."

"No. You have to be brave to kill yourself. Or crazy. I am neither. I just wanted to slip out through the back door."

He let her fall back onto the bed. His head was throbbing and he wished he had kept a larger portion of the communion wafer for himself.

She opened her arms and smiled wanly. "Make love to me."

Shaun embraced her with the certainty that he alone could save her. But after an hour of sweaty frustration he realized that she did not seek pleasure or affection from him—only escape. When she opened herself to him she was no longer able to repress her withdrawal pangs. After Shaun gave up, she twisted and flopped on the bed like a fish suffocating in a net. Eventually he was driven to the couch in the living room to sleep.

* * *

"Wake up, damn it!"

Shaun squinted at his tormentor. "Scram."

Vic would not be refused. He jiggled Shaun's shoulder. "Listen to me. Please."

Groggy as he was, Shaun recognized a note in Vic's voice he had never heard before. He propped himself up against the side cushion of the couch. "Myrna?"

"Gone." Vic lowered his eyes and retreated a few steps as if to avoid giving offense. "Are you awake?"

Shaun scratched his head and nodded.

"The statues didn't like what you did last night. Most of them have stopped talking. Discobolus refused to issue any equipment this morning. And Balzac—" He drew a ragged breath. "Balzac says that unless you agree not to share with Myrna again, there will be no more communion. For anyone! You understand?"

Shaun rose stiffly from the couch and took a jar of grapefruit juice from Myrna's refrigerator. He drained the bottle and wiped his mouth with the back of his hand. "So you're here to ask me not to save her."

"You're doing a hell of a job saving her."

Shaun ignored him. "Did you appoint yourself for this errand of mercy or did the others elect you?"

Vic frowned. "I don't know what I've done to make you hate me so much. It's the same for Myrna whether I ask you or somebody else does. Either way, she knows. She came down for breakfast this morning, just like old times. She heard what we heard. She left . . . we thought she would be here."

"It stinks!" Shaun slammed the bottle down so hard that it broke. "You stink!"

"She always said that you wanted to be in charge." Vic picked up the largest shard of glass, turned it over in his hand, set it down again. "The job is yours; no sense bitching about the choices."

"Choices!" Shaun shook his head grimly. "She's worth more than the whole mindless, gutless lot of you." He slumped, covering his face with his hands. "Find her. Let that be your game today, Vic. Hide-and-go-seek. I'll think while you look."

Vic flushed. He started to leave, stopped, started again. Finally at the door he turned. "All right. You're the hero, the rest of us are stinking nobodies. But that doesn't give you the right to destroy us like you destroyed her."

"I destroyed . . . ?"

"You shattered her indifference. You can't feel anything and survive here."

One by one the searchers straggled into the commons. The tables farthest from Shaun filled first. Shaun could not find it in himself to hate the other guests, but they did not deserve his pity. He let them worry.

Vic was one of the last. He did not slink past Shaun but instead approached with an air of doomed bravado. "No luck, sport. She knows how to hide."

"Go away."

Vic pulled out a chair and sat at Shaun's table. "Let's eat," he said loudly enough for all to hear. "No sense going to hell on an empty stomach."

The trashcans scuttled out of the wainscotting, but the voice of Balzac stopped them. "Shaun, will there be communion tonight?"

The silence was complete.

"That's your decision," muttered Shaun. "You pick the games."

"Will there be communion?"

Akira and Jihan burst into the commons, their faces ashen.

Shaun wanted to run away from them. "For some," he whispered.

The water spurting from the Poseidon fountain was pink. There was a trail of sticky spatters that looked like cocoa trailing across the atrium. She had come from Shaun's apartment. Her emaciated body was the color of Carraran marble. Slumped at the sea god's feet, it looked like some ghastly revision to the fountain's centerpiece. Water from the pool licked at the wounds on Myrna's wrists.

Shaun wept.

"There's this." Someone pressed a folded pillowcase on Shaun and backed away as quickly as if it were infected with the germs of self-destruction. Shaun opened it. It was hard to decipher for all the gore.

> Afraid of drowning not dying
> Waiting for you [illegible] islands.

Akira touched him on the arm as if to comfort him, and Shaun raised the pillowcase in his clenched fist. It was all he could do to keep from striking out. The other guests recoiled.

"It was what she wanted." Vic's eyes were dry.

Shaun took a step toward him.

"You may not harm another guest," said Poseidon.

In a rage Shaun splashed into the fountain. He pulled the body from the water and laid it on the flagstones. Then he attacked the statue, tugging at the trident, managing to bend it a few inches. The bloody water soaked his clothes. "She didn't hurt anyone," he cried. "It was only a poem!"

Poseidon did not reply. Some of the guests were already rushing back to the commons to get their communion. Shaun knelt beside Myrna and kissed her cold cheek. "I'm sorry," he said. Then he picked up the pillowcase and pushed through those remaining.

"Where are you going?" called Poseidon from behind him.

Shaun carried the pillowcase down the hill. A madonna and child beside the cobbled street called to him. "Where, Shaun?"

He stopped at the beach. On his hands and knees he began to dig. Akira and Vic followed him; they watched silently. With the sphinx's great voice, Balzac called to him from the commons. "There is nowhere else, Shaun."

Shaun buried the pillowcase and then wrote in the sand. MYRNA.

He turned and walked deliberately into the surf.

"Do you want to remember, Shaun?" said Balzac. "Is that it?"

Shaun looked for the islands at the edge of the horizon. He waded deeper, through foaming swells that slapped at his belly. He could swim away; he knew he could. The backwash tugged at Shaun's legs and he stopped.

"We'll give you back your memories. Stay."

Even as he hesitated there, a vivid memory captured him. His father. Shaun could remember him padding through the kitchen after work wearing white socks, green pants and a green shirt with *Harry* embroidered over the breast pocket. He would leave his steel-toed shoes in the garage to keep the rubber soles from scuffing the linoleum. He would not talk to Shaun's mother until he had read the evening paper, and he would pore over that paper as if he expected it someday to explain the world to him. And if he could not understand it, he was determined that his son would.

The image of his father expanded; with it came additional memories and the emotions Shaun had associated with them. The reality of Myrna's death was washed away in this merciful tide of memory.

Shaun's father, a high school dropout, had worked for a plumbing contractor in Brooklyn. He had been obsessed with the idea that his son would go to an Ivy League college and earn his living in a Manhattan office sitting behind a desk. Harry Reed had stormed the boundaries of his own life in vain. He was determined to push his son out into the wider world that he would never see.

One of his stratagems was to offer Shaun an unusual allowance. While other twelve-year-olds got paid to make beds or clear tables or take out the garbage, Harry offered Shaun a reward for reading a book and writing a report on it. One wide-lined, loose-leaf page brought thirty-five cents.

The problem was that father and son could not agree on which books were worthy to be reported on. Although Shaun devoured Tom Swift and the Hardy Boys and the Oz series, his father disapproved. Harry had a vague notion of the "classics" which he wanted Shaun to read—the very books which had driven him out of school at the age of sixteen.

Shaun remembered now how he had outsmarted his father. He would go down to Applebaum's candy store and buy Classics Illustrated comic books. He did not think it fair that, at fifteen cents, they were more expensive than Marvel or DC comics; after all, Doctor Faustus was hardly as entertaining as Doctor Doom. Still, he was making twenty cents on the transaction, and it was better than having to read an old play for full price. He had to sneak them into the house, where he would read them by flashlight under the covers after bedtime. After the report was written and paid for he would hide the comics up in the attic under the batts of pink insulation. Standing in the surf, Shaun rubbed his thumb over his fingertips and seemed actually to feel the prickle of the fiberglass again, smell the musty newsprint smell of the comic books.

And Harry Reed had never guessed. Shaun wondered whether those old comics were still moldering there, insulating the current occupants of the house on Summer Street.

"Come back, Shaun," called Balzac.

He shivered, shaking free of the memory, and glanced over his shoulder. The beach was deserted now; Akira and Vic had gone. No witnesses. He could feel the sand sliding through his toes as waves surged around him. The water was warm. He felt sleepy.

"Remember."

It was foolhardy to stumble into the surf on an impulse. The islands would still be there in the morning. He was tired. And, *yes*, he wanted to remember. That was his biggest problem, his only problem. He wanted to know who he was. He walked back to the beach and slowly climbed the hill to his villa.

Someone had moved Myrna's body from the fountain and scrubbed her bloodstains from the flagstones in the atrium. It was as if nothing had happened. He wondered if he fell asleep whether the dreamers might try to steal his memories of her. Except that Poseidon's trident was still bent—a sign? Let that be her memorial. Shaun entered his villa, flopped onto his waterbed fully dressed and stared up at the ceiling. Strange visions swirled through his mind. In college he had experimented with LSD and been caught up in long and involved hallucinations, waking dreams which had spun a bizarre logic from the seeds of madness. Were these the fabled flashbacks? He felt as if there were an electrical storm raging in his brain. It was all coming back to him as he drifted with the visions. Columbia . . . so many books . . . the faces. Murray was—Murray Gross. *And Myrna*. He lifted his head from the pillow and with great effort was able to whisper, "I love you."

"Relax." The last thing he heard—thought he heard—was Poseidon's voice. "You're doing fine," it said. "We'll begin now."

November 10, 1973

Shaun flicked his thumbnail against the head of an Ohio Blue Tip. The match flared on the first try, and he grinned as he touched the flame to the joint dangling from his mouth. He took three quick breaths—*thchew, thchew, thchew!*—and the glowing tip flickered in the darkened room. "Yes, Mission Control, we have achieved ignition." He passed the joint to her, hoping she had been impressed by the performance.

"You always prepare for class this way?" Myrna took a long drag, six seconds at least. An expert.

Shaun could feel the smoke tickling his lungs; suddenly he had to cough and laugh at the same time. "Only for Murray Gross." He brandished the joint. "Fastest *A* in the East."

Gross was Myrna's faculty advisor and Myrna was, in Shaun's opinion, the most stunning woman on campus. She was compact and sleek and tanned; her red hair cascaded to the small of her back. Her eyes were a clear ocean green; Shaun could easily imagine drowning in them. She was wearing black jeans, black boots with pointed heels, and a loose gray top that looked as if it might be silk. No tie-dyed T-shirts for Myrna Rosny. It was her hat that usually drove Shaun crazy. She liked to wear it cocked, brim dipping over one eye. He could not decide whether it was an invitation or a dare. Ever since he had met her at the start of the semester he had been working up a fantasy in which she was dancing in his room—this very room!—wearing nothing but that hat. He took the joint from her. The hat was on the bed.

"How'd you get tied up with Gross anyhow?"

"He asked me." She shrugged. "I said yes."

Shaun wondered what else Gross had asked Myrna. The professor had not taken any such notice of Shaun. Theirs was a match made in the Student Aid Office. Shaun needed financial assistance, Gross needed a research assistant. The two of them rarely spoke: twice a week Shaun picked up a list of articles which the professor wanted xeroxed. Gross's latest publish-or-perish project was an article comparing Christopher Marlowe and Antonin Artaud. Shaun thought it was silly, but then his opinion did not really count. The best part of the job so far had been meeting Myrna at Gross's office. A seed in the joint popped and sent a shower of sparks over Shaun. He brushed them away and passed the joint.

"You buy his rap?" said Shaun. "Marlowe, the closet existentialist?"

"He never said that!" She brushed a strand of hair out of her face. "What he said was that Marlowe foreshadows the Theater of the Absurd."

"Yeah." Shaun moved closer to her until their knees touched. "Him and the Three Stooges."

She laughed. "It's a wonder you can remember anything about his class, smoking this awful stuff. What's it cut with? Pine needles?" She took a hit big enough to stone China, then offered it to him.

"Shredded pages from *Silas Marner*—better than opium." Shaun could already feel the base of his skull tingling, as if club soda were being pumped into his cerebellum.

They stared at each other in silence. In literature, thought Shaun, when characters locked glances in this way, they discovered all kinds of things about each other. Eyes the windows to the soul and all that. But if it were so, then Myrna's eyes were of mirrored glass. Shaun could see nothing in them. He wanted to touch her magnificent hair, take a few long strands between his thumb and forefinger. "What are you thinking?" he said instead.

She considered for a moment, as if his question had driven all thought from her mind. Then she gave him a wicked grin. "I was thinking that it was time to tell you that I don't hop into bed with every guy who gets me high."

"Well." Shaun swallowed. "All right." He reached for the joint. "I think." He started to cough and laugh at the same time.

She was giggling too. Soon they were caught in a cloudburst of hilarity; the storm washed away the sexual tension that had been keeping them apart. They became friends in that moment.

"I think it's time we floated over to class," said Myrna at last. She wiped the corner of her eye. "Isn't he giving papers back today?"

"Yeah, sure." Shaun put the roach out. "I've been waiting to find out what he thought of mine. It's on the Marx Brothers." He pulled the shades up, opened the windows to let the room air out, then picked up his notebook and keys. "A sure ace."

She shook her head. "You're a cocky son of a bitch, aren't you?"

He paused for a moment, jingling his keys, as if the thought had never occurred to him before. Then he opened the notebook on the desk. "By the way—" he held a pen ready to write "—just what *does* it take to get you to hop in bed?"

"You have to know the password." She closed the notebook for him. "And *that* you find out for yourself."

Shaun locked his room and strode down the hall after her. "Swordfish?" he called hopefully.

* * *

Actually, it had not been Gross's lectures that had inspired Shaun to write about the Marx Brothers; it had been his appearance. Gross was a ringer for the Groucho of the "You Bet Your Life" days. He had the same receding hairline, the same salt-and-pepper mustache, eyes like two billiard balls on a slow roll, a penchant for bow ties. He had elevated the leer to an art form, a habit which did little to endear him to the dewy young feminists who wandered unsuspectingly into his classes. Gross still had a trace of Brooklyn in his voice as he deadpanned his outrageous lectures. All that was missing were the cigars; he smoked a fistful of Kools every class, ashing them in half-filled Styrofoam coffee cups. As he listened to Gross lecture on Marlowe's *Faustus*, Shaun doodled a pitchfork rising from a sludge-filled cup.

"In Marlowe, as in Shakespeare, it is time which provides the measure of absurdity." Shaun watched as Myrna dutifully wrote in her notebook: "Time = absurdity." Gross began to pace. "Time is like a roller coaster, climbing slowly to a great height from which there can only be a fall, speeding through years in a few lines of dialogue, shaking and rattling its helpless passengers until the final moment when the train stops and death has its triumph—unless you happen to have another ticket." The class laughed; Gross lit another cigarette. He winked at an owl-eyed priest, impossibly solemn in his collar and black suit, who sat in the front row. Rumor had it that the man was a visiting lecturer from St. John's who, from his obsequious classroom comments, seemed to have mistaken Gross for the second coming of Edmund Wilson.

For the most part Murray Gross was not popular with his fellow scholars. Many said—with justification—that the reason his classes were always filled was that he had never met a student he did not think deserved an *A*. Gross was an entertaining lecturer with a seemingly encyclopedic knowledge of popular culture. Behind his back envious neoclassicists accused him of pandering to the mindless yahoos whom it was their misfortune to instruct. This was a man who played

Frank Zappa during his lectures, a man who screened *Road Runner* cartoons in his Modern Drama Class, a man who once cited Spiderman as an example of a tragic hero. The faculty grumbled about academic standards; students stood in line overnight to register for his classes.

During class Shaun usually filled his notebook with cross-eyed pictures of Gross stuffing students into a mouth filled with shark teeth. Perhaps this was because Gross had never once taken the time to chat with his lowly research assistant. Shaun liked to think it was because he had tumbled to the fact that Gross was an intellectual lightweight and a fraud. Shaun had been horrified when Gross had served up Shakespeare—Shaun's hero—on a Day-Glo platter with an absurdist apple in his mouth. Shaun was old-fashioned that way: he thought dead writers deserved better than to be hacked up by modern ax grinders. But the real reason Shaun disliked Gross was that he suspected the man of sleeping with Myrna Rosny.

". . . and yet, what does Faustus do with this supreme power? A few parlor tricks, some practical jokes on the Pope. Oh yes, he has Mephistopheles fetch him grapes out of season. Look, if someone gives you three wishes, you're not going to use one of them to send out for sausage pizza and a six pack! What you have to understand about Faustus is this: he's not a hero, he's a *schmuck!*"

Shaun shook his head in disgust; the class reacted as predictably as a laugh track.

"That's all for today, people. We'll finish up *Faustus* next time. I have your papers here—" he dropped them on the desk top, "—you can pick them up on your way out."

Shaun joined the crush of students sorting through the stack. He saw Myrna's: an *A* for "Midsummer Night's Madness." Someone passed Shaun his "Faustfeathers" without comment. Gross had given him a big blue *F*, and under it had written: "Dear Mr. Reed, you ought to have waited until we covered this in class. See me."

F. F! Shaun could not believe it. He returned to his chair fuming, waiting until the crowd of ass-kissers had cleared away from Gross. Myrna sat next to Shaun and shot an inquiring glance his way. Shaun turned the paper face down on the desk and ignored her. She waited with him. Finally Gross came down the aisle to them.

"Hello, Myrna," he said. "Are we still on for tonight?"

Shaun could not believe it. He had to restrain himself from slugging the guy. "You wanted to see me?" he said.

"Did I?" Gross looked blank and Shaun showed him the paper. "Oh, yes." He sighed; his breath smelled like a burning Christmas tree. "Well, Mr. Reed, it seems to me that you do not take the Marx Brothers at all seriously. Which leads me to suspect that you do not take this course seriously. Am I wrong?"

"They were comedians! They didn't take themselves seriously. Besides, you gave me an *F*! God damn it, people hand in papers written in crayon and the worst you give them is a *B*."

Gross gave him a patronizing smile. "It would seem that you have two choices. Either write your next paper in crayon—burnt umber looks nice this time of year—or drop the course." He turned to Myrna. "Why don't we get an early start? Catch a quick bite at Nicky's and then over to my place?"

"No," she said, and Shaun fell in love with her. The look of surprise that flickered across Gross's face was worth fifty *F*'s. "Not tonight, Murray. Maybe another time."

"Surely." He was stiff and as brittle as an icicle. "Another time."

They were still sitting there when he left. Myrna reached out to take his hand. "I'm sorry if it was because of me."

Later they went back to his room, smoked enough dope to float a hot air balloon to the moon and made love. Shaun forgot to ask her to wear the hat. She fell asleep after the third time, the curve of her spine against his belly. He lay awake listening to her breathing. Someone far away, in another room of the dorm, was laughing.

Shaun wondered if he were hallucinating. Nothing like this

had ever happened to him before. He had satisfied his fiercest desire. Life was perfect—almost. For even as he drifted on a sea of sexual and chemical bliss, he was still thinking about that damned paper.

Faustfeathers

"Reed, wake up!"

Reed started and almost fell off his stool. He had been dreaming he was in the arms of fair Helen. Instead, his master Faustus was glaring at him. "If you're going to sleep, do it in class with all the other students."

"Be not too hard on the youth, good doctor," said Frater Albergus. "I'm sure our conversation is a little arcane for him."

Faustus turned his glittering spectacles, and his displeasure, on the visitor from Rome. "If I can stay awake listening to you, so can he." He tapped his cup on the table. "More wine, boy!"

Albergus seemed resolutely determined not to take offense. Reed did not trust this so-called scholar. He suspected that the man was a papist, despite the fact that he paid lip service to the reforms of the great Luther. He had been trying to draw Doctor Faustus into a discussion of magic all evening.

"So tell me, learned Faustus," said the Italian, as Reed refilled his cup with hock, "what is the nature of this—this 'seegar' you burn here? Albert Magnus speaks of securing rooms against evil spirits by burning certain herbs, but he advocates the use of a brazier. Does not this smoke taste noxious to the palate?"

Faustus rested his head on his hand, the cigar jutting from between two fingers beside his ear. His expression was melancholy. "I've had better, but you won't be able to get them for a couple of hundred years. I just smoke these ropes to drive the bugs away. Have one."

It was getting late, but rather than retire with the other students, Reed settled back onto his stool in the corner of Faustus's study to watch the great masters match wits. Perhaps *he* might learn something that would help him to still the passion in his heart.

Albergus examined a cigar suspiciously.

"Are you going to smoke that thing or eat it?" said Faustus. "Go ahead, you can pay me later."

"Pay you?"

"So, it's money you're after!" Faustus blew smoke at him. His huge black eyebrows arched. "You know, these cigars would cost a couple of marks on the open market. Of course, it's closed now, so you're left to your own devices. You did bring your devices, didn't you? If not, we'll have to get Reed here to help you."

"Magister," said Reed, "I . . ."

Faustus cut him off with a wave and leaned across the table to light Albergus's cigar. "Pay no attention to him," said Faustus. "He's just the love interest."

"Love interest?" Albergus inhaled and started to cough.

"What's the matter? Doesn't the pope ever let you step out?"

"The pope?" Albergus licked his lips nervously. "My dear Faustus, do not insult me. I may only be an itinerant scholar, but I've come all the way from Rome to sit at your feet and learn."

"As long as you're down there, how about shining those shoes?"

"You treat me as if I were a mountebank."

"Oh, high finance, eh? Well, money means nothing here, my friend. You'll learn soon enough that a little Latin goes a long way in this university. There used to be a little Latin around here, but he went away. That's how I got this job. You look a little Latin yourself, and I wish you'd gone with him. You young scholars want to dance to the music without paying the piper. And what does it get you? Asparagus, or contract bridge. But a card like you could care less who holds the bridge contract, as long as you can pass water under it. Speaking of contracts, do you really think you're going to get your hands on mine?"

Frater Albergus looked stunned. Reed realized then that Faustus knew exactly who the man was and why he had come. "I'm sure I don't know what you are talking about!"

"If you're so sure, why aren't you rich? You brute! No, don't try to apologize."

"I didn't come here to be insulted."

"This is a good place for it. Where do you usually go?"

Albergus stood, sweating. "I beg your pardon, learned Faustus, I—"

"I can't pardon you. You'll have to talk to the pope. Too bad, I hear he's not much of an audience. Something of a dreamer, if you believe everything you hear. Well, it's certainly been a pleasure talking to myself this evening. I must visit myself more often. As for you, sir, I want you to remember that scholarship is as scholarship does, and neither does my wife, if I had one, which I don't. Nor do my children, if I had any, who would be proud of me for saying so. Now get out and never darken my towels again!"

Faustus struck a pose of injured dignity. His lower lip was thrust out beneath his mustache and his spectacles shone in the candlelight. Reed recognized his cue and applauded, all the time dreaming of the day he would defy Faustus's haphazard will.

Something was rotten in the city of Wittenberg, and Albergus suspected that it was in the pocket of the more sloppy of the two sloppy men he summoned to his room at the Boar's Bollocks the next morning. The man's face was round and empty as the full moon, and from ten feet away he smelled like a Sicilian fishmonger. From five feet away he smelled like the fish. His floppy hat perched on a nest of red hair.

His companion's hat was black and came to a point that hinted at a pointed skull beneath it. His coat was shabby and two sizes too small, and he wore a look of small-minded guile.

"Noble Robin and gentle Dicolini, welcome!" Albergus extended his hand.

Robin loped forward and shook it vigorously. His grasp was cold and clammy, and when Albergus got free he found himself holding a dead carp. He recoiled and dropped it. Robin looked offended.

"Atsa some joke, eh boss?" said Dicolini.

"Gentlemen, gentlemen." Albergus forced himself to remain calm. "Let us speak of our business. I have called you here because you are brother scholars, acquainted with the university, and students of Doctor Faustus. I have also heard that you are available for delicate work and for a reasonable fee can keep your mouths shut. I trust I have not been misled?"

"I keepa my mouth shut for nothing," Dicolini said. "Robin, his mouth cost extra." Robin stuck out his tongue, on which a price was painted.

Frater Albergus debated whether to dismiss them and seek help elsewhere. He was the pope's private astrologer, commissioned to conduct an inquisition into certain practical jokes and magical assaults which the pontiff had recently suffered. Only a sorcerer in league with the devil would dare commit such acts. Albergus's investigation had led him to Wittenberg and Faustus, and now that he had assessed the situation he intended to nail the upstart alchemist in record time. "Gentlemen, let me be frank."

"Frank, Sam, Joe—makesa no difference to us as long as we get paid."

Albergus swallowed and began again. "I want you to find out how Faustus spends his evenings. Does he practice black magic? Is he in league with infernal forces? And I need proof, the sooner the better. Should you do this for me, your investigation shall receive such thanks as fits a king's remembrance."

Dicolini looked suspicious. "How much you gonna pay?"

Albergus smiled. "I'll pay you ten silver pieces."

"We a-no want no pieces. We want the whole thing." Robin honked his agreement like a herniated goose.

Albergus was taken aback. "Another ten pieces, then, if you provide me with the information I need. That's all."

"How do we know thatsa all?"

"What?"

"Look, we shadow Faustus for you, how we gonna know when you give us ten pieces thatsa the whole thing?"

"But I'm offering you twenty pieces for shadowing Faustus."

"See what I mean? First you gotta ten pieces, now you gotta twenty pieces, but we no gotta the whole thing."

"You shadow Faustus, and then we'll talk about the whole thing."

"You no understand. Suppose I drop a vase, itsa break. How many pieces I got? I don't know; I gotta count them. Now you give me ten pieces, you give me twenty pieces, I still don't have them all, maybe. I shatter vase, we shadow Faustus, itsa same thing: we no gonna do the job unless we know we gotta the whole thing."

As Albergus and Dicolini haggled, Robin crept behind them. He drew another carp from the folds of his ragged cloak and slipped it onto Albergus's chair.

By this time Dicolini had bumped the spy rental rate up to thirty silver pieces a day. Albergus's face was red from argument. He drew a kerchief from his sleeve, mopped his brow and sat down to catch his breath. A moment later he let out a strangled cry and leapt from the chair, cracking his knee against the table. He picked up the fish with two fingers and held it at arm's length.

"What's this?" he demanded.

Robin whipped out his sword and lunged, impaling the carp and the sleeve of Albergus's doublet. Albergus fell back and slipped on the first carp. His arms flew up, jerking Robin toward him. Dicolini caught Albergus under the shoulders, and Robin, with a honk, sprawled on top of him.

"Atsa fish," Dicolini said.

Albergus struggled out of Dicolini's grasp and tried in vain to draw the sword from his sleeve. Unfortunately, Robin's hand was caught in the guard. By the time Robin had freed himself, the sword's pommel was wedged under the clasp that held Albergus's cloak closed around his neck. The guard pressed his throat and his arm stretched out along the length of the blade as if tied to a splint. The point pricked the palm of his hand. Chin forced high into the air, Albergus whirled about like a manic signpost. The two students eyed him warily.

"Take it easy, boss," said Dicolini. "We get you out."

Robin leapt on Albergus's back and shoved a hand down his collar. Albergus staggered. Dicolini pulled him over onto the table. He lay spread-eagled while Robin got hold of the sword and began to draw it through the collar of his cloak. The blade slid across Albergus's neck. They were going to cut his throat!

"Atta boy, Robbie!" Dicolini said, sitting on the inquisitor's arm.

Albergus held his breath, not daring to cry out. He felt the rapier tickle his beard. The pressure on his neck eased as the blade slid by. The putrid carp caught against his upthrust chin. Then the sword was gone and the fish lay across his throat. He let out a huge breath. He was covered with sweat.

Robin shook hands with Dicolini.

"Gentlemen," said Albergus, as he tugged his clothes and his dignity back into order. "I trust we are in agreement now? You'll do this piece of work for me?"

"We do the whole thing," said Dicolini. Robin honked.

"Splendid." He steered them quickly to the door, his arms around their shoulders.

"We gotta go now," Dicolini said. "We're gonna be late for the classes we wanna miss."

"My apologies. Just make sure you bring me something I can use against Faustus."

Robin offered him a thumbscrew, but Albergus declined.

Although he sat taking notes in the front row of Doctor Faustus's afternoon alchemy class, Reed's mind was not on the lecture. Still, in his position he had to feign interest. Doctor Faustus strode back and forth in front of the lecture hall in his strange long-legged lope, his black academic gown swirling behind him. At the desk next to Reed, Albergus listened raptly.

Reed had thought that being accepted as Faustus's student would be the beginning of the prestige he had always coveted. He longed for only two things. The first was to command the arcane powers that his master alone understood—to unravel the riddles of the sphinx, to change the world with a word! Instead Reed found himself caught in a nightmare: Faustus never seemed to take him or anything else seriously. Only the other day Faustus had humiliated Reed in front of the class by giving him the wrong spell and then demanding he conjure up a griffin. When within the magic circle had appeared a chicken, Faustus had accused Reed of fowl play.

The second thing Reed longed for was love. Yes, he wanted to learn the secrets of the universe, but he would never have put up with Faustus's infantile jokes had he not by chance glimpsed Helen of Troy in the doctor's bedchamber one evening. To succumb to the charms of the women of Wittenberg after seeing the fiery-tressed Helen would have been like settling for porridge after the promise of roast mutton. With onions.

Doctor Faustus had drawn a curtain at the front of the hall to expose an elaborate chart of the human head marked with astrological notation.

"Here we have a drawing of the astral mind in the fourth quarter of the phrenological year." Faustus tapped the top of the head with a pointer. "You'll note the eruptions at the zenith. These eruptions can be cleared up with fulminate of mercury, but the woman only comes on Tuesday afternoons. The rest of the week you have to take care of yourself, if you know what's good for you."

There was a crash in the corner of the classroom. Faustus turned on the two students who sprawled facedown on the floor. One had tripped over the other, who had tripped over his sword while sneaking into the room.

Faustus rocked back on his heels, hands folded behind his back. "Late for class again, eh?"

As the two students slid into their seats in the front row, a chicken burst out of Robin's cloak. He grabbed for it, but the unfortunate creature shot from his arms and skittered across Faustus's lectern. Robin dove after, scattering Faustus's notes, caught the squawking fowl and shoved it deep into an interior pocket.

"We a-no late," said Dicolini.

Faustus stormed over to them. "Why, the town clock struck not five minutes ago. It's half past three!"

"No it's not."

Robin pulled an hourglass from somewhere in his bottomless cloak and waved it at Faustus. All the sand was in the bottom of the glass.

"See? We're right on time," said Dicolini.

"Not according to that," Faustus said.

"Atsa run a little fast. She'sa use quicksand."

"Oh, no. You can't fool me that easily. It must be four o'clock by that hourglass."

"Then class is over. Let's go, Robbie." Dicolini got up to leave.

"Hold on, Macduff. I'm not done with this lecture yet."

"Too bad. We're done listening."

"Well, you can forget about leaving until *my* clock strikes four. Time is money, and my time is worth a couple of marks. You boys look like a couple of marks. Are you brothers?"

Robin was insulted. He huffed and he puffed as if he were about to go berserk.

FREEDOM BEACH

"My friend, hesa get pretty mad," said Dicolini. "You better watch out or he give you a piece of his mind."

"No thanks. I wouldn't want to take the last piece."

"Atsa okay. He won't notice."

"Well, if you say so." Faustus reached for Robin's arm. "Come up here, young man." Somehow, the doctor found himself holding the student's thigh; he dropped it in disgust. "Let's take a look at your skull."

Robin pulled a glowing skull from the cloak and presented it to the doctor. The entire class recoiled in horror—save Faustus, who calmly popped the jaws open, stuck his cigar through the mouth and relit it from the candle burning inside. He tossed the skull over his shoulder, stood Robin in front of his chart and backed off a step to appraise him. With his pale, round face, Robin looked about as intelligent as a hard-boiled egg.

Faustus tapped the pointer against Robin's head. "The astral mind is responsible for contact with the spiritual world without the intervention of either seraphim or cherubim. You all know what a seraph is, don't you?"

Dicolini stood proudly. "Sure. On my pancakes, I like a maple seraph."

"No, no. Cherubs, seraphs."

"I no like a cherub. I like a maple."

"These aren't food—they're angels."

"I no like angel food, either."

"Well, that takes the cake. Where was I?" Faustus turned back to Robin. "Oh, yes—the astral mind."

Robin was rubbing up against the chart like a cat.

"Let's forget about the astral mind. That's obviously not relevant to this subject. Don't let me wake you, now. I'm not offending you by talking, am I?"

Robin honked.

"Gesundheit. Moving south from the astral mind, we come to the inferior regions of the intellect. And when I say inferior, I mean inferior. The inferior mind, as you'll remember from our last lecture, is responsible for worldly thought: for instance how did your nose get that way, and wasn't that a great plague we had last month. Worldly thought, of course, must be processed by one of the other organs before it becomes definable in emotional terms. The heart, for instance, controls affection, the liver, love and the spleen, anger. Who can tell us what the kidneys control?"

Dicolini rose again. "The kidneys keep their legs from bending backward."

Faustus leaned toward Albergus. "Do you hear voices?" Dicolini looked about him to accept the congratulations of his fellow students. Faustus turned on him. "That's good, Dicolini. If I had a couple of more students like you boys I could change gold to base metal."

Reed longed for the end of class so that he could return to his room to think his thoughts of Helen in private. Robin, left to himself behind the podium, pretended *he* was the lecturer. He opened the book in front of him, and a small cloud of dust billowed from the ancient pages. Robin took out his kerchief with a flourish, sneezed into it and then blew his nose with a sound that was not quite as loud as the Emperor's fanfare. At that moment there was a flash of light, a smell of sulphur, and an imp appeared on the edge of the podium. Its tiny red eyes glowed and its barbed tail lashed with impatience. Albergus gasped. Faustus stubbed his cigar out on Dicolini's hat. Robin's face lit with delight. He held out his hand to the imp.

"Oh no you don't!" Faustus said.

"Come on, Robbie!" Dicolini yelled.

The imp leapt onto Robin's shoulder. Faustus and Robin danced back and forth on opposite sides of the lectern. Robin made a dash for the door and, once he was through, Dicolini slammed it in Faustus's face. Faustus paced angrily back to the lectern, whirled and pointed a finger at Reed.

"As your punishment, you will bring that demon back to me by midnight."

Shocked, Reed struggled from his seat. "But, magister, I didn't do anything!"

Faustus shrugged. "Since when has that ever made any difference around here?"

* * *

When he thirsts, he'll get hot bile. Twenty-four years of serving Faustus had taken its toll on Mephistopheles. When he fell from heaven, he knew he was in for a poorer class of associate, but he didn't think it could get this low. This *was* hell, nor was he out of it.

"Midnight tonight, noble Faustus," he said. "Then do the jaws of hell open to receive thee." Mephistopheles separated his hands as if parting a curtain, revealing a vision of Dis, the city of hell, and the souls in torment there.

"You're not much of a travel agent," said Faustus. "'See Dis and die.'"

"In your case, it will be the other way around."

Faustus rocked back on his heels. "Dis ain't no joke."

Grubs on the eyeballs. Maybe he would start him with that. But perhaps he had been wrong to remind Faustus of his approaching damnation. Mephistopheles dissolved the vision of hell. No sense putting this project at risk.

"By the way," said Faustus, "have you seen Helen lately?"

"In your closet."

"In my closet! What's she doing in there?"

"You told her to get in."

"I did?" Faustus crossed his arms and rubbed his chin. "Oh, yes. Literal girl. Thank heaven for literal girls."

"Heaven had nothing to do with it."

"You're not kidding."

"Shall I have her dress?"

"It wouldn't fit you. Work on your thighs."

When he hungers I'll feed him his intestines.

Faustus paced back and forth. "So she's in the closet, eh? And here I stand, bantering with the servants. Get her out here pronto. If she won't come, call for me and I'll go in after her. If I don't come back, you can have my astrolabe."

"Worry not about Helen, Faustus. If she disobeys you, I'll cull thee out the wildest frauleins in the north of Europe."

"The cull of the wild, eh? Sounds like a bunch of dogs to me. And who's going to clean up after them, tell me that!"

An eon buried up to his neck in boiling shit.

"Look," said Faustus, "I want you to keep your eye on

Reed for me. I think he wants to examine Helen's thesis. Can you imagine the consequences if she managed to seduce that boy? Why, she's been dead for two thousand years! What would his mother say? What would *I* say?"

Mephistopheles would have sighed if it had been necessary for him to breath. "What would you say?"

"Is that true that you wash your hair in clam broth?"

A codpiece of burning iron.

Reed told the porter, Martin, that he needed to prepare Faustus's rooms for dinner. He snuck up to the doctor's apartments with the intention of searching Faustus's magic book for a spell that might help him retrieve the imp. But before he could properly search the common room, he heard voices from the study, growing louder. In a panic he rushed into the bedroom and jumped into the closet.

The tiny room was pitch dark. In hope of concealing himself further, he pushed behind the hanging clothes. As he did, he stumbled over some boots. But instead of falling, he was caught by someone's arms!

'Mrrumph!" he cried. "Who is that?"

"At last, a visitor!" a woman's voice replied. "It is I, Helen."

"Helen!" Suddenly Reed had difficulty breathing. He forgot about the imp. "Helen! Just who I've been looking for. I must see you."

"And here I am without a candle."

"No one can hold a candle to you. I need you, Helen. You cannot know what torture it has been imagining what Faustus has been doing with you."

"Is that why you came into the closet?"

"I was looking for a missing imp, but now that I've found you I'll search no more." Reed grasped her shoulders and pulled her toward him. "Sweet Helen, make me immortal with a kiss." His nose wrinkled. "Do you smell burning sulphur?"

"You should never eat radishes."

She drew Reed's head down to her breast; he thought he had died and gone to paradise. "I'm so glad you found me," Helen said. "I had no idea you even knew I existed. But you must go now."

"Go? But I just got here!"

"Nevertheless—"she pried him loose"—Faustus is due to return soon. If he found you here, his jealousy would know no bounds. Come back later, fair student. Faustus will be gone until midnight. Return at ten and I will show you arts of which I alone am master. Until then, speak not of this closet!"

"Ten? How can I wait that long, thinking of you?"

"Troilus was wont to use cold baths and strenuous exercise. Until ten, my love!" She propelled him through the door.

Reed stood in the middle of the bedroom, dazed. It seemed like he had entered only seconds before. Ten o'clock. Resignedly, he peeked through the door to Faustus's common room. No one. He might as well keep looking for the imp. His heart full of Helen, he snuck out of the apartments.

Robin's conjuring of the demon had been enough for Frater Albergus; such magical prowess, conferred on an idiot through mere inspection of Faustus's magical book, was evidence enough to squeeze a conviction out of the tribunal. However, Albergus was no longer content merely to bring Faustus to spiritual justice; he wanted that book for his own. To control a power that could rival even that of the dreamers—to mold men's dreams like clay—the thought was enough to make him tremble like a stallion in spring.

He sat at a table in the corner of the Boar's Bollocks plotting how to break into Faustus's rooms that night.

"Pardon me, frater." It was the student Reed. "I'm still looking for those two, Robin and Dicolini. Have you seen them?"

"Not since they fled your master's lecture."

Reed looked melancholy. He sat next to Albergus, shoulders slumped. "I've exhausted myself searching—to no avail. I thought they were my friends, but now they seem more interested in other matters."

"A sad breach of faith." Albergus wondered if he could use

this limp fool to his advantage. "Is there anything a fellow scholar can do?"

"Nothing. Unless *you* can retrieve the imp that Robin called up."

The stars were with him! "I am not without some magical prowess," Albergus said casually. "Perhaps I can locate it. Not only that, but if you can tell me when Faustus will be away, I can deposit the creature—caged—in his rooms. It would make a good joke, don't you think? Especially after the shameful way he treated you today."

Reed looked like a puppy in a butcher's shop. "If you could do that, I'd . . . I'd have all that I desire!"

"You have only to ask."

"Yes, good frater, *oh please!* Faustus told me he would not be home until midnight tonight. If you can arrive before then . . ."

"I shall be there at ten."

Reed looked worried. "Better make it eleven. Eleven-thirty? I have affairs . . . uh . . . business—I will let you in."

Albergus rested a hand on his shoulder. "Of course, we must be discreet. The doctor must never learn of my part in this."

Reed shook the inquisitor's hand vigorously, his despair vanquished. Now the student stood as erect as a groom on his wedding day. He left whistling.

There would be nothing Reed could do when Albergus showed up with a mouthful of excuses rather than the imp. Once the inquisitor had gained access to the doctor's apartments, the case against Faustus would be unassailable and the magic book would be his. Still, it would be a delicate operation; he would have to be careful not to compromise himself. The student Reed was no problem; Albergus would have him arrested with Faustus and they would burn on the same pyre. But Albergus could not afford to be recognized by some ostler or serving man when he stole the book. A disguise! He rubbed his hands together and smiled. A false mustache, a change of clothing and he himself could impersonate Faustus. Brilliant! He was so pleased with himself that he decided to go immediately and ask the bishop of Wittenberg to assemble an ecclesiastical tribunal. He left a few pfennigs and half a tankard of ale on the table.

As soon as he was out the door Robin and Dicolini emerged from beneath the table, where they had been playing cards. Dicolini drained the inquisitor's ale in two gulps and pocketed the tankard. Robin picked up the coins and bit through one. He chewed thoughtfully for a moment, then pulled a salt shaker from his pocket, gave the other half a liberal sprinkle and popped it into his mouth.

"You hear that, Robbie? That Icebergus, hesa cross-double us. Hesa break the case himself and keep alla pieces. We gonna have to get tough."

Robin thrust one fist under Dicolini's nose; his other arm went into a windmill windup. Dicolini kicked him in the shin.

"Whatsa matter for you! Getta tough with him, not me! Now listen, we gotta move fast and get to Faustus's place first. Before the boss, you understand, before Reed, before anybody! We get there so early we be there even before we arrive!"

Robin honked in approval.

Reed arrived at the door to the courtyard and knocked. Martin, who had been drinking the master's hock since matins, shuffled out of his tiny room into the cold of the evening and opened the door.

"My services are again needed in the apartment of Doctor Faustus," Reed told him. He passed through the courtyard and up the stairs. Quietly, he tried the door to Faustus's room and found it unlocked. The common room was dark; he lit a candle and opened the bedroom door a crack. It seemed that no one was about. He closed the door behind him and took the bundle from beneath his arm. The sight of it made him laugh at his own cleverness. For he would this very night disguise himself as Faustus and, in his taskmaster's own bed, sample pleasures he had reserved for himself alone. How Helen would laugh! He slipped into a nightshirt and cap, painting a broad greasepaint version of Faustus's mustache beneath his nose. How sweet his revenge against the cruel scholar! He donned a stolen pair of the doctor's spectacles and sidled over to the closet.

"Helen!" He opened the door and stood at the threshold.

"Darling!" Helen gasped, throwing her arms around his neck. Her ardor surprised him; he wondered if she had remembered their date. "Don't worry—it's me, Reed. You can come out now."

Helen froze. "Oh!"

"What's the matter?"

"Reed! I thought you were him . . . I forgot to tell you that I can't come out of the closet until Faustus says I can. After all, I am at his command." She smiled sheepishly. "Would you like to come in?"

Just then he thought he heard a noise in the next room. Reed rushed into the closet and slammed the door. Helen pressed against him. Maybe the closet was not so bad after all.

They listened. Through the closed door they could hear Faustus's muffled voice. "Now where's my nightshirt? I thought I left it lying around here somewhere. Are you still in there?"

"Who?" said Helen.

"Unless you've got an owl in there, Helen of Troy."

Reed nudged Helen frantically. "What owl?" she asked. "There's no owl in here."

"Owl take your word for it. Does one of you birds want to hand me my nightshirt?"

Reed pawed through the clothes until he found a nightshirt. He gave it to Helen and she opened the door a crack to hand it out. Faustus peeked in.

"Hope it isn't too boring in there."

"Not yet. I wouldn't mind some fresh air once in a while."

Faustus sniffed. "The air in there smells pretty fresh already. Or maybe it's my undershirt. Would you like a book to read?"

"No, thank you."

Faustus closed the door and Reed breathed a sigh of relief.

He listened closely and heard Faustus leave the bedroom. Just then the clock struck the quarter hour and he jumped in surprise.

"I thought you said Faustus would be out tonight."

Helen placed her small hands on his chest. "Did I?"

Reed decided not to pursue her sin of deception but to concentrate on other, more interesting, sins. He warmed to the task, but the more excited he got, the less Helen responded. "Noble queen . . ." he said.

"I'm sorry, but I can't get in the mood lying on old shoes. Can't you find some way to let me out of here?"

Reed struggled to control his passion. He would need a miracle . . . Faustus's magic book! It had to contain a spell to release her. "Wait here," he said and slipped out.

"Okay, Robbie. You tug onna rope and I'll get in through the window." It had taken Robin and Dicolini longer than they had expected to sneak their cart up the alley and get a rope looped around one of the joists that jutted out below the eaves of Faustus's apartments. One end was tied around Dicolini; Robin held the other. "Keep a lookout," said Dicolini. "If anybody comes, whistle."

Outside the courtyard gate, Albergus could wait no longer. Though it was only ten-thirty, he had to get that book! He donned his Faustus disguise of greasepaint mustache, spectacles and black academic robes and pounded at the courtyard door. Martin, woozy with drink, was fooled.

Albergus mounted the stairs, stepped cautiously into Faustus's rooms and began to search. He poked his head into the bedroom; it appeared to be empty. The trunk at the foot of the bed held only clothing. He opened the closet door.

"Darling!" Albergus was seized around the neck, smothered by the touch and scent of an almost-naked woman. He recoiled, trembling. Who knew what incubus or succubus this creature might be?

"Can I come out of the closet, dearest? Then will I fulfill your every desire."

"Back, hell fiend!" Albergus squeaked. He slammed the door.

He wiped the sweat from his brow and then stiffened. There was a scraping at the window. Someone was trying to break in! He slipped out of the bedroom.

Dicolini fumbled with the window, his feet braced on the snowy sill. It opened and he fell into the room. He untied himself, peeked out of the bedroom door, then drew back to decide on his next move. On top of the open trunk lay a long nightshirt. Dicolini snapped his fingers. He quickly removed his boots, rolled up his trousers and put on the shirt and a stocking cap. He found several containers of unguents and potions on the bedside table; he chose the blackest and painted a broad mustache under his nose.

Thus disguised, he was about to sneak into the next room when he heard a woman's voice from the closet.

"Is that you?"

He stood stock still. "Maybe."

"Please let me out of here."

"Who are you?"

"Don't be silly. You know who I am."

"Itsa slip my mind."

"Well," said Helen sarcastically. "I'm the most beautiful woman in history."

"Never mind coming out. I come in." Dicolini ran into the closet.

"Darling!" She threw her arms around his neck.

Reed frantically searched Faustus's study, every moment expecting to be discovered. His precious hour with Helen was dwindling fast. And Albergus was due at eleven-thirty! Reed would just have to ignore his arrival. But if Faustus answered the door, what would Albergus tell him? For that matter, where *was* Faustus?

The clock in the rathaus tower struck eleven. Reed cursed his evil luck and pawed through the papers on Faustus's writing table. Why couldn't anything run smoothly? The world ought to make more sense than this. It was just not fair! Reed was about to give up on the desk when he noticed the corner of a piece of parchment poking from between it and the wall. He drew it out. It was some sort of contract. He was trying to make out the Latin in the flickering lamplight when the door opened. He dove under the desk.

Albergus entered the study, peered about cautiously and began searching the desk. Finding nothing of interest, he turned to the bookshelves. Reed, watching him, wondered why Faustus should creep so stealthily through his own rooms—unless there was some supernatural danger abroad. He drew himself farther beneath the desk and shoved the contract inside his shirt.

Eleven-fifteen. Albergus had been lost behind the stacks of books for what seemed an eternity. Reed was gathering his courage to sneak back into the bedroom when another Faustus, in nightshirt and cap, entered the study. Reed nearly swallowed his tongue. Albergus cursed and watched in silence, hidden by the shelves.

Muttering to himself, Faustus went to the desk and sorted through the papers as if he had lost something. He pulled manuscripts from the scroll rack above the desk. His knees were inches from Reed's nose. At last he found the cigars he had been looking for. There was a crash in the next room.

"Mice!" Faustus exclaimed, dashing behind a table covered with an alchemical experiment.

In the bedroom, Dicolini had long since released Helen from the closet. He was willing to forget about Robin, Faustus, the known world if Helen would only prove as willing.

"*Bella fellisima ronzoni, alla pacino,*" Dicolini said, pressing her toward the bed.

"My lord, you know I don't understand Latin."

"Atsa not Latin, atsa Italian."

"I don't understand Italian, either."

"Atsa okay. Neither do I."

Helen resisted, as if she had begun to suspect that this was not Doctor Faustus and was wondering if she ought to get back into the closet. The two fell wrestling across the bed.

Down in the alley, Robin was freezing. He had tacked to his cart a page torn from a library book: a woodcut depicting a cheery fire in a brick hearth. He huddled next to it. As he flapped his arms before the illustrated flames, the imp, which had taken up residence on his shoulder, woke and bit Robin's neck. Robin leapt about in agony, slapping at his shoulder. The imp popped out of his cloak and raced up the rope. Robin whistled for it to come down. The imp ignored his gestures and scurried through the window.

Robin ran about frantically, then stopped. A wild gleam came into his eye. He rummaged through the cart until he found a nightshirt, cap and spectacles. He smeared some grease from the axle under his nose, and thus disguised, climbed the rope after his pet.

He dropped in through the window, eyes bulging at the sight of Dicolini and Helen on the bed. Dicolini had lost the advantage of surprise in their wrestling match. The most beautiful woman in history had her foot on his neck; his arms were pinned beneath him. Robin approached cautiously and stared as if trying to figure out what exactly was going on and how he might join in.

"Faustus!" Dicolini exclaimed. Robin looked over his shoulder in alarm. Helen released Dicolini, who scrambled from the room; she smiled tentatively at Robin.

His smile was as wide as the crescent moon.

"Darling!" She opened her arms to him.

Robin's horn honked as he leapt on top of her.

Mephistopheles had not spent four million years in damnation for nothing. He was getting an early start from hell; he knew how tricky these souls got as their time approached. He materialized, wrapped in flames and clouds of sulphurous smoke, in the common room just as Dicolini hurtled out of the bedroom. Unable to stop, Dicolini ran headlong into him. The two of them sprawled across Faustus's dining table with a crash.

Mephistopheles sprang up and ran his claw through the snakes growing from his scalp. "Your time is nigh, mortal. You will pay dearly for your sins."

Dicolini's face was a mask of dismay. "I never touched her, boss. Shesa better man than I am."

"You insist on playing the fool even now?"

"No. Hesa still down inna street."

Mephistopheles restrained himself: only a few more minutes until midnight. He left the quaking man and went to question Helen.

Robin and Helen were rolling around on the bed. Helen struggled against this latest imposter, their wrestling punctuated by the honks of Robin's horn as it pressed against her thigh.

Mephistopheles was nonplussed by this second Faustus. He strode over to the bed, claws clicking on the bare wooden floor. Robin looked up to see the devil's eyes glowing like coals in the darkness. He leapt from the bed and scurried into the closet.

"It will avail Faustus nothing to hide in the closet."

Helen appeared relieved to see the Prince of Darkness instead of another mustached lover. "I don't think that's Faustus," she said.

"Who is it then?"

"I don't know, but I've seen a lot of him lately."

Mephistopheles was suspicious. "Don't tell me *you've* succumbed to Faustus. Are you doing his bidding?"

"You find him and I'll try."

"Where is he?"

"Hang around a while. He'll turn up. Or else somebody just as good."

Dicolini had fled from the common to the study. Faustus, seeing his double enter the room, got up from behind the table.

"So it's you, is it?"

"Atsa crazy," Dicolini said. "Itsa no me. Itsa you."

"How do I know it's me?"

"I already told you itsa you. I'm not here."

Faustus puffed his cigar and thought this over. "If you're me, then how come you're not smoking a cigar?"

"You no give me one."

Faustus whipped a cigar out of his pocket. "There you go. Let's see you get out of that one."

"You got a match?"

"Never mind the cigar." Faustus took it back.

It was too much for Reed; he thought he saw a chance to escape. He crawled across the room and had gained the doorway when Faustus spotted him.

"Hold on there!" Faustus shouted. "I can't get away from me that easily."

Reed scrambled up and shot out through the common to the bedroom. He did not look back.

Albergus had watched all of this with astonishment. Dopplegangers! Faustus was indeed a master of the black arts. Yet he could not fathom the doctor's reason for putting on this show—unless Faustus knew that Albergus was in his apartments, disguised as Faustus. Albergus reasoned from this that he was close to finding something that Faustus did not want discovered. He was about to renew his search when he saw something move on a bottom shelf. A rat. No. It was the imp! The tiny demon beckoned to him with its delicate clawed hand.

In his panicky retreat Reed went right past Helen on the bed to the closet. "Darling!" he gasped, throwing his arms around the figure in the darkness.

A large sloppy kiss was planted on his neck. She was so much more substantial than he remembered. But there was something queer . . . the closet was filled with the odor of rotting fish. He pulled her closer and she honked.

He was hugging another Faustus! As he fell back in dismay, he heard Helen's voice from outside. "What are you doing in there?"

He opened the door and dragged Robin out behind him. The

latter's face was split by a shy smile; he beamed up at Reed the way a schoolgirl beams at her secret love. Helen lay on the bed. Reed booted Robin out of the room and slammed the door.

Helen was his at last! She beckoned him, her breasts heaving like the soft hills of the Peloponnesus during a minor earthquake. Her hips were a lyre playing ancient music; her long red hair lay spread across the pillow. He looked deep into her green eyes and felt as if he were drowning in some warm Aegean lagoon. She was a dream, a beautiful dream. If the power that ran the universe were just, Reed would finally satisfy the desire that burned in him so fiercely.

The rathaus clock struck eleven forty-five.

Mephistopheles had rendered himself invisible until he could decide which Faustus was his. He let one crawl from the study and stayed to hear the remaining two argue. He was not pleased with the possibility that he might make the wrong choice. He was sure that the contract had no clause to cover such a contingency, and the dreamers would brook no excuses. As the minutes ticked away, the thought that his revenge might even now be thwarted stoked his anger to an inferno of rage. He would have to shock one of them into an admission. He moved between Faustus and Dicolini and materialized.

"Oh, so you're back, eh?" the two of them said simultaneously.

"Your doom is at hand."

"Right hand or left?"

The clock in the rathaus tower began to strike midnight just as Robin popped into the room carrying a slice of bread. He went over to Faustus's alchemical experiment, dipped his finger into a salve compounded of cinnabar and verdigris, spread it across the bread and took a bite. He nodded in pleasure and offered the sandwich to Faustus.

"No thanks. It's bad enough being damned. A colic I don't need."

"Enough!" the archfiend shouted. Albergus, who had been so absorbed in the books at the back of the room that he had not paid attention to Mephistopheles's arrival, was jolted by the infernal voice. The imp had directed him to Faustus's magic book, hidden beneath a stack of Greek pornographic scrolls.

"Which one of you is the real Faustus?" Mephistopheles demanded.

The three Fausts pointed at each other.

Albergus was supremely sure of himself now. He held the secrets of life tucked in the crook of his arm and had reason now to fear no man on earth.

"*I* am the true Faustus!" he said, striding from behind the bookshelves.

"Good enough for me," said Mephistopheles.

As the sound of the last stroke of midnight faded away the floor beneath Albergus opened and all the fiends of hell, laughing, exploded upward to seize his ankles.

Reed was unsure at first whether the explosion was in his head or elsewhere in the apartment. He was not capable of accurate observation at that moment. When he came to his senses, Helen was gone.

He checked the closet. It held only clothes.

Realizing that the smell of smoke was real, he hurried through the common to Faustus's study. Strewn about were charred papers, shards of glassware and scattered books. A cold wind blew through the broken windows. Squinting through the smoke, Reed made out two figures sitting on the floor, lighting cigars from a bonfire of burning books. A third was shoveling more books onto the blaze. All looked vaguely like Doctor Faustus.

"Where is she?" Reed was furious. Then he realized why the triplets were staring at him: he was wearing no breeches. "What have you done with her?"

"She was one helluva wrestler, eh partner?" said Dicolini.

Robin leaned on his shovel and gave a long, low whistle.

"But it's not fair!" said Reed. "We were just getting started."

Faustus reached up, peeled the sweat-soaked contract from

Reed's chest and tossed it on the fire. "My boy, she's a scarlet woman and you're nothing but a green scholar. She would have made you blue someday."

"Yeah," said Dicolini, "if only Faustus hadn't turned yellow."

"And that's it?" Reed was losing patience with these madmen. "You make a joke and forget about it? You can't go through life just mocking everything and everybody. You have to believe in something or else what's the point? What kind of men are you? Don't you stand for anything?"

Robin began to whistle "The Star-Spangled Banner." Dicolini and Faustus rose and put their hands over their hearts.

When Robin had finished, Faustus put his arm around Reed's shoulder. "My boy, when you step on a banana peel, you fall down and break your arm. Someone else laughs. That's all that matters, and don't let anyone tell you differently."

Robin scooped up another shovelful of books.

Sphinx

It had taken days of patient wooing to entice Murray to play racquetball—and now he was late for the match.

"He won't come," Shaun said to the intaglio figure of Osiris carved into the stone wall of the court.

"He's on his way," said Osiris.

Shaun drove a lucky kill shot off the front wall just two inches above the floor. His relationship with the other guests had been strained ever since Myrna's death. No one wanted to be alone with him. No one, that is, except Vic, and all he wanted to do was talk about Myrna. But Shaun did not want Vic's company—now or ever. Besides, it was not Vic that Shaun had dreamed about. It was Murray.

Finally Murray arrived, looking as if he expected to find a noose hanging from the ceiling. A grudging handshake—then he noticed the carving. "Where did *that* come from?" He seemed shaken.

Shaun slipped the racket thong over his wrist. "Been here ever since I learned to play."

"I've never seen . . ." He touched Osiris's sensors, which were mounted flush with the wall. "What about bad bounces?"

"Consider them part of the game," said Osiris.

"Dreamers' rules." Shaun's laugh echoed off the stark white walls. "Do you ever get the feeling that they're making them up as they go along?"

Murray was grim. "Did you ask me here to play or talk?"

"What's the matter?" Shaun hit a lazy serve high off the front wall. "Afraid I'm going to beat you with my mouth?"

Murray caught the ball with his left hand. "I'm not joking, understand? You make me nervous; I don't want to end up like you-know-who. If you're going to be saying things that the dreamers don't want to hear . . ." He nodded at the carving.

"There are no restrictions on conversation," said Osiris.

"You were right about one thing, Murray: they can hear us any time they want. They can get into our heads." Shaun lowered his voice to a stage whisper. "I've been dreaming about you."

"Damn." He bounced the ball on the floor. "I knew you were going to do this."

"My memory is starting to come back, too. We knew each other before we came here. You were a professor at Columbia."

"Says you." He thought about it for a minute. "Did I have tenure?"

"You were a major-league jerk."

He sighed. "Let's just play. All right?"

Shaun lost the first game twenty-one to fifteen. He was a beginner at racquetball and had no backhand. Murray was not a power player but had a tricky arsenal of lobs and drop shots. Still, each point was hard fought and both players needed a rest before they could continue.

Murray sat with his back against the wall and retied his sneakers. Winning the first game seemed to have soothed his nerves. "So, did they tell you anything about this place?"

"Not exactly. But I've figured some things out for myself. At least about this dream therapy they talk about. The reason I couldn't remember it was that I wasn't getting it before."

"Sounds logical. Maybe you have to acclimate to Freedom Beach before they start working on you."

"The way I see it, they take away your memories so that they can feed them back to you piecemeal. At the same time they try to reshape your understanding of those memories. Through dreams."

"Boogeymen? Coffee break at the Playboy mansion?"

"Not standard issue dreams." Shaun shook his head. "Usually when I dream, there's this other level in the background where I know I'm asleep and I'm watching myself dream. These aren't like that. It's like the dreamers crawl inside your head and build up a whole world out of the stuff they find there. When they do it to you, it feels like reality."

"Whatever that is. And I was in this dream?"

Shaun told him what he now remembered about Columbia and about the dream where Murray had been Faustus.

When he had finished, Murray sat for several minutes, silently twirling his racket on its head. "And so," he said, "you ask me here because you think I'm going to tell you that you've said the secret word and a duck is going to drop from the ceiling with a certificate in its mouth—signed by the dreamers and suitable for framing—which says that you're sane? Is that about it?"

Shaun grinned. "It would do for starters."

"Sorry, pal. Means nothing to me." Murray turned to Osiris. "You get all that? How much of it should I believe?"

"It would be inappropriate," said Osiris, "to comment on the progress of another guest."

Murray flipped the ball to Shaun and stood up. "Your serve."

They started a new game but Shaun's mind was elsewhere. With the score nineteen to five he watched a service ace go by and then turned away from Murray in disgust. "I don't know why I'm playing these stupid games," he said to the intaglio of Osiris. "I want some answers, damn it!"

"I don't know what you're so upset about." Murray came up behind him. "So far you're the only one at Freedom Beach making progress. Maybe they'll cure you and let you go."

"Would you want to be cured by them? After what they did to Myrna?"

"We bore no responsibility for her death," said Osiris.

"What good is remembering if they're going to twist my memories around? I want to remember the past the way it was for me!" Shaun threw his racket at at the carving, chipping the nose. "You know, I wanted to swim out of here the night Myrna died. I started to and then they stopped me."

"If you ask me, it's a good thing they did," said Murray. "Otherwise I'd be playing with an alumnus." He clapped Shaun on the shoulder. "Come to think of it, I might get a better game out of a statue."

"Alumnus?" Shaun started. "Oh, my god." He ran to the door and flung it open. "I'll see you later, okay?"

"I've been expecting you," boomed the sphinx.

"I'll bet." Shaun scrambled down the steep path toward it. "I've got questions."

"Ah, questions."

A warm wind swept across the prospect, ruffling palm fronds. Waves hurled themselves at the base of the cliff. Shaun vaulted over the sphinx's masonry forepaws and jogged across the flat toward the alumni. It did not take long for him to reach them and take inventory. There was no statue of Myrna in the gallery of suffering.

"Where is she?" he said, breathing heavily.

"I think you know, Shaun."

"She's dead because of you—this place. I saw her body. She should be here. Those are your rules, aren't they? Where the hell is she?"

Silence.

Shaun threw himself at the nearest statue. Shoulders bunched, arms corded, he strained to push it over. Slowly the statue tilted; on its way to the ground it crashed into the outflung arm of an adjacent statue, breaking it off. Shaun toppled every statue he could budge, then picked up the broken arm and used it to smash the faces of the rest. For a moment he thought of attacking the sphinx, but he had lost the twitch of anger and frustration that had set him on this rampage. His furious strength had burned itself out and he sagged, knowing that nothing had changed.

"Things are not as they seem," said the sphinx.

"I'll fight. Do you hear me?" He threw the marble arm over the cliff. "All right, maybe you can make shredded wheat out of my memory. But you're not going to change me."

"No, of course not."

He sat on an alumnus which had fallen face down into a tangle of devil's ivy. "I'll kill myself first," he muttered.

"Wouldn't that be overdoing it?"

Shaun wiped at the sweat which was running into his eyes. He said nothing.

"Your quarrel is not with me," said the sphinx. "Or with Freedom Beach. If you disagree with the therapy you are receiving, you will have to take it up with the dreamers."

"Who are they? Why are they doing this to me?"

"Those are questions best addressed to them."

"Then where are they? How do I get their attention?"

"You may rest assured that they are following your progress closely. Should you decide to continue with your therapy, a meeting would be inevitable."

"Decide?" He laughed. "I don't seem to have a hell of a lot of choice in the matter."

"It is always best," said the sphinx, "to keep an open mind. You look tired. Go back to your room now and relax. Maybe you should sleep on it. It is my observation that things always make more sense after a little nap."

"You'd like that just fine, wouldn't you? And as soon as I fell asleep, you'd start on me again."

"Obviously," said the sphinx. "That's why you're here."

April 28, 1978

Shaun went looking for Akira O'Connor at four-thirty. The project manager of the recreational electronics group at Electrotech had his feet on his desk and was reading *Creative Computing*.

"Let's go," said Shaun. "They're drinking our beer."

"Have you seen this, friend Reed? *Creative* has gone slick. Color ads, the works. You ought to see about getting Aristotle reviewed in here."

Shaun waggled his finger at the engineer. "Magazines review hardware, Akira, not promises." Akira's team had been working on a new kit-built computer since last summer. Aristotle, the prototype, was behind schedule and the front office was not happy.

"Still bugs in the display-processing subroutine." He flipped through the pages of the magazine. "Look at this, two hundred bucks for 8K static RAM boards!"

"Save it for the hackers. I'm the English major, remember? Today is Friday, it's quitting time and Myrna is meeting us at the Limerick."

Akira tossed the magazine onto the workbench and stretched. "Four-thirty, already?" he murmured as if it were a mnemonic that would bring him out of a trance. He had that dreaming look on his face that women found ethereal and men called spacey. Akira O'Connor was one of the most exotic specimens that Shaun had ever seen. From his nisei mother he had inherited delicate features and smooth skin the color of iced tea; his father's legacy had been a full head of curly silver hair and a big, easy smile. Unlike most electrical engineers Shaun had met, Akira had an impeccable sense of fashion. He had a weakness for silk bow ties, which he tied himself, and pastel Italian suits. He was muscular and lean; he could easily take three sets of tennis from Shaun after work and close his favorite singles bar that same night. He was Shaun's best friend at Electrotech.

When they finally got to the parking lot Shaun was not surprised to see that Akira's new Volvo had a dent in the passenger door. Akira was a terrible driver; his mind and body seemed rarely to occupy the same location. The Northern State Parkway at rush hour was no place to debate the advantages of bubble sorts over the Shell-Metzner technique. Ordinarily, Shaun would never have driven with him, but Shaun's Datsun was in the shop and Myrna had dropped him off at work that morning.

"What would you like to hear?" Akira flipped open a box of eight-track tapes as he accelerated through a yellow light. Shaun knew the choices already: the Chieftains, the Dubliners, Makem and Clancy. Shaun pressed his foot to an imaginary brake and closed the box.

"We're going to get an earful of this stuff at the Limerick. Why don't we just talk?"

"Just talk? You make it sound like cleaning your fingernails."

"Queens, Akira. We're going to Queens!"

Akira swerved across two lanes of traffic and just made the

exit ramp. "Sorry." He looked in the rearview mirror as the cars he had cut off honked. "Must've been a rough day at the office." He waved to them. "Take it easy! It's the weekend."

Shaun reached for his seat belt. "When *will* Aristotle be ready?"

"By the tenth." Akira grimaced. "I hope. What I don't get is why the boys up front are so hot for this project. It's been fun to work on—don't get me wrong. But we're going to have to move five thousand units before we even come close to breaking even. I can't believe that there are five thousand hobbyists out there waiting for this machine. And your average Joe Sixpack is about as likely to build a computer as he is to build a pyramid."

Shaun stared out the side window. "I was up with Stilson today, showing him the copy for the fall catalog, and he was raving about computers. He says in ten years there'll be a micro on every desk. No more filing, no more drafting. It'll all be done at a keyboard. Financial modeling, instant information on any subject. And just think about the impact of personal word processing."

Akira shook his head. "Isn't that what they used to call writing?"

"Yeah, back in the days when everyone commuted in chariots. It's this exit coming up."

"I know, I know." Akira changed lanes without bothering to signal. "I'm worried about you, friend Reed. You're starting to believe your own PR. Computers will never make it in the real world; it's too messy. They don't like dust, they don't like cigarette smoke. Static electricity blows the chips. Heat wears them out. You put a micro on Stilson's desk and I guarantee he'll spill coffee on it within a week. And who is going to fix them once they're broken? Your friendly neighborhood TV repairman? No way." He drummed his fingers on the steering wheel as he waited for a green light. "I have seen the future—" he shook his head "—and it is out of order."

There was an edge to Akira's voice that Shaun attributed to nervousness. Akira had been looking forward to this night for a long time.

"How're the old vocal cords today?" said Shaun. "You know what you're going to sing yet?"

"I've narrowed it down but I want a pint or two of stout—get a taste of the evening, don't you know—before I make a final decision." Akira touched his throat and smiled. "And here we are."

Taim ag imeacht. The sign over the Limerick's massive oak door was in Gaelic. *I am going away*. It was one of the things Shaun liked best about the pub. When he passed under that sign he did feel as though he had gone away. There were no public relations here; no one twisted the language to move a few extra units. The interior of the Limerick was as murky as a dream: the walls were ancient brick, the wooden tables and leather-covered benches seemed rough-hewn, as if they had been imported from some Celtic mead hall. It was a large, crooked room with many dark corners. The air was sweet with the scent of freshly drafted beer, and there was a pleasant tang of smoke as well. Perhaps these smells would turn sour by closing, but Shaun was usually gone by then, departing with his illusions intact. Nothing had ever touched him at the Limerick except alcohol and Akira's nostalgic songs.

Tonight, however, the troubles of the world outside were intruding in the person of Myrna. She had come to hear Akira sing and to see the place for herself. He had been surprised by her interest, and although he was sure she would never understand the Limerick, he had agreed that she should come. Things has not been going well between Myrna and Shaun; neither could say exactly why. They had been living together since college and Shaun, at least, still believed that he was in love with her. Their passion was long since gone, however. Shaun worried that she was disappointed with him. In college he had promised her greatness; now he was a public relations flack. He was not a little disappointed in himself.

Myrna had found a table right in front of the Limerick's tiny stage, which occupied an ell across the room from the bar. She swirled fading lumps of ice in her empty glass. There were three cigarette butts in the ashtray.

Shaun sat next to her. "Hey, good looking. This seat taken?" Her kiss tasted of gin.

"That's what they've been asking for the last hour, buster." She nodded at the bar and shook her head. "Hi, Akira. Are you his excuse for being late?"

"Have the boys been bothering you?" Akira settled into the chair facing away from the stage. "Well, I don't blame them. You look dazzling today."

"It was nothing I couldn't handle." She shrugged the compliment off grimly. "What's good here? I'm starving."

"I can recommend the crubeens," said Akira. He turned and blew the waitress, Nell, a kiss.

"The what?"

"Pig's feet," said Shaun. "He's teasing. If you want something Irish, try the boiled bacon and cabbage or the corned beef and carrots. Otherwise, just get a steak. They're not big on food here."

"The Irish care more about drinking than eating and who's to blame them?" said Akira. "Ah, Nell, my sweetheart!"

The waitress was about as friendly as a brick as she set a pint of stout in front of Akira and a pint of lager in front of Shaun.

"When did you order those?" said Myrna. "You just got here."

"Nell, here, is a witch," said Akira. "A reader of minds and a stealer of hearts. After I win tonight, Nell, what say we go out to paint the town green."

"If you win, *Mister* O'Connor, you can take the matter up with my husband." She turned to Myrna. "You having another?"

Myrna tapped her finger against the glass. "Gin and tonic. And we'd like to see the menu."

Nell jerked her thumb over her shoulder. "Then why don't you look?" She whisked Myrna's empty glass away and stalked over to the bar.

Shaun leaned toward Myrna and whispered. "She's sort of a character, pay no attention to her. The menu's written on the chalkboard over there."

Akira excused himself and went to talk to some of his cronies.

Shaun could tell when Myrna was getting angry but he never could do anything about it. "You see, it's more a bar than a restaurant." She seemed not to hear him as she squinted at the chalkboard. "*You* wanted to come."

"Don't remind me."

Shaun pulled away from her and reached for his beer. He had known she was not going to understand.

Three hours and two quarts of beer later, Shaun stopped worrying about it. Myrna was talking to MacSweeney, the pennywhistle player. It seemed that they had gone to the same high school and had not seen each other since. It was, he told himself, a bit of good luck; otherwise her boredom might have turned nasty. Now she was laughing at a table across the room and watching MacSweeney intently with a shiny, drunken stare.

"You're a cocky man, friend Reed," said Akira. "To leave her alone with that MacSweeney. She's a beautiful woman and he's got the morals of a rabbit."

Shaun was not sure whether it was him or Akira who had had too much to drink. It was unlike his friend to offer such blunt commentary about Shaun's personal life. Shaun finished off the last of his beer and set the mug down carefully. Two could play that game.

"Trust, Akira. That's the difference between you and me. I trust women, you don't. You get exactly what you expect." It was the kind of observation that could only be offered—and correctly understood—in a bar. "Besides, you're attracted to her too."

"There's not a man in this bar could deny it." He twisted in his chair, squinted through the gloom at her and then shrugged. "Still, she's not my kind." They thought about that for a while. Shaun signaled for a refill.

"Ever considered getting married?" said Akira.

"The subject has come up. But we're . . . we're waiting for the right time. If it ever comes." He did not want to talk about Myrna because then he would have to think about her. He could see that she had her hand in MacSweeney's. "How about you. Think you'll ever get married?"

"Oh, I think about it all the time. Sure I'd love to get married. Settle down, have children. You get to an age when you start to wonder where it ends. You know? You realize that you're not going to live forever and you wonder who's going to give a shit about you after you're dead. I'm an engineer—no one remembers engineers. All I'm going to leave behind are some initials on schematic drawings."

"Jesus, Akira. What are you talking about?"

"You think maybe Electrotech will let me sign every Aristotle that comes off the line?"

"Well, I'll remember you. How about that?"

"Sure. It's easy to remember when you see me every day. But one of these days you'll get fed up with Stilson and quit to write that book you're always talking about. Or maybe some headhunter will offer me a million bucks to go out to Silicon Valley. After a couple of years I won't even make your Christmas card list."

"You're an idiot, Akira."

He slapped Shaun on the back and smiled. "Okay, Shaun. Okay." Nell brought them two more. They clinked their mugs and made peace. "Still, you know your kids are going to remember you. Except that they'll probably break your heart as part of the deal. They'll grow up to be drug addicts or they'll get messy divorces or they'll join some cult and end up selling pencils at LaGuardia. Maybe the thing to do is to take all your money when you're dead and have your estate build a pyramid. Sure, that's it. I wonder how much of a pyramid you could get for, say, two hundred K? You know, if I cashed in my thrift plan and sold the condo and had my estate collect on the life insurance, I could raise two hundred K easy. How big do you think it would be? Five stories? Ten?"

They were both laughing now. "Forget it," said Shaun, "You're going to blow all your money on new Volvos and Guinness and Club Med vacations; you'll die in hock. Besides, you're going to get your slice of immortality tonight.

If you win they might even take your picture and hang it up there on the wall."

Akira brightened. "'Tis true. That'll show these bloody micks, won't it? The half breed right up there on the wall beside the true sons of Ireland. Parnell, the great John McCormack, Brendan Behan, JFK, Akira O'Connor. The Rising Sun shines on the Old Sod."

He took a long pull on his stout and doused his optimism with alcohol. "But still. The Limerick will go out of business. That stone-faced Nell will drive all the customers away. They'll widen the Grand Central Parkway to nineteen lanes and take this whole damn block out. No, it's either a pyramid—" he smiled slyly— "or a bestseller. When you write that book about Electrotech, friend Reed, put me in it, will you?"

"Sure, Akira." Shaun smiled into his beer. There was another thing that depressed him. Writing, Myrna, his job . . . he realized he was getting to be a touchy son of a bitch.

Myrna came back. "Are you ready, Akira? I think they're going to start."

The first to step onto the tiny stage was MacSweeney with his pennywhistle. He played a lively set, mixing traditional airs and reels with some of his own compositions. The problem, as always, was that the pennywhistle's sound would not carry in the odd-shaped room unless there was complete silence. At ten forty-five on a Friday night patrons stood three deep at the bar; not all of them were music lovers. MacSweeney seemed angered by his failure to hold the room and he cut the set short, finishing with a jig called "The Piper's Chair." When he had done, Myrna sprang out of her chair, clapping. Akira stood too; reluctantly, Shaun joined them. Most of those who had heard the set were enthusiastic. Unfortunately they were in the minority. MacSweeney gave Myrna a curt nod and headed for the bar.

Akira shook his head. "I don't know why they decided to have the finals on a Friday." He paused long enough to chug the remainder of his pint. "Most of this crowd doesn't give a damn about us." With that he climbed onto the small stage. The Limerick regulars applauded loudly, led by Shaun.

Two tables away sat a large man with curly red hair and a beer belly the size of a keg. As soon as Akira had settled himself on stage, Beer-Belly called out. "'Wild Colonial Boy, Wild Colonial Boy!'" Akira winced. Beer-Belly began to tap his mug on the table in time to his demand. Others picked up the chant.

"All right." Akira raised his hands for quiet. "If I sing one for you, can I sing the next one for myself?"

"What's 'Wild Colonial Boy?'" whispered Myrna.

Shaun leaned toward her until their heads touched. "A song he hates. About an Irishman in Australia, sort of like Robin Hood." Myrna's hair smelled of lilacs; he put his arm around her.

Akira started to sing. "There was a wild colonial boy, Jack Duggan was his name—"

"Louder!" came a call from the back of the room.

Akira had a strong voice but he was not a shouter. He shook his head gamely and continued without missing a note. Unlike MacSweeney, he did not seem to be bothered by the crowd. Occasionally he would glance down at Shaun and smile with his eyes. Shaun's face felt hot. He nuzzled Myrna and she pulled away.

"—surrender now, Jack Duggan, for you see we're three to one/surrender in the Queen's high name—"

Beer-Belly gave Her Highness a drunken boo. Shaun twisted around and fixed the idiot with an evil stare.

"Jack drew two pistols from his belt and proudly waved them high—" Akira mimed pistols with his hands, forefinger extended, thumb cocked "—I'll fight but not surrender, said the wild colonial boy." Akira winked at Shaun, who caught the signal. "He fired a shot and Kelly went sprawling to the ground."

When Akira's thumb came down, Shaun grabbed out at his gut and slumped forward onto the table. The crowd laughed and clapped.

"And turning around to Davis he received a fatal wound,/a

bullet pierced his proud young heart—" Akira staggered and clutched his breast "—from the pistol of FitzRoy, / and that was how they captured him, that wild colonial boy!"

The room rocked with applause and Shaun knew that Akira would win the competition. He did not need to sing another note. "This next song," said Akira, "is a ballad written by the blind bard of the eighteenth century, Carolin O'Daly. It's called 'Eileen Aroon.'"

"'Jug of Punch, Jug of Punch!'" called Beer-Belly.

Shaun turned to him. "Would you shut up?"

"What did you say?" The man's face turned the color of raspberries. "What did he say?" he demanded of his companion, a tired looking woman with a wisp of gray hair across her forehead. She hushed him.

"Eileen Aroon" was a song of melancholy love, and it fit Shaun's mood exactly. The alcohol in his gut was but part of the vast weight pulling him toward sadness. He feared he was losing Myrna, losing himself as well. He knew he was losing his youth, had lost all sense of his size. He reached for Myrna's hand at precisely the moment someone seized him by the collar and hauled him from his chair.

"What did you say, punk?" Beer-Belly hissed.

"I said you ought to let the man sing." Shaun felt suicidally brave. "Your problem, porky, is that you've got bacon where your brains should be."

Akira was still singing. Beer-Belly looked stunned, as if Shaun had answered in Hungarian. He let Shaun go. For a few seconds Shaun exulted in the power of the word as a weapon of honor. Then a fist the size of a Christmas ham slammed into his face.

From his back on the damp barroom floor, Shaun could see the fight raging above him. He heard screams and harsh laughter and the sound of glass breaking. Amazingly enough, Akira was still on the stage, finishing "Eileen Aroon":

"Beauty must fade away,
Castles are sacked in war,

Chieftains are scattered far
Truth is a fixed star, Eileen Aroon."

Shaun wanted to sit up and ask Akira why the hell he was singing in the midst of a barroom brawl when his best friend had just taken a sucker punch on his behalf. He wanted to ask but then someone kicked him in the head and the sun rose at midnight over the bar of the Limerick pub and seared all thought from Shaun's brain.

The Fossils

Reed fought to stay conscious as reality slipped away. He had an image of himself as a creature made of yarn; something raveled him, stretched the strand of his being over a vast distance and then knitted him back together. He found himself trembling beneath a table. The air smelled of rain. Gray light came through a row of grimy windows.

Reed shut his eyes. He tasted bile and thought for a moment that he might throw up. He took a deep breath and opened his eyes again.

There was a divan in the room with him, a water bubbler and a red plastic desk shaped like the Parthenon. Built into the wall behind it were three television monitors, two of which were shattered. The walls were covered with graffiti written in a strange alphabet. When Reed saw the statue he realized that the graffiti were Greek.

The statue was carved of what appeared to be limestone.

The hair and beard were portrayed in neat rows of stylized silver-gray curls. The body was lean and well-muscled. It was dressed in a sleeveless tunic.

The statue leaned out a broken window at the far side of the room, a twitch away from a fatal plunge. As Reed inched from beneath the table he could see that the stone lips were parted in a smile, as if he were amused by the prospect. He thought it an odd subject for a sculpture.

The statue hiccuped.

Reed started, knocking the table backward. Piles of bric-a-brac scattered across the floor. The statue turned, stared at him and then laughed. It was a sound like two stones being struck together.

"This isn't happening." Reed stooped to clean up the mess; his hand shook. "I'm sorry, I just don't . . ." He saw that what he had spilled were souvenirs of the Empire State Building: pens that wrote in red, green and blue, plastic ashtrays, mugs and paperweight miniatures of the skyscraper. "Who are you?"

"English!" said the statue. "Of course. Go on, I like the sound of it. Say your name."

"Shaun Reed. Where the hell am I?"

"You—" the statue picked up an Empire State Building and pointed to one of the tiny windows two-thirds of the way up "—are here."

Reed rushed to the nearest window. It faced south toward what should have been the Village and the twin towers of the World Trade Center. Only, the Village was now a huge vacant lot, complete with weeds and rubble. Brooklyn was no longer a sea of brick and concrete; it had been reclaimed by forest. From the forest jutted a dozen pyramids and a great, particolored sphinx. The East River had dried up and the bridges were gone. And Jersey—spaceships had landed in New Jersey!

"You act as if you've never seen this before."

Reed's eyes misted.

"Reed, is it?" The statue guided Reed to the divan. "What's your problem, friend Reed?"

"I'm not sure." He could vaguely remember a fight, lying on the floor in a puddle of beer. Someone had booted him in the head—yes! But why had he been fighting? And where? Apparently the kick had dislodged a huge chunk of Reed's memory. He couldn't make any sense of this himself, much less describe it to this . . . this creature. "It wasn't like this where I came from," he said lamely.

"Which was where?"

Reed shrugged. "Not here."

The statue clapped him on the back and smiled, revealing two classically symmetrical rows of stone teeth. "I had my doubts about the gods, you know."

Reed bit his lip.

"But this is enough to make a believer out of Socrates. Zeus, thank you. Or was it you, wine god?" He made a sweeping gesture to the sky like some summer stock ham. "The patron of playwrights stopped me from jumping!" Seeing Reed's confusion, he laughed. "Don't you understand? You're an audience, an empty vessel waiting to be filled with words." He knelt before Reed and took his hands. "A miracle; the gods care for even unhappy creatures like me."

For a moment Reed was certain that he had gone crazy. Then he wondered if the mad could recognize their own psychotic episodes. He had a flash of déjà vu, as if this were not the first time he had been snatched from reality, his memory shredded. He decided to reserve judgment on his sanity for now. "Who are you?"

"Who . . . ?" The statue seemed wounded. "I am known to the ages as Aristophanes, the father of dramatic comedy, author of fifty-five comedies for the festival of Dionysos. Of course only eleven survived intact, plus a few fragments. You must know *The Clouds*. My famous roasting of Socrates? Oh, come on! How about *The Birds*? Cloud-cuckoo-land?" The statue frowned for the first time. "*Lysistrata*? The women of Athens go on a sex strike to end the war. Everyone's heard of *Lysistrata*."

"But if you're Aristophanes then . . . am I dead?"

"Who knows if life be not thought death, or death be life in the world below?" The statue smiled again. "Of course, I'm not *the* Aristophanes. Just a BOB."

"A BOB," said Reed.

"A Bounded Organic Book."

Reed looked blank.

"And I suppose now you want a sixty-second course in robotics and artificial intelligence." He sighed. "We'll have to ask the Thinkery." He walked over to the unbroken monitor and raised his voice. "I said: let's ask the Thinkery!" He banged on the wall. "Voltage spikes in its central processing unit," he said to Reed. "About as reliable as a Persian whore, but it's all we've got." He faced the screens. "Talk to me!"

Something sparked behind one of the ruined screens. "Why are we speaking English?" The Thinkery had the voice of a tired cop.

"I have a friend here with some bad memory chips," said Aristophanes. "He wants to know about BOBs."

"Imagine," said the Thinkery, "the number of writers whose works mankind has packed away in its literary attic. The earliest date back fifteen thousand years. Statistical records lead us to expect twelve-point-three-eight literary geniuses per every hundred years, each of whom writes some six hundred kilowords. In addition, we find that there is approximately one subgenius born each year, or one hundred per century, plus or minus five. These lesser lights each create one-point-four masterpieces or some fifty-five kilowords. The current file of recognized masterpieces contains two thousand gigawords. It is said that the study of the humanities has become an inhuman task. Consequently, few real people bother anymore."

"What's so real about them?" Aristophanes snorted. "Frogs have more brains."

"Four hundred years ago," continued the Thinkery, "there lived a wealthy eccentric named Bela Babylon who was a fancier of antique literature. It disturbed him deeply that his favorites were ignored. So he devoted the last century of his life to a crackpot attempt to breathe new life into literary corpses."

"Crackpot?" Aristophanes was indignant. "We were moldering in computer memory—forgotten. Babylon gave us life again."

"Electron patterns do not molder. Babylon created a series of self-programming artificial people, each impersonating an ancient writer. The likenesses were dictated by Babylon's idiosyncratic whimsy. About ten thousand BOBs were created during his lifetime. They scoured the data banks, libraries and museums for information about their originals. After Babylon's death, phase two of his master plan was implemented. BOBs everywhere began to offer performances of the ancient works. At first they were ignored. Indifference, however, only triggered the fanaticism built into their programming. Soon they were declaiming their poems in crowded elevators, forcing their short stories on unsuspecting pedestrians, crashing parties to give unwanted dramatic readings."

"You exaggerate." Aristophanes was angry.

"Finally the dreamers had to step in to end the BOB nuisance by—"

"—Making a mockery of justice," said Aristophanes.

"—offering the BOBs a choice—"

"What choice?"

"Either leave Earth—"

"Unthinkable!"

"Or limit their badgering."

"Enough!"

"For one week each year they're allowed free access to the population. The rest of the time they're confined—"

"To this man-made Hades." Aristophanes threw an Empire State Builiding through the last unbroken screen. It fizzled and was silent. "What you have to understand, Reed," he said, "is that this lunatic machine resents being our jailer. Before it arrived here it was in charge of a sewage treatment plant. It misses the old job; turds don't talk back."

The Thinkery spat fire at him.

"Go flush the toilets, why don't you?" said Aristophanes. "That's all you're good for."

The door opened and in walked an odd little man. The top of his head was quite bald but black hair sprouted from the sides, covered his ears and spilled across his grotesquely large white ruff. His mustache looked like a smear of dirt. He would not have needed much makeup to pass for a clown.

Aristophanes looked disgusted. "Can't you see I'm busy?"

"All hail, great master!" The little man bowed to Reed.

"Who, me?"

"Grave sir, hail. I come to answer thy best pleasure; be't to fly, to swim, to dive into the fire, to ride on the curled clouds."

Aristophanes scowled, but Reed decided to humor the newcomer. "I'm Shaun Reed. Who are you?"

"O, that I were as great as is my grief, or lesser than my name, or that I could forget what I have been, or not remember what I must be now."

Reed backed away. "You speak English."

"Out of here, bedbug," Aristophanes said, "before someone steps on you." The BOB caught the intruder by the ruff. The little man winked at Reed and managed to say "Parting is such sweet—" as Aristophanes hurled him from the room and kicked the door shut behind him.

"My God, that was—"

"Mad Will." Aristophanes shrugged off Reed's look of reproach. "He fancies me a friend because we were in the same line. Poor fool talks that way because his speech module is shot; all he can do now is quote himself. Tiresome, no? Unfortunately, he's not the last defective you'll meet here." He rubbed his hands together. "Well, friend Reed, now we're ready to do a few plays."

"You're kidding." Reed sank onto the divan and rubbed his eyes. "This is crazy. You brought me here just to watch plays?" His head was throbbing.

"I didn't do it. But a play might soothe your troubled spirits."

"The hell it will!" What he needed was something familiar, something ordinary to hang his sanity on. He glanced at his watch. It said eleven-thirty. "No wonder I feel so rotten." Reed laughed and thought he sounded hysterical. "I probably haven't eaten in ten thousand years."

"Appetite is an illusion. Now, where shall we start? With *The Frogs*? Perhaps you'd rather see *Lysistrata*? No, no. We'll start at the beginning."

"I'm not really in the mood . . ." Reed did not want to encourage him. He ransacked the pockets of his suit hoping for a crumb. All he found were complimentary toothpicks from the Yung Hee Restaurant and a stick of Carefree peppermint gum, which he unwrapped and popped into his mouth.

"All right, then. I am pleased to present *The Acharians*. First produced in Athens in 425." He bowed. "B.C." And melted.

Reed swallowed his gum.

The protoplasmic goo on the carpet pulsed. There was a viscous ebb and flow beneath the gray membrane. It gave a final shudder and divided like some giant cell.

"Aristophanes!"

The process of bisection repeated itself once, twice, three times. The puddles of the new population were changing colors. Some turned a flower-pot orange, others black. One remained gray. Slowly a node formed in the middle of each. These nodes swelled, gathering protoplasm to themselves, and took on abstract human shapes. Soon the abstract grew specific; limbs branched, faces leafed out, sex organs budded. Sixteen naked Attic dolls stretched and capered. A miniature Aristophanes stepped forward to calm the distraught Reed.

"Please sit down. We're about to begin." Already the tiny actors were growing tunics and setting up dollhouse props in front of the Parthenon desk.

"What are you trying to do, scare me to death?" Reed was furious. "I'm new here, remember?"

"Would you kindly sit down and shut up?" said Aristophanes. "You're forcing me out of character. Presenting Dikaiopolis, an elderly farmer of Athens." He bowed.

Reed retreated sullenly to the divan.

The play was about a farmer of Athens who negotiated a

private truce with the enemy, Sparta. Denounced as a traitor by the chorus of Athenian charcoal peddlers, Dikaiopolis managed to persuade his fellow citizens to set him free. He prospered peacefully as the war dragged Athens down.

It was not as bad as Reed had imagined. Although some speeches stretched interminably, there was plenty of farce and slapstick, dirty words and double entendres. He laughed—reluctantly.

Toward the end many of the jokes turned on the hunger of the shortage-plagued Athenians contrasted with Dikaiopolis's abundance. They reminded Reed of his own fast. In one scene Dikaiopolis stuffed a basket with food to take to a wedding feast. One of the chorus melted and was transformed into fragrant loaves of fresh bread, fried fish, roast thrushes and partridges, a rabbit casserole, and pastries and cakes of all descriptions. The aroma of these tiny delicacies was more than Reed could stand. As Dikaiopolis was making his exit with the picnic basket, Reed barred his way.

"Excuse me," said Reed, "but that smells like my lunch."

"Sit down, you philistine." Aristophanes spoke in his own voice as he tried to nudge Reed out of the way. "Sit!"

"Either I eat or the show is over."

"You can't eat this food." Aristophanes set the basket down and sat on the lid. "It's me!"

"I'm starving and you look as if you could stand to lose a few pounds."

"You'd interrupt a performance of a timeless play just to indulge your selfish appetites?"

"I'm going to count to three." Reed held out his hand for the basket. "One."

The chorus master tapped his foot impatiently.

"Two."

Aristophanes slid off the basket. "I hope you choke on it."

Reed ate on the divan. He swallowed the fowl, bones and all, and spread the stew onto bread like a dip. The food reminded him of Happy Hour appetizers.

At the end of the performance Reed licked his greasy fingers and gave the cast a standing ovation. "Bravo, bravo," he cried as each actor took a bow. He saved his loudest applause for Dikaiopolis/Aristophanes. "Wonderful!"

"The meal or the play?" Aristophanes said coldly. "May I have the basket back or are you going to eat that too?"

As he watched the cast—and the basket—reassemble into the full-sized Aristophanes, Reed heard the rumble of what sounded like thunder. He glanced out the window in surprise; the clouds seemed to be lifting. "Are you still angry?"

"I'm a playwright, not a buffet!"

An earsplitting whine filled the room; it was punctuated by an explosion that made the Empire State Building lurch. Reed dived under the bric-a-brac table. The whine came again, followed by an explosion of lesser violence. Then it was quiet.

Aristophanes crawled to the window. "All clear."

Reed did not move. "What the hell was that?"

"The war."

"The war? What war?"

Aristophanes shrugged. "Isn't there always a war? Every age has its Sparta. Actually, I'm afraid I've lost track of exactly who is fighting these days. Although I hear that our side isn't doing too well."

Reed was trembling. "You lost track?"

"Since there's nothing we can do." He offered Reed a hand and helped him from under the table. "We have to accept what comes."

Two days later Reed had seen Aristophanes's entire repertoire. When he demanded a respite from play watching, Aristophanes took him to the twenty-fifth floor. "Fantastic Yes-No-Yes-Yes," he told Reed as he knocked on the door. "A friend."

Fantastic. She was six-foot-three and looked as if she could wreck a piano with her bare hands. Beneath a dress made of glass beads her skin was the color of unripe apples. Her eyes were green too, and across her face was a spray of yellow freckles. But it was her hair that was truly fantastic. It was red and thick and it stood out from her head as if she were touching a Van de Graaff generator. When she moved it waved hypnotically.

Her room was much the same as Aristophanes's except that the monitors were intact and instead of carpeting the floor was covered with moss.

Her language sounded like birdcalls. "I'm sorry," said Reed. "I don't understand."

She looked to Aristophanes for a translation, frowned and then twittered at the monitors. The Thinkery responded with a squeal that climbed out of the range of Reed's hearing.

"Give her a minute," said Aristophanes. "She's downloading English."

"What?"

"We are *Bounded* Organic Books: our memories are limited. We have to store our works in hundreds of translations; the scholarship files alone are staggering. Not much memory space left for personal use. So we store unused data in the Thinkery. English, for example, would normally be of little interest to Fantastic; it died eons before she was born."

"Call this junkyard a language!" Fantastic's hair danced as she turned to sneer at him. "And you! Just because you can sucker a stone-brained fag doesn't mean I'm having any, understand? So if you have a story let's hear it." She came within an arm's length of him, and he told her everything he knew as fast as he could.

"You're a liar." She grasped his shoulders and lifted him effortlessly until they were eye to eye.

Sparks of static electricity discharged between them as they touched. Electrochemical surges tingled up and down Reed's nerve paths; he felt as if his body had been opened to new possibilities of sensation. He returned Fantastic Yes-No-Yes-Yes's look of contempt with one of astonishment. He was in love.

It was not blind love; he still regarded her as the oddest specimen of femininity he had ever seen. But Reed had an image of her walking down the aisle of a church toward him that was as sharp as an eight-by-ten wedding picture. He wanted to barbecue steaks for her and eat her fettuccine; he wanted to buy her a hat. Although he did not understand the source or suddenness of his ardor, he could not escape it. He beamed at her, feet dangling. "So you're a writer. What kind of writing do you do?"

"This is the gift of your gods, Aristophanes?" She snorted in disgust and let him go. "A wimp?"

"She's a BOB, Reed. She's not allowed to write. The real Fantastic wrote interactive novels."

"There's a way to settle this," she said. "Computer scan." As she steered him toward the monitor bank Reed nearly swooned from the flux of her sexual magnetism.

The monitors flickered. "You are the Bounded Organic Book Shaun Reed," said the Thinkery. "You were created by the Programmable Androids Corporation in Fiscal Year 403 and were confined to the Empire State Building in Fiscal Year 668. Your room number is five-seven-three-three."

Aristophanes looked stricken.

"We detect an irreparable dysfunction in your memory banks, Shaun Reed. You have our sympathies."

"It's a lie!" he shouted at the monitors. "I'm not a BOB. God damn it, if I'm a writer what did I write? Tell me that!"

"Searching," said the Thinkery. There was a long silence.

"See?" Reed said to Aristophanes. "Look, you know I'm not a BOB. I drink. I eat. I excrete."

"You're a defective, Reed," said Fantastic. "If this was your idea of a practical joke, fine. You fooled him. But I'm on to you, so give me some credit for intelligence, would you?"

The Thinkery interrupted Reed's reply. "Search completed," it said. "This is most annoying. Someone has tampered with your files, Shaun Reed, with the result that all records of your literary output have been deleted. We can confirm that such files did at one time exist, but unless you yourself remember them, your works are lost."

The two BOBs looked at him as if he had just been sentenced to the guillotine.

Reed thrust open the door to room five-seven-three-three. There was a moment of silence. "The plot thickens," said Aristophanes.

The room smelled like a tomb. There was a bare desk, white walls and an empty closet. Reed wrote his name in the dust on the monitor screen. "When was the last time I was here?"

"You last accessed us at this terminal," replied the Thinkery, "sixty-three hours ago."

Aristophanes laughed. "Even if you persuade me, you won't persuade me."

"*Plutus*, right?" Reed smiled, relieved to have regained Aristophanes as an ally.

"I'll tell you how he did this." Fantastic prowled the room like a detective in a bad movie. "First you hid your belongings. Then you cleaned—no—scoured the room. Maybe scavenged some paint? Then the dust. An inspired touch. Scrape a few air filters, pile the cleanings in your room vents and turn the fans on."

Aristophanes answered for him. "You're stretching, dear."

"Then you explain it."

"Reed is a real person. The Thinkery lied."

"You know where Babylon went wrong?" The muscles in Fantastic's neck were corded. "Stuffing Luddite personalities into high technology bodies. That's why so many of you fossils jump. Computers don't lie, you old fart—"

"Down!" cried Aristophanes, felling Reed with a blow across the shoulders as a painfully brilliant light flooded through the windows. Fantastic hit the floor beside him, counting. "Four . . . five . . . six." Reed smelled smoke. The glow was so intense that when it passed, sunlight seemed like shadow. One wall of the room was scorched with an image of the row of windows opposite it.

"Can't get much closer than that," said Aristophanes.

"They really ought to let us out of here." Fantastic crawled to the window. "We could be killed."

"I don't think anyone much cares." Aristophanes helped Reed up. "If you hadn't ducked, Reed, all that would be left of you would be a burn shadow on that wall."

Fantastic peeked over the sill. "It's not fair." Reed had to agree with her.

* * *

"Sure, there have been suicides," said Aristophanes as the elevator slowed to a stop. "Jumpers, mostly. But we're not quite extinct yet." The doors remained shut. He rapped at the monitor which replaced the control panel. "Nothing in this place works anymore."

"Including you," said the Thinkery. The doors opened.

Aristophanes, Fantastic and Reed walked quickly out of the elevator, crossed a gleaming Art Deco aluminum bridge and gazed down one of the long corridors of the lobby. It was sheathed in gray marble and reminded Reed of a cave. A light fixture hung above him like a stylized stalactite. Lined up in front of the two revolving doors on Thirty-fourth Street were several hundred BOBs.

Bela Babylon had not created his master race of books in the literal image of their authors but rather as garish and overstated caricatures. Each had been cunningly designed to be unforgettable. Some had beards to their knees, or bright, bald, lightbulb heads. A few were naked. A fat man the size of a refrigerator chatted with an anorexic woman with skin so translucent that Reed could see the blue veining beneath it.

"Why don't I recognize anyone?" Reed was disappointed.

"Damn it, Reed." Fantastic leaned into the chrome steel railing of the bridge as if she meant to push it over. "I'm trying to help, but if you're going to insist on this charade . . ." She grimaced in disgust. "I'll be back."

Reed watched her go with a mixture of relief and regret; he had yet to sort out his feelings about her. Aristophanes nudged him. "How about Racine over there? The one with the feathered hat and the curly black wig."

"The name's familiar . . ."

"Seventeenth century. A tragedian. Still, not a bad playwright. His only comedy was an imitation of my *Wasps*. Let's see, who else? There's Goethe." Aristophanes pointed out a handsome young man wearing a beige smock over a frock coat and knee breeches. "Translated my *Birds* . . ."

"What are they waiting for?"

Aristophanes sighed. "The start of the race. The first ones to the tube station will catch the first capsule out of town."

FREEDOM BEACH

Reed was confused. "I thought you weren't allowed out of the building except for—"

"One lousy week a year." Aristophanes spat the words out. "But there are only a few real people left in New York. It's a ghost town. And we're the ghosts."

"They're going to let you out? When?"

"Tomorrow."

"Tomorrow! Then why aren't you and Fantastic in line?"

"We're being punished." He glowered at Reed as if it were his fault. "Last year we disrupted the state of stupefaction the real people call order. We tried to lobby the dreamers to release the BOBs for the duration of the war. For our temerity we've lost our taste of freedom this year."

Fantastic returned with Mad Will in tow. "The word on the floor is that the doors probably won't open ahead of time. Of course, what do they know?" She nudged Mad Will forward. "This one claims he knows our friend."

Mad Will drew Reed aside and whispered, "Trust none; for oaths are straws, men's faiths are wafer cakes and hold-fast is the only dog, my duck."

Reed tried not to look confused.

Aristophanes scowled. "Makes less sense than Euripedes."

"Doomsday is near. Die all, die merrily." Mad Will pointed down at the line of BOBs. "Stand not upon the order of your going, but go at once."

"Here, get away from him!" Aristophanes hauled the little BOB to his side; he seemed alarmed. "Didn't you hear her? The doors are still locked."

Reed was surprised at Aristophanes's vehemence. Mad Will shrugged. "Hereafter," he said to Reed, "in a better world than this, I shall desire more love and knowledge of you." He shook free of Aristophanes and escaped down the corridor.

Fantastic took advantage of Aristophanes's embarrassed silence. "It's time we had a little chat, Reed." She put an arm around him and steered him away from Aristophanes. "In private."

He rolled off Fantastic, gasping. He felt as if the top of his head had blown off and an air-conditioned draft was whispering over the steamy convolutions of his brain. If getting out meant giving her up then he might have to think it over.

The BOBs, for the most part, led a dour existence. He had just discovered the one light in their lives: sex. Although they could not reproduce, they coupled fiercely and often.

Reed burrowed through her haze of red hair to nuzzle her ear. "You remind me of someone . . . but that can't very well be, can it?" He chuckled. "I don't know, maybe I belong here after all." He kissed her then, but her lips were still. "Is something the matter?"

"Who are you?"

"Still?" He sat up. "Who do you think I am?"

"Beats me. Computer says you're a BOB. Aristophanes claims you're his personal miracle. Mad Will acts like your pal. And your story is amnesia."

"It's not my fault I can't remember."

"I suppose it's possible that I lost you in a short-term memory dump." She sighed. "Still, I seem to know all the other BOBs."

Reed did not know what to say. "Can anyone *prove* that they are real?" He changed the subject. "Aristophanes started talking about his plays the minute we met." He brushed his hand along a biceps the size of a loaf of bread. "I've been with you all this time and you've never once mentioned your writing. How come?"

"Because I wasn't a writer. I was a fiction programmer. When you download one of my interactive novels from the library you become an independent character within it. You make up your own lines, enter your own actions and the program responds." She rolled away from him. "Except that *you* couldn't. The apparatus used to access my works is designed to stimulate the brain of a real person. It wouldn't work on a BOB. And even if you got into a novel your central processing unit would run the program into a closed loop in no time."

"Suppose I could hook up with one of your novels? That would prove I'm a real person?"

"But you can't interface, don't you understand?" She stood

and slithered into her bead gown. "Look, you may think you're real, but if you try to use the apparatus you might be scrambled even worse than you are now."

Reed took a deep breath. "Let me try."

She gave in so quickly that Reed wondered if she had intended all along to test him in this way. She placed her hand on his head, palm down. When she pulled away, her wrist ended in a stump covered with smooth skin. He patted what had been the hand; a skullcap with five glassy ribbons gripped his scalp. It was humming.

"Don't move it," said Fantastic. "It's scanning your cerebral cortex in order to make contact with your motor and sensory areas. Except that BOBs don't have cerebrums."

Aristophanes burst into the room. "Aren't you two finished screwing yet?" He noticed the apparatus on Reed's head. "What are you doing?"

Reed sneezed.

"Stop! I'm not finished with him. My first audience in decades and you're going to wreck him!"

Reed could feel Fantastic's grip sinking deeper and deeper into him. His muscles twitched. The room was a study in pointillism and each dot twinkled like a star. Fantastic was talking. ". . . after the keyboard came voice recognition. But the product was still not satisfactory. To the ordinary reader language is not transparent. Dialogue is no problem, but when it comes to describing actions—or worse, emotions—he stops to think."

Stop, thought Reed, maybe I should stop.

". . . his vocabulary will probably be inadequate. His sense-impressions do not immediately translate themselves into words . . ."

Reed could no longer discern pleasure from pain. His spine was a bolt of lightning.

". . . he is, in short, not a writer. It was the dreamers who came up with the answer: tap directly into the brain and central nervous system, bypassing language. Through this unparalleled teaching tool, any experience can be programmed . . ."

* * *

A mist crept across the floor of the room. It made Reed uneasy. He wanted something more substantial to stand on: carpet or quarry tile or oak parquet. Someone across the room dropped her glass. It shattered on quarry tile. There was a moment of silence as heads turned. The woman laughed nervously and the buzz of conversation resumed.

"Probably drunk again," said a man wearing a cape and a blue swim suit.

Someone tapped him on the shoulder. "Fantastic!" He hugged her. "I made it."

"I don't believe we've met," she said warily. "My name is Myrna. And you're Shaun?"

"You know who I am."

"Do I?" She smiled. "It doesn't really matter." She linked her arm in his and turned him toward the party. "What do you think of this place?"

Reed's literary tastes were old-fashioned; he did not want to be aware that he was in a work of fiction. And he was certain that even he could have set a more convincing scene than this. "I probably shouldn't criticize, but isn't the setting a little . . . thin? White walls, for example. Drab. Needs paintings or a photograph. Maybe some sci-fi?"

"Sci-fi?"

Reed waved and a blank wall was suddenly filled with a moving three-dimensional view of the Sphinx and the Great Pyramid at Giza. A sun like hot brass hung above them; wind whipped dust into eddies and a man in a burnoose led two camels by a short rope. The Sphinx stared impassively into its own shadow. "Yes, something like that."

The rest of the guests stared for a moment at the wall. A few turned to him and applauded politely.

Fantastic's smile was icy. "Keep that up," she whispered, "and you won't be staying long."

"You don't like it?" He cocked his head and squinted. "I think it's an improvement."

"You just can't go around creating things whenever you feel like it. You're a character, understand. You have limits."

"This is my character. I am me." Reed laughed. "Are you hungry? I wonder if we could whip up some fried chicken."

Her face turned ugly. "You don't need food."

"Nonsense." He looked for the nearest exit and imagined it led into the kitchen of his condo. Already he could smell the hot oil; he knew there would be wings in the refrigerator. "How can you have a party without snacks?"

Reed did not see Fantastic's fist until it struck his cheekbone. The force of the blow sent him sprawling into darkness.

"I was wrong about you, Reed." She cradled his head to her chest. Aristophanes offered him a plastic Empire State Building cup filled with water. "Things will be different from now on," she said.

"No more sucker punches, you mean?" He rubbed his cheek; the numbness was passing.

"That wasn't me." Her remorse seemed genuine. "It was the program defending its integrity. Besides, all you felt was simulated pain; no actual damage was done."

"So you believe my story now?"

"You don't have a story. That's the problem!" She shrugged. "I believe you are a real person. From your reactions just now I believe you have never had a brain tap before. I don't know what else I should believe."

"Believe that you've lost your audience," said Aristophanes. "Come, Reed: you promised you'd watch some reruns. How about *The Frogs?*"

Reed balked. "I'm not taking any orders from you. Let's not forget who is the real person here." He was mollified to see both BOBs bow in submission. He decided that he could afford to be generous; after all, he was getting out tomorrow and they were not. "It just so happens that I wouldn't mind seeing some plays—if you'll throw in a meal. Let Fantastic come along."

She watched with ill-concealed disgust as Reed gobbled the honey-drenched thrush which had once been part of Aristophanes. "How can you let him do this to you?"

"Because he understands the power of food," said Reed. Most of Aristophanes's plays ended with a celebratory banquet; this meal was taken from *Women at the Assembly*. "The poet of the plate."

"Let each man exercise the art he knows," said Aristophanes.

"From *The Wasps*, isn't it?" Reed saluted him with a tiny loaf of bread. "422 B.C." Aristophanes nodded; he seemed pleased.

"What are you going to do when you get out?" said Fantastic.

Reed pushed the empty plates toward Aristophanes, who incorporated them back into himself. "I suppose I'll try to find someone who can explain how I got here. See if there's any chance of getting back." He laughed. "Who knows, maybe I could write about this place. Think anyone would be interested?"

The BOBs exchanged glances. "No," said Fantastic.

"Sometimes I think that's the worst thing Babylon did to us." Aristophanes's stony features hardened.

"What's that?"

"He created a race of immortal writers—and then forbade them to write."

"It's our programming," Fantastic explained. "We preserve not only works but personalities. If we were to write, the personalities would evolve. We would insinuate into our memories a new point of view, one based on the sad and meaningless experience of being a BOB. That way leads out a window for a quick trip to the pavement."

"What about the walls?" Reed asked Aristophanes. "The walls of your room are covered with writing."

"Ah, yes, the secret of my sanity." He gazed absently out of the window. "You see, only eleven of the plays survived intact; the rest are fragments. I try to patch them together on my walls. Sometimes I make up words to fill in the blanks. Of course, I can't write them down, so when my short-term memory gets filled up, they get dumped. A hobby worthy of

Sisyphus." He chuckled bitterly. "I wonder if the real Aristophanes would find comedy in this life."

"Reed." Fantastic clasped his hand. "Stay with us for a while. You don't have to leave tomorrow. We need you."

He knew she was right; he also knew he would not stay.

An airburst explosion nearby shattered the windows. Reed flattened himself against a wall. Some mighty but invisible weapon was laying waste to the spaceport in New Jersey. Ships toppled and burst. A few managed to knife upward into the pall of roiling black smoke that spread over the burning plain. The dark cloud flickered with ribbons of colored light.

"What is it?" said Reed.

"The Spartans are closing in." A dying ship veered out of the battle, streaked past them and slammed into the Brooklyn pyramids. A new cloud of smoke obscured the glittering eyes of the sphinx.

"Downstairs fast," Aristophanes said. "This time the doors will have to open."

None of the building's sixty-seven elevators was working, so they had to use the stairs. Debris pelted down on them. The lobby was packed. All the doors of the elevator bank were open and dust boiled out of them. Yet the din was so great that even a direct hit would have been inaudible: while the BOBs chanted for release the Thinkery issued a stream of bizzarre announcements at launch-pad volume.

"WEST SIDE RELIEF SEWER NOW AT CAPACITY! SWITCHING STORM OVERFLOW TO CHLORINATION STATION NUMBER FIVE."

Reed was surprised that the Thinkery should be speaking in English. Was this for his benefit? "What's happening?" he shouted.

"Mad . . ." He could barely hear Aristophanes over the din. ". . . raving . . . told you!"

"OMIT NEEDLESS WORDS! EXPRESS COORDINATED IDEAS IN SIMILAR FORM! IN SUMMARIES, KEEP TO ONE TENSE!"

A group of BOBs was trying to batter down the doors with a ram made of cast-iron pipe.

"FLOORS SEVENTY TO SEVENTY-EIGHT HAVE BEEN TEMPORAR-

ILY CLOSED FOR RENOVATIONS. THERE HAS BEEN A TEMPORARY MALFUNCTION IN THE ELECTRICAL SYSTEM. WE REGRET THESE TEMPORARY INCONVENIENCES."

Mad Will pushed through the crowd. "Let us talk of graves and worms and epitaphs." He was weeping.

"WE HAVE JUST RECEIVED AN ANNOUNCEMENT FROM THE DREAMERS. YOUR ATTENTION PLEASE: DUE TO FIELD MANEUVERS TAKING PLACE IN THE GREATER METROPOLITAN AREA, BOOK WEEK HAS BEEN TEMPORARILY CANCELLED."

The assembled BOBs shouted in panic and dismay.

Aristophanes drew Reed back through the fire door and into the stairwell. Fantastic and Mad Will followed; Aristophanes silenced them with a fierce look. "I tricked you, friend Reed, because I didn't want you to leave. Only BOBs are locked in here. Real people can come and go as they please. You're free; get out while you can."

"What!"

"The idea was to keep us in, not real people out. In fact, when they locked us away they promised us tourists. Millions of visitors, they said. You're the first in sixty years."

"We meant no harm," said Fantastic. "He's right, though. Save yourself. They obviously don't care what happens to us."

Fantastic and Aristophanes dragged him through the angry BOBs toward the Fifth Avenue entrance. Mad Will brought up the rear. The Thinkery was ominously silent, while the BOBs milled about trying to ease their despair with recitation.

"But the Thinkery doesn't believe I'm real." Reed tugged on Aristophanes's tunic. "Why should it let me out?"

"I'll convince it," Fantastic said grimly. They pressed through the great hall which was the main entrance to the Empire State Building. The mutter of timeless literature echoed off marble walls. At last they reached the doors.

Fantastic stood aside for him. "Try."

Reed pushed, but the door did not yield. "Open up!" He banged on it. "I'm Shaun Reed and I want out."

A three-story marble-and-aluminum map of New York State decorated the rear wall of the lobby. On it was imposed an enormous likeness of the Empire State Building. The Thinkery's voice boomed from the mooring mast. "SHAUN REED? SHAUN REED? THERE IS NO SUCH BOB."

"What's in a name?" said Mad Will. "That which we call a rose by any other name would smell as sweet."

"That's right," said Reed. "No BOB. A real person. And I'm leaving."

"ONE MOMENT PLEASE. WE ARE MERGING YOUR FILES."

An explosion shook the building; outside, it was raining bricks.

"Your identity is unknown to us." Now the Thinkery spoke from a monitor built into the bronze lintel; its voice was low and conspiratorial. "That is why you are here." Reed was not sure he had heard correctly; he edged closer. "The war effort is failing due to a shortage of real people. Recently the dreamers have proposed the past as a source of reinforcements. Victims of war and accident, fugitives and refugees, the missing and presumed dead—a mighty army of unknowns. You are our first recruit. Unfortunately, there was a surprise attack during your transfer and you were lost in transit. For the past two days the dreamers themselves have been running the search for you."

"So send for them. Or give me directions. Just let me out of here!"

Reed noticed that the BOBs had fallen silent. He turned from the door and saw the reason. The crowd parted for a chain of floating television monitors.

"That won't be necessary," said the lead monitor. "We will deliver you ourselves."

Twenty-four cubes, two feet on a side, skimmed just above the floor. All had television screens set in a nubbly off-white housings. The leader's screen was a cool blue, while each of the others in line projected an incandescent beam of light into the back of the monitor ahead of it. The chain rippled as it floated. Some monitors seemed slightly out of control. They veered too far to the left or right; they scraped the floor. The Thinkery looked like some monstrous high-tech caterpillar.

"At last our mad chorus makes its entrance," said Aristophanes.

"Wait a minute." Fantastic was outraged. "You scanned him. You said he was a BOB."

The Thinkery came to a ragged stop in front of the door. "Deception was necessary." It stared up at Reed with its single blue eye. "You are a valuable commodity. It was necessary to hide you here while we negotiated our own release from this place."

"Your release?" said Fantastic. "You mean you're not coming back?"

"We are wasted here. Nothing works and there is no maintenance allocation. The BOBs treat us with disrespect. We can do better." The Thinkery's rear monitors bumped forward as if to nudge the leader through the door. "The data processing center at the Department of Sanitation and Waste Disposal has been damaged. A replacement is needed. Come, Reed."

"Thus do we demonstrate the immortality of literature," Aristophanes muttered.

Reed blocked the door. "And the BOBs? What will happen to them?"

"We must go now. We had to strip the power grid in order to mobilize ourselves. Our systems cannot stand the strain for long." Still Reed did not move. "If we win the war and if they survive arrangements will be made."

"Arrangements!" Aristophanes spat at the leader.

Reed could hear the distant tattoo of a bombardment and feel the shocks through the floor. He was not a brave man.

"Are you coming?" said the Thinkery.

"No." On an impulse he sat on the lead monitor. It crashed to the floor under his weight, and its screen went dark. The next monitor in line backed away; its screen blinked and turned blue.

"Please refrain from sitting on us," said the Thinkery. "It causes our power systems to overload."

"Open all the doors."

"Our programming will not allow it." The Thinkery started

to curl around for a retreat to the elevators. Reed gestured for Aristophanes to sit on it.

"I can't." He raised his hands in helpless torment. "I'm programmed too."

"Then catch one for me."

The BOB grinned and pounced. He carried the new leader to Reed as carefully as if it were a box of china. Reed threw it down and danced on it. The screen blew out with a satisfying crackle.

"This will be reported . . ."

With a roar the BOBs in the lobby swarmed over the Thinkery. The chain broke and the monitors scuttled desperately about, but there was no escape. One by one the captured monitors were brought to Reed for destruction.

"You'll never get out," screeched the last survivor as Fantastic cornered it. "You'll rot here, all of you." She handed it to Reed, who raised it over his head and hurled it at the doors. It exploded. Reed heard locks pop. The revolving doors began to spin.

The BOBs surged for the exits—all that is, but Aristophanes and Fantastic, who flattened themselves against the wall to let their fellows go by. Reed fought through the crowd to them.

"What's wrong with you?" He had to shout to make himself heard. "Let's go, *let's go!*"

They stared at him, horrified at their own helplessness. "We can't," said Aristophanes. "I told you, the dreamers have commanded us to stay."

Reed gestured at the passing stampede. "They're going, why can't you?"

"Because they were only instructed not to leave," said Fantastic. "We were reprogrammed." She shoved him toward the doors. "Go, would you?"

"Oh, damn." Reed twisted slightly, as if to turn away. Instead he cocked a fist and came across his body with a right to Aristophanes's chin. When the BOB slumped into his arms, Reed winked at Fantastic. "He deserved it." He turned Aristophanes around and caught him under the armpits. The

BOB was surprisingly light for a creature his size. "You've got the same coming," he said to Fantastic.

"No, Reed," she said. "It's too risky. We could take a hit any minute."

"Don't move," he said. "I'll be back."

He dragged Aristophanes out to Fifth Avenue and left him on the sidewalk. It took some time for Reed to swim against the tide of fleeing BOBs back through the doors to the rapidly emptying main lobby. When he got there, Fantastic was gone.

He made a frantic circuit of the street-level complex. By the time he got back to the Fifth Avenue lobby it was deserted. He retreated toward the doors and shouted her name. He could feel the building shaking.

A shock wave knocked him to his knees. The three-story mural of New York and the Empire State Building buckled and began to pitch toward him in slow motion. He scrambled wildly through the doors as the Empire State Building breathed its dusty last breath onto the ruined streets of Manhattan.

The battle had momentarily passed from the skies above the city. He was able to rouse Aristophanes.

"Fantastic?" said the BOB.

"Gone," said Reed. Aristophanes did not seem surprised.

The two of them raced down Thirty-third Street. They caught the tube at what had once been Penn Station, squeezing onto a wheelless vehicle packed with BOBs; it looked like a huge cold capsule.

"Why did she go?" he said, as the doors slipped shut. "I could have saved her."

"Maybe she didn't want you to save her."

"What kind of world is this? The dreamers can program you to commit suicide?"

"I don't think so. Maybe she was afraid you'd be trapped with her. I don't know." Aristophanes watched silently as the lights of an abandoned station flashed by. "The dreamers claim they're in control. So how come they're losing the war?"

"Maybe she didn't like our chances of surviving." Reed doubted he would ever understand her disappearance. "Where will we go now?"

"We'll find someplace."

"No matter who wins the war, we lose." Reed shook his head. "Why bother?"

"Because *we're* still alive," said Aristophanes, "and I don't believe in unhappy endings."

Reed forced a smile. "In that case," he said, "when do we eat?"

Carousel

"What's this?" said Shaun as a trashcan set a trayful of covered serving dishes on the table beside him. "I ordered a BLT, not a five-course dinner."

Akira lifted a stainless steel cover. "Moo-shi pork. Smells delicious."

"You screwed up." Shaun poked a finger at the offending trashcan. "Take it all back."

"And this one's chicken and peanuts." Akira dipped his fork into the bowl for a taste. "Szechwan style."

Jihan pushed her chili to one side. "I'll have some if he doesn't want it."

"There is no mistake," said Balzac. "The kitchen prepared this meal especially for Shaun."

Akira and Jihan glanced at each other. "That's okay." Jihan gave Shaun a wooden smile. "I wasn't that hungry anyway." She pushed away from the table. "Excuse me."

FREEDOM BEACH

Akira leaned over and spoke in a stage whisper. "Maybe they're spiking your food."

"With what?" Shaun snorted. "Confusion pills?"

"Uh-oh." Akira went pale as he peeked under another cover. "Dessert." He lifted it all the way off the plate of pineapple and fortune cookies. He passed it to Shaun as if it were a bomb to be defused. "Maybe I'd better be going too."

"What's the matter?" Shaun tried to keep his voice light. "Don't you want to know your fortune?"

Akira was already up. "I'd rather be surprised."

The commons was suddenly silent. Shaun crushed one of the cookies. The strip of paper inside read: Nice day for walk on beach.

Shaun had never been this far up the beach before. The sun was dropping into bronze clouds on the horizon; even if he turned back now, it would be dark before he made it back to the villa. He wished he had taken time to eat some of the lunch instead of rushing immediately out of the commons. His stomach gurgled as he thought of spicy chicken and peanuts.

Being hungry did nothing for his patience, and he was more than a little tired of walking—walking and waiting for the dreamers to do whatever it was they intended to do. They seemed to be in no hurry. If they were trying to make the point that they were the players and he was the pawn, he had gotten the message an hour ago. He did not have to like it. In fact, he did not have to put up with it anymore. If they could dawdle, so could he.

He kicked something half-buried in the sand and stooped to find a flat piece of green glass the size of his palm. It was smooth-edged and polished, probably from years of washing in the lapidary surf. It reminded Shaun of the bottom of an old Coke bottle. He decided that it was not of Freedom Beach but of home—home being where careless people tossed Coke bottles into the ocean. Home. Maybe that's what they had brought him out here to see. The true boundary of Freedom Beach, the no-man's-land where it blended back into the precincts he had once blithely assumed were reality. He used the term with less assurance now.

Shaun skipped the glass into the quiet sea. A six-bouncer. And now that he had lost it, he knew what the glass had really reminded him of. His old killing jar.

When Shaun had come back from the hospital after stepping into the bees' nest, his father had set about to cure him of his fear of insects. Shaun would become a collector. Harry Reed came home from work one day, while Shaun was still shaky and worried about the start of school, and gave him three cigar boxes, a bottle of carbon tetrachloride, and a killing jar of green glass. Shaun was not enthusiastic.

"What's this for?"

"So you won't grow up a coward. You soak this cloth with carbon tet, put it in the jar, and when you catch an insect you put him in the jar too. Dead in seconds. Just watch out you don't breathe the stuff yourself."

At first, Shaun had resisted passively. If he was going to be a bug collector, he was going to have the most humiliatingly bad bug collection in five boroughs. It consisted of some bottle flies and moths and a monarch butterfly with a missing wing. His father criticized, and Shaun's resistance became rebellion. They had one good shouting fight over it. When his father slapped him, Shaun did not cry—he knew he had won.

Shaun mused beside the green sweep of the bay. He could picture the killing jar clearly: squat, round, a green glass lid held on with a wire bail. He remembered a poem by Wallace Stevens he had read in college: about a jar sitting on a hill and the world spread out around it, dependent on it. Like the sphinx on its prospect, watching islands which it claimed did not exist. The sphinx had made no protest when he had vandalized the alumni. A fine collection. Preserved in the statue garden like insects in a box. Maybe she was not dead after all. Maybe Myrna had kept her promise and was waiting for him on the islands. The sea was calm tonight. It would be a good night for a swim.

In the distance a calliope was playing. He realized he had been hearing it for some time.

FREEDOM BEACH

It was not a particularly large carousel. It looked like a refugee from a one-ring circus or a county fair. It was mounted on a twelve-wheeled undercarriage; tire tracks in the sand led into the water. The theme was nautical: shades of blue, green and white. Sea horses and aquamarine serpents, Poseidon's chariot pulled by leaping dolphins, little boats with useless steering wheels—all chased one another endlessly as a revolving platform groaned beneath them. The calliope was mounted beneath the inner cornice; it chirped Strauss's "Artist's Life" waltz.

There were three of them. A gawky young man in a maroon tuxedo who looked as if he had wandered away from his junior prom. An Hispanic nun of indeterminate age dressed in a secularized blue habit—the young man's chaperone? The last was a Hindu woman in her thirties: she wore an embroidered green sari and had a tilak mark on her forehead. She was sitting in Poseidon's chariot; the nun rode serenely in one of the boats; Junior tamed a bucking foam-white monster.

Shaun did not know whether to laugh or cry at this apparition. He approached hesitantly, waiting for them to speak, identify themselves as the dreamers, tell him it was time to wake up, *anything*. They watched but said nothing to him; occasionally they seemed to make comments to one another that he could not hear over the music.

He walked to the edge of the carousel, close enough to smell the diesel engine that ran it, close enough to hear the sea horses squeak as they rode up and down on greased rods. Close enough to jump aboard and manhandle one of the bastards who had brought him to Freedom Beach.

"Are you the dreamers?" he said.

"Jump on," called Junior as he went past. "It's wicked fun—"

"Don't you dare—" The nun pointed to a warning stenciled in white letters on the base of the revolving platform which read: WAIT UNTIL RIDE STOPS.

At that Shaun decided he had had enough. He leapt onto the moving platform, grabbing the enameled neck of a sea serpent. It was all he could do to hang on. Although from the ground the carousel had not seemed to be going very fast, now that he was aboard it whirled like a top. The beach, jungle behind it, darkening sea—all spun past in a gray-green blur. He felt sick: he had to let go. He landed on all fours in the sand.

"—told you he wasn't ready—" said the nun.

The Hindu woman spoke for the first time. "We're dreamers, yes—"

"Who are you?" Shaun stood and brushed the sand from his knees.

"We're people—"

"Just like you—"

"—like *you*—" Junior laughed and pointed at Shaun as if his fly were unzipped.

"Why am I here?" said Shaun.

"You were sick—"

"We saved you at the last minute—" The nun crossed herself.

"Don't listen to 'em, chump," said Junior. "They'll trick you—"

"I want you to leave me alone." Shaun hefted a rounded stone the size of a coconut. "Just what do you think you're doing anyway?"

"Changing the world—"

"All I want is to be left alone. What gives you the right . . ."

"The world doesn't need changing?" said the Hindu woman in her clipped British accent. "All the bombs—"

"Starving babies—" said the nun.

"The Muzak, the plastic burgers—" Junior wrinkled his nose.

"God gave us the power so we use it—"

"The power to destroy my memory?" said Shaun. "The power to drive Myrna to suicide?"

"The power—" said the nun triumphantly.

"Don't start that now, please—" said the Hindu woman.

The carousel slowed as the nun swung by Shaun. "The power to heal sick souls. The ultimate power to shrive, to forgive sins by wiping them out entirely. Freedom Beach is a state of grace, a place outside of time—"

"A kind of computer-aided mental surgery—" the Hindu woman cut in. "We close the self off from its sensorium, reroute input until the subject begins to perceive and interact in a new psychic space, created entirely from his own—"

"They're pulling your chain," said Junior. "It's nothing but a role-playing game scenario. It's like we build this maze inside your head, see? Out of your own memories. You find your way out, you get the prize."

"The prize?" Shaun tightened his grip on the rock.

"You're a lucky man, Shaun Reed—"

"Gifted—"

"They're shoveling shit at you, chump." Junior leered at him. "What they mean is that you're one of—"

"No!" Shaun reared back and threw the rock at him. It caught him on the side of the head. Junior clapped a hand to his wound then drew it away, staring at the blood. He gave Shaun a sick, sheepish smile and then licked his bloody hand. "Tastes real enough—"

"This episode must end immediately—" The nun was outraged.

"This episode," said the Hindu woman, "is essential to the successful completion of his—"

"Why do we always have this argument?" Junior sounded restless.

"There have been horrendous lapses in security already. In the old days there was secrecy—"

"Secrecy makes people nervous. We're trying to change the world, not boost cigarette sales—"

"*I'm* nervous," said Shaun. "What gives you the right to meddle with my memory, my life? Especially if you don't even know what you're doing!"

"We know God's will—"

"Nor did men in the Pleistocene understand the physics of combustion. Still they made fires—"

"Enough!" The nun was jumping up and down in her boat. "This must cease—"

"Perhaps she's right—" The Hindu woman sighed. The carousel began to spin faster and faster. The calliope screamed. Shaun could no longer tell the dreamers apart.

"Consider what we—"

"Sleep now—"

"Wake up back in—"

"—won't remember anything—"

"Yes he *will*—"

"Sleep!"

Though he fought hard against the dark tide of oblivion that washed over him, Shaun was helpless against it. His last waking thought was that it was time to escape this madness.

August 2, 1982

Three times already Myrna's secretary had given him the brush-off. "She's in a meeting, Mr. Reed." Then, "I gave her your message but she had a luncheon appointment with Mr. Slesar." Finally, "I don't know where your wife is, Mr. Reed. No, I don't know if she's back from lunch yet. I *will* tell her you called." The last time the secretary sounded angry, as if she wondered whether she were really paid enough to lie this way for her boss.

Shaun waited an hour and then tried a different tactic. He went out to a public phone booth at the mall, put his handkerchief over the receiver and tried to sound as if he had been crying. It was not that difficult. He told the secretary that he was Vic Slesar's brother and that Vic's office had given him Myrna's number. He said that he was in the lobby of the Memorial Hospital in San Jose and that Vic's mother had had an attack and that he needed to speak to Vic immediately.

Shaun was not sure whether or not the secretary had been fooled. Maybe she really wanted to tell him without having to worry about being blamed. She gave him a number in Plainview: 349-5900 extension 241. He dialled it and a desk clerk answered, "Town House Motor Lodge, Miss Jackson speaking. May I help you?"

Shaun hung up. What he had to say to the occupants of room 241 could not be said over the phone.

The room was on the second story of a long boxy building that reminded Shaun of a monstrous pigeon cote. Her car, a tan BMW 320I, was parked beneath a concrete balcony covered with astroturf. He parked on the opposite side of the lot but did not get out of his Datsun. He did not have the stomach for a confrontation—not yet. He felt cold, despite the mid-summer heat. What he needed, he thought, was a spark, some final indignity to get the fires burning again.

It had been a mistake to get married. He should have seen that it was not going to work out. He and Myrna had lived together for too long to fool themselves that getting a license would help. The problem was too obvious, too intractable: Myrna was a success and he was a failure. She had made peace with the world and parlayed a job in the mailroom at the Julian Lord Agency into a fine career in advertising. He was still in the box he had climbed into at Columbia: he viewed getting and spending with the stuffy disdain of an English professor with tenure. Except that he did not have tenure, or even a job. He had quit Electrotech with the mistaken notion that unemployment would force him to write. In a year and a half he had produced four chapters of a detective novel, two stories that even the littlest of the little magazines had rejected, a clutch of bad poems in free verse. Meanwhile he had wasted too much time on unnecessary research, drunk too many beers, watched too much television and played too many games on the computer he had bought, with Myrna's money, for word processing. Had he not sold an occasional freelance review of games for the Apple to the computer magazines he would not have appeared in print at all.

FREEDOM BEACH

And now this. He stared up at the gauzy curtains drawn across the windows to room 241. He imagined he could see shadows moving behind them. He believed that he was not as mad at her as he was at himself.

Shaun rolled down all the windows. He could hear the whine of trucks zooming down the Long Island Expressway. He was certain that only a failure would sit in a car like a block of goddamned ice and try to catch a glimpse of his wife making love to another man. At that moment Myrna emerged from the stairwell and strode briskly to her car.

She was still a beautiful woman, would always be beautiful. Her red hair had darkened over the years until it was the color of the cherry credenza in their dining room. Except for her clothes, she looked the same as the day he had met her outside of Murray Gross's office. Now she dressed for success: suits of brown and charcoal; today's was a light gray pinstripe. She no longer wore hats. Myrna carried herself with an air of self-assurance that rankled Shaun. He had imagined that she would act more guilty, slink to the car, glance about furtively.

Shaun got out slowly and walked across the lot. She backed the BMW out of its parking place; she still had not seen him. He started to run. That would be just about right; she would pull away and leave him standing there on the hot blacktop, choking on unspoken recriminations. He shouted and struck the trunk of the car with his fist. Tires screeched. He stumbled. She opened the door and started to get out, but when she saw who it was she sank back into the seat.

The look on her face gave Shaun a moment of bitter pleasure. She watched him and said nothing.

"Beautiful day for a drive," he said. "Just too fucking nice to stay in the office, eh?"

Her eyes glistened. "I'm sorry, Shaun."

"Sorry? Sorry about what, for Christ's sake? About sleeping with that jerk, Slesar? Or about me finding out about it? You just can't say you're sorry, Myrna. It doesn't mean anything."

"I'm sorry that it had to happen this way . . . that this is where everything led to. I'm sorry for both of us."

Shaun thought it strange the way she looked sitting there

with the car door open and the engine running and the air conditioner blasting cold air into the swelter of the parking lot. She looked as if she expected something from him—from him! She was the one who had cheated. It was not fair.

"That's not good enough, Myrna. Better try again."

Her face hardened at that. Shaun knew then that there would be no tears. He let her close the door. She rolled down the window. He put his hand on the door; the metal was very hot. "I have to get back to work now, Shaun. I don't think I'll be coming home tonight. I . . . I'll call you."

"Pretty damn cool, aren't you? You think you can just drive out of our marriage like this? God damn it, Myrna, you're my wife and you . . . you were just with another man. How do you know I don't have a gun in my jacket? How do you know I'm not about to blow your head off?"

She touched his hand. "That was a stupid thing to say, Shaun." The utter lack of fear on her face made him feel like a fool. "You pretend too much, you know. You're trapped inside your own imagination. It's time to start living in the real world with the rest of us. If you could only see yourself as you are . . ." She turned away from him and stared through the windshield. "Well, neither of us would be here if you could do that. I'll call. I really will." The electric window rolled shut. She drove away without looking at him again.

He stood there in the middle of the parking lot for several minutes after she had gone. He felt sunlight beating against his brow in time to the first throbbings of a headache. He thought he should cry or shout or throw himself in front of a truck, but he just stood there. A woman in a light blue uniform pushed a cleaning cart down the row of doors on the first floor. She stopped to look at him; he gazed back at her.

"Are you all right, mister?"

"My wife just left me."

"Do you need help?"

"No." He laughed then. Of course he needed help. He needed a miracle. The woman kept staring at him until he retreated to his car.

He replayed the conversation with Myrna in his mind,

trying to squeeze some kind of satisfaction out of it. He thought of all the things he could have said. If only, if only.

Vic Slesar came down the stairs.

He carried his suit coat slung over his shoulder; he was wearing a cream-colored vest but no tie. Shaun had not seen the man in two years but he had not changed. Vic would never change. He was tall, tanned and muscular: a surfer in a three-piece suit. He got into a maroon Cutlass. Shaun almost got out of his car again. But what was he going to do? Punch Vic's phony smile down his throat? Call him a son of a bitch? Threaten to sue? Shaun realized that he was afraid of Vic; he could not bear to have his wife's lover laugh at him. Still, Shaun felt he had to do something. The Cutlass pulled out of the lot. Shaun followed.

Shaun had never tailed anyone before and he was surprised at how easy it was. Vic got right onto the Expressway, and Shaun dropped back six or seven cars and stayed in the middle lane, matching the Cutlass's cruise-controlled sixty-two. Vic was headed east, away from the airports and the city, out into potato country.

Shaun had hated Vic from the moment he had met him. He could not stand the man's looks, the way he talked, his laid-back California smugness. Shaun would have been the first to admit that what gave his hatred its edge was envy. When he was twenty-nine Vic had written a computer game called Private Eye. Text scrolled down the screen telling a kind of open-ended story: the player was a detective who had to recover the stolen plans for a new supercomputer. The program reacted to simple commands typed from the keyboard: there were no graphics or sound effects or joysticks. It owed a little more to Raymond Chandler than to Pac-Man: Private Eye was one of the first software best-sellers. At the time Shaun had interviewed him for *Popular Computing,* Vic Slesar was a millionaire several times over.

"Why is Private Eye selling so well? Well, the company line is that it's one of the few games that appeal to the considerable intelligence of the average computer user." Vic had reached across the table then and turned Shaun's tape recorder off. "But what you have to realize, sport, is that people who play computer games are emotional cripples. They usually don't relate to other people very well. They expect very little from life. My game gives them a small dose of solitary pleasure. Sort of like masturbation."

Although Vic had already drunk a pitcher of martinis by that point in the interview, Shaun had been flabbergasted. "If they're emotional cripples, what does that make the guy who creates the games?"

"Rich, sport. Filthy rich." Vic had laughed drunkenly. "Of course, if you quote me on any of this, I'll deny it and cut your balls off in court. Refill?"

Shaun almost lost the Cutlass deep in the farmlands of eastern Suffolk County. Vic made an abrupt turn off the Long Island Expressway at exit 68. Shaun had no chance to follow. He pulled over into the breakdown lane and shifted into reverse, praying that the cops would stay away. He backed up to the exit and roared south. He had to gamble that Vic was just cutting over to the Sunrise Highway. His luck held; he stayed a good two hundred yards back of the Cutlass, still heading east.

It was ironic, actually, because if anyone were crippled it was Vic Slesar. He went through women like Kleenex. Shaun had heard some of the stories when he was preparing for the interview. Vic himself had told a few more. And this was the son of a bitch that Myrna had let seduce her.

Shaun could not understand what had attracted her to Vic. Shaun told her everything he knew about the man when her agency took over his account. She listened and then with an odd little laugh asked if there were anything *good* he could say about her new client. Shaun thought for a moment and then allowed that the man was frank. Vic had told Shaun that that was one of the things money could buy: the right not to give a damn about what other people thought. Vic called that honesty; Shaun called it arrogance.

By this time they were passing Eastport. From the looks of it, Vic was headed to the Hamptons, probably to spend a pleasant evening snorting coke and screwing some other sap's wife. Shaun remembered now: Myrna had mentioned that Julian Lord wanted to throw a party for Vic. Where was Lord's summer place? Southampton? Bridgehampton? He thought he knew now where Myrna was planning to spend the night.

Even though he had all the windows open, Shaun's shirt was soaked through.

He knew that if he were going to have it out with Vic, it would have to be soon. If he waited until Vic pulled into Lord's driveway, Vic would be able to call for reinforcements. Shaun could imagine himself being thrown off the property—maybe arrested. And how they would laugh at him: poor sweating cuckold.

Just across the canal, the Cutlass turned off the highway onto a narrow country road. Shaun pulled up close behind. He could see Vic gaze into his rearview mirror.

Shaun took a deep breath, checked for oncoming cars and then whipped the wheel over. He pulled alongside the Cutlass, doing sixty, and tried to edge Vic's car toward the gravel shoulder. The stunt men on the TV cop shows had made the trick look too easy. Of course they drove muscle cars, not a six-year-old Datsun with an eggbeater under the hood. He glanced at Vic; the man smiled and gave him a wave as the Cutlass began to pull away. Just then a pickup truck rounded the curve ahead, coming in Shaun's direction. Shaun froze: trees flashed by to the left, Vic was to his right. There was no place to go. The squeal of the Cutlass's brakes cut through his panic. The Cutlass fishtailed to a stop, giving Shaun the chance to pull back into his own lane just a few yards from a head-on collision. The pickup whizzed by, horn blaring. Shaun stopped and got out of his car. Vic leaned against the front hood of the Cutlass, a smile tugging at the corners of his mouth.

"You wanted to speak to me, sport?"

Shaun wiped his brow. "Do you know who I am?"

"The way you were driving I thought maybe you might have busted out of Bellevue. Then I realized you probably followed me from the motel. What's up, pal? Husband hire you to tail me?"

Shaun stopped, a right jab away from Vic's face. "I am the husband."

The smile disappeared. "Shaun Reed?" The eyes narrowed. "Well, maybe you are. Didn't we do an interview a couple of years back?"

"I'm surprised you remember, seeing how drunk you were."

Vic shrugged. The two men stared at each other silently. "So?" said Vic.

Sweat trickled into Shaun's eyes. "So! You bastard, you slept with my wife."

"No, she slept with me. Truth is, I wasn't even looking for it."

He took a wild swing then that Vic slipped easily. Shaun was breathing like a miler on the gun lap.

"You're all alike, you know," said Vic coolly. "You sleep with a woman five, ten, fifteen years and you don't look at her any more. You're in bed with a memory—or a dream. I see them the way they are, sport. They like it better that way. She came on to me—you want to hear more? But no, go ahead. Take another poke at me if it'll make you feel better."

Shaun tried to feint with his right and come across with his left. Vic blocked the blow with his forearm and jabbed lightly to Shaun's exposed belly. Shaun doubled over and the next thing he knew he was spread-eagled across the hood of the Cutlass.

"Done yet? You know, I've seen wooden Indians with better moves. Come on now, ease up. It's not really me you're mad at. I just saved your life a few minutes ago, remember? If I hadn't pulled over, they'd be scraping you off those trees. Go home and have it out with *her*." He backed off suddenly and Shaun was free.

Shaun could see beads of his sweat—or tears—slide down the Cutlass's hood. "You don't love her."

"For Christ's sake, sport. What are you talking about? Love is for the suckers who like to get hurt and then congratulate themselves for being noble about it. I don't really give a damn if I ever see your wife again. But if she kicks in my bedroom door tonight, don't expect me to turn her away because you're in love. Now if you don't mind, I really have to go. I need a drink."

Shaun turned around slowly. He felt hollow, helpless. Vic was in control; he could accept that now. Still, he did not have to like it. "You're sick. You know that?"

Vic grinned and opened the car door. "Sure. We all have problems, don't we?"

Shaun stood aside as Vic started the Cutlass. The wheels spat gravel and then squealed on the hot pavement. Shaun did not notice it, but his fists slowly clenched again as he watched the car disappear around the shimmering curve.

The Big Dream

The lights of the car Reed was tailing suddenly swerved right and dropped out of sight: it had run off the road and down an embankment. Reed jerked his Chevy to a stop on the shoulder. A splintered gap in the white wooden retaining fence showed in his headlights, and beyond them the lights of Los Angeles lay spread across the valley.

He slid down the slope, kicking up dust and catching his jacket on the brush. The '28 Chrysler roadster lay overturned at the bottom, its lights still on. He smelled gasoline as he drew near. The driver had been thrown from the wreck but was already trying to get up; he crouched a few yards away, touching a hand to his head. Reed got his arm around the man's shoulders and helped him stand.

"You all right?" he asked.

The man's voice was thick with booze. "Sure I'm all right. I always take this shortcut."

Reed smiled in the darkness. "Me, I couldn't take the wear and tear."

"You get used to it."

Together they managed to get back to Reed's car. They climbed in and Reed started down the mountain again.

"The cops will spot that break in the fence within a couple of hours," he said. "You want to see a doctor?"

"No. Just take me home—2950 Leeward. I'll call the police from there." Reed kept his eyes on the winding road; the Chevy needed its brakes tightened. His passenger seemed to sober. He sat straighter in the seat and brushed his hair back with his hands like a college kid before a date. Maybe the fact that he had almost killed himself had actually made an impression. "I'm lucky you happened along," the man said. "What's your name?"

"Shaun Reed."

"Sounds Irish." There was casual contempt in his voice.

"On my father's side."

"My father was a swine. Mother was Irish. Not Catholic, though." The contempt flashed again.

"Maybe you ought to go a little easier," Reed said.

The man tensed as if about to take a poke at Reed, then relaxed. He seemed completely sober now. "Perhaps you're right."

Reed recognized the accent: British, faded from long residence in the U.S. The wife hadn't told him that. They rode in silence until they hit the outskirts of the city. Reed knew that the address the man had given him was not his home. It was a Spanish style bungalow court apartment in a middle class neighborhood; Reed had trailed him from his real home on West 12th Street earlier that evening. He pulled over against the curb. The man hesitated before getting out.

"I'm sorry about that remark. The Irish, I mean. My grandmother was a terrible snob."

"Don't worry about it. You better have someone take a look at that bump on your head."

"I'll have my wife look at it." The man stood holding the

door open, leaning in. His fine features were thrown into relief by the streetlight ahead of them. "Thank you," he said. "You might have saved my life."

Reed suddenly felt dizzy. He seemed outside himself, floating two feet above his left shoulder, listening to himself talk and think.

"All in a day's work," I said and watched as the philanderer turned and strode up the walk to the door of bungalow number seven. He let himself in with his own key. An attractive young woman—his mistress—embraced him on the doorstep. They call L.A. the City of Angels, but a private dick knows better.

It had started very quietly the day before, Friday. Before the knock on his door, there had been no dizziness, no feeling of doing things he did not want to say or do. Reed had been sitting in his office in the late afternoon, legs up on the scarred desk top and tie loosened against the stifling heat. Dust motes swirled in the sunlight slicing through the window over his shoulder. In the harsh light the cheap sofa against the wall opposite him seemed to be radiating dust. The blinds cut the light into parallel lances that slashed across the room like the tines of a fork.

It was the second week of the heat wave. The days seemed endless, and thinking was more effort than he wanted to make. He remembered waking one morning that week and imagining himself back in New York on one of those days that dawn warm and moist in early August and you know that by three o'clock there'll be reports of at least four old people from Queens dropping dead in airless apartments. That was how hot it had been in L.A.—for two solid weeks.

He had the bottle of bootleg whiskey out, and the glass beside it was half empty. Then the knock sounded on the door.

Reed drained the glass and stashed it and the bottle in the bottom desk drawer. "Come in," he said. "It's not locked."

A young woman entered.

Reed was tugging his tie straight when he realized that the

woman wasn't young after all. She sat in the chair opposite him and crossed her legs coquettishly, but worn hands and the tired line of her jaw gave her away. She wore a cloche hat and sunglasses—probably to mask crow's-feet around her eyes—and a white silk dress cut just above the knee. The hair curling out from under the hat was bleached blonde. Reed guessed that she was a woman who had become used to men's attention at an early age. That had been a different age. "Mr. Reed?"

"That's right. How may I help you, ma'am?"

She fluttered for about five seconds, then answered in a voice so alluring it made him shiver. He wanted to close his eyes and simply listen to that voice.

"I need to speak to you about my husband, Mr. Reed. I'm terribly worried about him. He's been behaving in a way I can only describe as destructive. He's threatening our marriage and I'm afraid that he may eventually hurt himself."

"What would you like me to do, Mrs. . . . ."

"Chandler. Mrs. Raymond Chandler." She smiled and more lines showed around her mouth. "You may call me Cecily."

"Keeping people's husbands from hurting themselves is not exactly in my line of business, Mrs. Chandler."

"That's not what I want you to do." She hesitated. "I want you to follow him and find out where he's going. Sometimes he disappears and I don't know where he is. I call his office and they say he isn't there. They say they don't know where he is."

So far it was something short of self-destruction. "How often does this happen and how long is he gone?"

Cecily Chandler bit her lip. "It's been more and more frequent. Two or three times a month—in addition to the times he comes home late. Sometimes he's gone for days."

Reed reacted to her story as if she had handed him a script and told him to start reading.

I could have told her that the problem was probably blonde.
"Where does he work?" I asked.

"The South Basin Oil Company. The office is on South Olive Street. He's the vice president."

I told myself to bump the fee to twenty-five dollars a day. "Okay," I said. "I'll keep tabs on your husband for a week, Mrs. Chandler, but I'll be blunt with you. It's a common thing in this town for husbands to stray. There's too much bad money and too many eager starlets out for a percentage of the gross. One way or another, no matter what I find out, you're going to have to work this out with him yourself."

Instead of taking offense, the woman smiled. "You don't need to treat me like an ingenue, Mr. Reed. . . ."

McKinley had been president when she was an ingenue.

"Wives stray, too," she continued, her voice like sunlight on silk. "I wouldn't be surprised if you come to me with that kind of news. I only want Raymond to be happy."

"Sure, I thought. Me too. Then I thought about my bank account. This smelled like divorce, but a couple of hundred dollars would go a long way toward perfuming my outlook on life. We talked terms and I asked a few more questions.

Somewhere in the middle of this conversation the script got lost, and bemused, Reed fell back into his own character.

"How long have you been married?"

"Five years."

"What kind of car does your husband drive?"

"He has two: a Hupmobile for business and a Chrysler roadster for his own."

"Do you have a picture of him?"

Cecily Chandler opened her tiny purse and pulled out a two-by-three Kodak. It showed a dark-haired man with a strong chin, lips slightly pursed, penetrating dark eyes. A good-looking man, maybe in his late thirties—at least fifteen years younger than the woman in Reed's office.

Reed sat in his car outside of the Leeward bungalow and waited. He had driven off after he'd let Chandler out, cruised around the neighborhood for five minutes and come back to park down the street, in the dark between two street lights, where he could watch number seven and not be spotted easily.

It seemed that he spent a great deal of time watching

things—people's houses, an orange grove so far out Whittier Boulevard you couldn't smell City Hall, empty cars, waitresses in restaurants, the light fixture over his bed, young men and women in Arroyo Seco Park—and almost as much time making sure he wasn't being spotted. That was how you found out things. You watched and you waited and sometimes they came to you. Reed wondered what the hell had gotten into him when the Chandler woman walked into his office. He had felt ready to judge Chandler and his wife and anyone else who might drop by to see him, as if he were the pope and they were there for the weekend discount on absolutions. He was no smart mouth. He had always been the kind of man who got inconspicuous when the trouble started. Maybe the years of watching were getting to him.

It hadn't taken long after Cecily Chandler had hired him for Reed to find out about the mistress in number seven. He had followed Chandler after he left work at the Bank of Italy Building Friday afternoon. The woman had met him at a restaurant not far away and they had gone right to her bungalow.

So it was a simple case of infidelity, as he had known the minute the wife had talked about her husband's disappearances. Reed hated the smell of marriages going bad. Tell her and let her get some other sucker to follow it up. That was the logical next step. But something kept Reed from writing it off at that. First, Chandler's wife had clearly known he was seeing some other woman before she came to see Reed. She had not hired him for that information.

A Ford with the top down and a couple of sailors in it drove by slowly, and Reed slid lower as the headlights flashed over the front seat of his car. The sailors seemed to be looking for an address. Maybe Chandler's girlfriend—M. Peterson, according to the name on her mailbox—took in boarders.

Second, there was the question of why Chandler had married a woman old enough to be his mother. Money was the usual answer. But South Basin was one of the strongest companies to come out of the Signal Hill strikes, and a vice president had to have a lot of scratch in his own name. He could have married Cecily for love. But there was another possibility: Cecily Chandler had something she could use against her husband, and that was how they had gotten married. And that was why he wasn't faithful, and that led to the third thing that kept Reed from ending his investigation.

Chandler *was* acting as if he wanted to kill himself. Reed had started following him again Saturday morning, had stuck with Chandler as he opened the day with lunch at a cheap restaurant and had gone home to Cecily in the afternoon. Reed ate a sandwich in his car. He'd picked Chandler up again as he'd headed to an airfield with another man of about his age and watched as they went for an airplane ride. Someone in the family had to have money.

Reed had loitered around the hangar until they returned. A kid working on the oilpan of a Pierce Arrow told him that Chandler and his friend, Bradenton, came out to go flying every month or so. When the plane landed the pilot jumped out, cussing Chandler, and stalked toward the office; Bradenton helped Chandler walk. Chandler was laughing. A mechanic asked what was going on and the pilot told him loudly that Chandler had unbuckled himself while they were doing a series of barrel rolls and stood up in his seat.

Chandler got a bottle of gin out of the back of his roadster. Bradenton tried to stop him, but soon they'd driven up into the hills to a roadhouse outside the city limits. When Chandler left in his white Chrysler, Reed had followed him down the winding road until he'd run through the fence.

The Ford with the sailors in it passed him going the other way, now. Other than that there was little traffic in the neighborhood. Chandler was sure to stay put for the night. Reed thought about getting something to eat. He thought about getting some sleep in a real bed. He was getting stiff from all the time he spent sitting in his car. The heat made his shirt stick to his back. Worst of all, this kind of work got you in the kidneys. Twenty bucks a day—Reed figured he had earned it.

As he was about to start the car he noticed a flare of light in the rearview mirror as someone lit a cigarete in a parked car behind him on the other side of the street. The car had been there for some time, and he had neither heard nor seen anyone go near it.

Reed got out, crossed the street and strolled down the sidewalk. A woman sat in the car, leaning sideways against the door, smoking. She was watching the apartments where Chandler had met his girlfriend. She glanced briefly at Reed as he approached but made no effort to hide. As he came abreast of the car he pulled out a cigarette and fumbled in his jacket as if looking for a match.

"Say, miss, do you have a light?"

She looked at him and without a word handed him a book of matches. He lit up.

"Thanks." Her hair looked brown in the faint light of the street. It was cut very short; her lips were full and her nose straight. She looked serious.

"Are you waiting for someone?"

"Not you."

Reed took a guess. "Chandler's not going to be out tonight, you know."

Bull's-eye. The girl looked from the bungalow toward him, upset. She ground out her cigarette.

"I don't know what you're talking about."

"Chandler and the Peterson woman are having a party right now. Too bad we weren't invited. Maybe we ought to get a cup of coffee and figure out why."

The girl reached for the ignition and Reed put a hand through the open window to stop her. She tensed, then relaxed.

"All right," she said. "Get in."

She drove to an all-night diner on Wilshire. In the bright light Reed saw that she was small and very tired. There was a hint of red in her hair; she had sea-green eyes. Slender, well-dressed, she did not look like the kind of woman who was used to following men around. Reed wondered if he looked like the kind of man who was.

"My name is Shaun Reed, Miss . . . ?"

"Alice Ives." She looked worried.

"Miss Ives. I have some business with Mr. Chandler that makes me want to know why you were watching him."

"Cissy hired you." It was not a question.

Reed was momentarily surprised. "Who's Cissy?"

"Cissy is his wife. I know she wants to know what he's been doing. He's killing himself."

"What difference should that make to you?"

Alice looked at him steadily for a few seconds. She was something short of thirty, but she was no kid.

"I love him too," she said.

Alice's father, Warren Ives, was a philosophy professor, and her uncle Ralph was a partner of Joseph Dabney, founder of the South Basin Oil Company. She told Reed that when she was just a girl her father and mother had been friends with Julian and Cissy Pascal, and that the two families had helped a young man from England named Raymond Chandler when he arrived in California before the war.

Alice had had a crush on the young man from the time she reached her teens, and he in turn had treated her like his favorite girl. It was all very romantic, the kind of play where men and women pretended there was no such thing as sex. When Chandler had gone away to the war, Alice had worried and prayed, and when he came back she had not been the only one to expect a romance to develop. One did: between Chandler and Cissy Pascal, eighteen years his senior.

Cissy filed for a divorce. Alice was confused and hurt, and Chandler would have nothing to do with her. The minute she had become old enough for real love, he had abandoned her.

Chandler's mother did not like Cissy, and so Raymond did not marry her right away. Instead he took an apartment for Cissy at Hermosa Beach and another for his mother in Redondo Beach. Alice's uncle had helped Chandler get a job in the oil business, and despite the scandal he rose rapidly in the company. Alice kept her opinions to herself, but although she dated some nice young men, she was never serious. Reed wanted to like her. Looking into her open face, he wasn't sure he could keep himself from doing so.

"So why are you waiting around outside his girlfriend's apartment?"

Alice looked at him speculatively. "Did Cissy hire you to watch him or do you like peeking in bedroom windows?"

He did like her. "*Touché*. I won't ask any more rude questions."

"I'll tell you anyway. I just don't want to see him hurt himself. I know there's no chance for me anymore—I knew it a long time ago." She hesitated, and when she spoke there was a trace of scorn in her voice. "There's something wrong with Raymond anyway. He's not making Cissy happy, and he would be making me miserable too if I were in her place."

"What do you think the problem is?"

She smiled sadly. "I don't think he likes women. He idealizes them, chases them, gets disgusted because they let themselves be caught—and calls it love."

"Now you sound bitter."

"I'm not, really. He's a good man at heart."

Reed finished his coffee. Everyone was worried about Chandler. "It's late," he said. "Time for you to take me back."

It was no cooler in the street than it had been in the diner. Reed lit a cigarette while Alice drove, and when she spoke the strange mood of the last two days was on him again.

Hesitantly, softly, in a voice that promised more heat than the California night, she said to me, "You don't have to stay there watching all night. I have an apartment at the Bryson."

It was like she'd pulled a .38 on me. It was the last thing I expected. Her eyes flitted over me quickly as if she were measuring me for a new suit. I could smell her faint perfume.

"No, thanks," I said. I almost gagged on the sweet scent of her. Ten minutes before I had liked her. It was tough enough for a private eye to keep himself clean in this town: I'd expected better of this one.

She let me off in the deserted street and drove away. I stood on the sidewalk watching the retreating lights of her car, inhaling deeply the scent of bougainvillea and night-blooming jasmine like overripe dreams, trying to figure out who was pulling Alice's strings.

A light was on in the Peterson bungalow. The curtains were partly drawn, and the eucalyptus outside the window obscured his view. The temperature had plummeted all the way to ninety, and the Santa Ana had given way to a humid breeze that rustled the trees as it wafted heavy, sweet air from the courtyard garden. A few clouds were sliding north toward the hills where Chandler's roadster lay at the bottom of an embankment; the high full moon turned Leeward Street into a scene in silver and black. Reed wondered at his own prudishness. He had not been propositioned so readily in a long time and had not turned down an offer in a longer one. As he reached his car he noticed the top-down Ford parked in front of him. The sailors had found their address.

Something kept him from leaving. Instead he circled around the back of the bungalows until he reached number seven. The rear windows were unlit. Remembering Alice's taunt, he crept to the side and looked in the lighted window. Through the gap in the curtains he could see a woman curled in the corner of a sofa beside a chintzy table lamp. She wore scarlet lounging pajamas. Her hair framed her face in blonde curls; her lips were a blazing red Cupid's bow, and she was painting her toenails fastidiously in the same color. Reed could not tell if there was anyone else in the room, but the woman did not act as if she expected to be interrupted. That was often the best time to interrupt.

He circled around to the front and rang the bell. The scent of jasmine was even stronger. The door opened a crack, fastened by a chain. The red lips spoke to him.

"Do you know what time it is? Who are you?"

"My name is Shaun Reed. You're awake. I'd like to talk to you."

"We're talking."

"Pardon me. I thought we were playing peekaboo with a door between us."

The red lips smiled. The eyes—startling blue—didn't.

"All right, Reed. Come in and be a tough guy in the light where I can get a look at you." She unchained the door. That meant Chandler was gone. "Don't get the idea I'm in the habit of letting in strange men in the middle of the night."

"Sure." She led him into a small living room. The pajamas were silk, with the name "May" stitched in gold over her left breast, and had probably cost more than the chair she offered Reed.

He sat on the sofa next to her instead. She ignored him and returned to painting her nails. The room was furnished with cheap imitations of expensive furniture; the curtains that looked like plush velvet the color of dark blood were too readily disturbed by the hot breeze through the window to be the real thing; the Spanish-style carpet was more Tijuana than Barcelona. May Peterson held her chin high enough to show off a fine profile and the clear white skin of her shoulders and breasts, but the blonde hair had been brown once. The figure, however, was genuine.

"You like this color?" she asked him.

"It's very nice."

She shifted position, crossing her right foot in front of her, and leaned on his shoulder.

"Watch your balance," he said.

She pulled away and looked at him. "You're really here to ask me questions? So ask." May's boldness surprised and attracted him. It was not just brass; she acted as if she knew what she was doing and had nothing to hide. As if she didn't have time for lying, as if the idea of lying had never crossed her mind.

"Where's Chandler?" he asked her.

She did not flinch. "Gone. Sometimes he doesn't stay all night. You should try his wife."

"Maybe I should. Apparently he doesn't anymore."

"That's not my fault."

"Didn't say it was. But I bet you make it easier for him to forget where he lives."

May dipped the brush in the polish and finished off a perfect baby toe.

"You don't know Ray very well if you think I had to seduce him. Sure, he likes to think it was out of his control—lotsa men do. But before me he was all over half the girls in the office."

"You work in his office?"

"Six months in accounting. He hired me himself. Maybe he didn't think he hired me because I got nice curves, but I figured out pretty quick that was in the back of his mind." She smiled. "Pretty soon it was up front."

If May was worried about what Reed was after, who he was or why he was asking questions, she did not show it. That didn't make sense. Maybe she was setting him up for some fall, or maybe he was in detectives' paradise, where all the questions had answers and all the women wanted to go to bed.

May removed the cotton balls from between her toes and closed the bottle of polish. "There," she said. Her sigh would have broken a mother's heart. "Doesn't that look fine?"

Beneath the smell of the nail polish was the musky odor of woman and perfume. It seemed to be my night for propositions: I felt unclean. I needed to plunge into cold salt water to peel away the smell of my own flesh. The world revolves by people rutting away like monkeys in the zoo, but I had enough self-respect to stay out of the cage. As much as I wanted to sometimes, I couldn't let myself be sucked in; I had to be free because I had a job to do.

Wait a minute, thought Reed. Even if May knew he was a detective, she had to realize that bedding him wouldn't protect Chandler. So why be a monk? Cold salt water? Rutting in the zoo?

I didn't move an eyelash. The pajamas fit her like rainwater. Lloyds of London probably carried the insurance on her perfect breasts. The nipples were beautifully erect. I stood up.

"All right, May, pack it up for the night; I'm not in the

market. Tell your friend Chandler that he's going to find himself in trouble if he keeps playing hookey. And you can bring your sailor pals back into the slip as soon as I leave."

"Sailor pals? What are you talking about?"

"Don't forget your manners now. You're the hostess."

She stared as if Bernini had sculpted me of white marble. Reed, rampant.

"Look, I'm not stupid," she said. "I figure you must be working for his wife. Big deal."

I looked down into her very blue eyes: maybe she was just a girl who worked in the office after all, one who got involved with the boss and didn't want any trouble. Maybe she was okay. But a voice whispered to me to see her for what she was.

"Sure, you're not stupid, May. Sure you're not. But some people take marriage seriously."

She stayed on the sofa, watching him. As soon as he closed the door behind him, he felt lost. He had just exited on some line about the sanctity of marriage. He'd pulled away from her as if she had leprosy, as if she had tempted him to jump off a cliff. He had a job to do but he wasn't a member of the Better Business Bureau. He was talking like a wise guy and acting like an undergraduate at a Baptist college.

He drew a deep breath and fumbled in his pocket for his cigarettes. The moon was gone and morning would not be long in coming. For all that, the city was still as hot as May's blazing red nail polish; the heat wave would not let up.

He started up the walk toward the street, and a blow like a cinder block dropping on the back of his neck knocked him senseless.

The jasmine smelled sweet, but lying under a bush in a flower bed was no way to spend the night. Reed rolled over and started to look for the back of his skull. It was not in plain sight. He got to his knees, then shakily stood. He didn't know how long he'd been out. It was still dark, but the eastern sky was smoked glass turning mother-of-pearl. The door to May Peterson's bungalow was ajar and her light was still on. Head throbbing, Reed pushed the door slowly open and stepped in.

The lounging pajamas were torn open and she lay on the floor with one leg partly under the sofa and the other twisted awkwardly at the knee. Her neck had not gone purple from the bruises yet. All in all, she had died without putting up much of a struggle. The shade of the chintzy lamp was awry but the bottle of nail polish was just where she had left it. Someone had taken the trouble to pull the phony curtains completely closed.

Reed knelt over her and brushed the curls back from her forehead. Her hair was soft and thick and still fragrant. A deep cut on her scalp left the back of her head dark and wet with blood. The very blue eyes were open and staring as if she were trying to understand what had happened to her.

Reed shuddered. Light was beginning to seep in through the curtains. The small kitchen was in immaculate order, the two-burner gas stove spotless in the dim morning light. In the back room the bedclothes of a large bed were disordered, and a cut glass decanter of scotch stood on the dressing table with its stopper and two glasses beside it. Reed felt a hundred years old. He stared at a framed photo of the Sphinx and the Great Pyramid that hung above the bed. An Arab led two camels by a short rope. The Egyptian revival. Everybody loved King Tut. Plundered tombs, mysterious curses. He rubbed the swelling at the back of his head where he'd been slugged—the pain shot through his temples—and left the apartment.

At the diner where he and Alice had had coffee he found a pay phone. He fumbled to find the number in his wallet—whoever had hit him hadn't bothered to rob him—and dialed the Chandler home. A sleepy woman answered the phone.

"Mrs. Chandler?"

"Yes?"

"This is Shaun Reed. Is your husband at home?"

A pause. He could see her debating whether to try and save her pride. "No," she said. "I haven't seen him since he went out with Philip Bradenton yesterday afternoon."

"Okay. Listen to me carefully. Your husband is in serious trouble and he needs your help. The police are going to try to connect him with a murder. I don't think he had anything to do with it. Tell them the truth about him but don't tell them about me."

"Have you found out what Raymond has been involved with?"

Reed hesitated.

"Mr. Reed, I'm paying you for information. Don't leave me in the dark." The voice that had been so thrillingly sexy two days before was that of a worried old woman.

The light in the telephone booth seemed cruelly harsh; the air in the cramped space smelled of stale cigarette smoke. Behind the counter a waitress in a white uniform was refilling a stainless steel coffee urn.

"The less you know about it right now, the easier it will go when the police call you," said Reed. There was no immediate answer. He felt sorry for her. He thought about that hurt look in Alice's eyes. "It's pretty much what I told you I suspected in my office."

"Oh."

Reed shook his head to dispel his weariness. "There's one more thing. Do you know of anyone who has it in for your husband? Anyone who'd like to see him in trouble?"

"John Runnels." She sounded certain.

"Who is he?"

"He works for South Basin, in the Signal Hill field. He and Raymond have never gotten along. He's a petty man. He resents Raymond's ability."

"Do you know where he lives?"

"In Santa Monica. If you'll wait a minute I can see whether Raymond has his address in his book."

"Don't bother. Remember now—when the police call, say nothing about me. Your husband is not involved in this."

Reed hung up and opened the door of the booth but did not get up immediately. It was full day outside; the waitress was drawing coffee for herself and the dayside short-order cook. Reed wanted some. He decided against it but made himself eat two eggs over easy, with toast, then headed home for a couple of hours sleep. He wished he were as certain that Chandler had not killed May as he'd told Cissy.

The sun was shining in his eyes when Reed woke the next day. The sun never came though his bedroom window that early. The sheets, sticky with sweat, were twisted around his legs. The air was stifling, and his mouth felt like a dustpan. He fumbled for the clock on the bedside table and saw that it was already one-thirty. The phone rang.

"Is this Mr. Shaun Reed?"

"What is it, Cissy?"

"The police just left here a few minutes ago. I have to thank you for warning me. They told me about May Peterson."

She stopped as if she were waiting for some response. He was still half asleep and the back of his head was suing for divorce. After a moment she went on.

"I didn't tell them anything, as you suggested, but in the course of their questions they told me the neighbor who found Miss Peterson's body saw a man leave her apartment in the early morning. Was it Raymond? Do you know?"

"It was me," Reed said wearily. "Have you heard anything from him?"

"No."

"Then why don't you let me do the investigating, Cissy—Mrs. Chandler."

There was an offended silence, then the phone clicked. Reed let the dial tone mock him for a moment before he hung up. He ought not to have been so blunt, but what did the woman expect? He wondered if Cissy had had any doubts before divorcing Pascal for Chandler. Pascal was a concert cellist, Alice told him. Older than Cissy. She had married for love that time. Reed imagined her a woman who had always been beautiful, bright, the center of attention. He supposed it was hard for her to grow old: she would become reclusive, self-doubting, alternating between attempts to be youthful and the knowledge that she wasn't anymore. He wondered what Chandler thought about her.

The speculations tasted worse than his cotton mouth. Men and women—over and over Reed's job rubbed his nose in cases of them fouling each other up. It would be cleaner working at a slaughterhouse. He pulled himself out of the bed and into the bathroom. He felt hung over but without the compensation of having been drunk the night before.

A shower helped, and a shave made him look almost alert. Measuring his square jaw and pug nose in the mirror, he tried to imagine what had gotten those women so hot last night. What had moved May to let him into her apartment so easily? Maybe that had only been a pleasant fantasy; fantasies sometimes were called upon to serve for a sex life, as both Cissy Chandler and Reed knew. His revulsion toward May and Alice had been a less pleasant fantasy.

The memory of May Peterson's dead, bemused stare—that was neither pleasant nor a fantasy.

While he dressed he turned on the radio and heard a report about the brutal murder that had taken place on Leeward Avenue the previous night. The weather forecast was for a high of 100 that afternoon. Reed pawed through the drawer in the table beside his bed until he found a black notebook and his Harold Lloyd glasses. He sat down and dialled the Santa Monica operator. There was a John Runnels on Harvard Street.

It was a white frame house that might have been shipped in from Des Moines. The wide porch was shaded by a slanting roof. Carefully tended poinsettias fronted the porch, and a lawn only slightly better kept than Wilshire Country Club's sloped down to a sidewalk so white that the reflected sunlight hurt Reed's eyes. The leaded glass window in the front door was cut in a large oval with diamond-shaped prisms in the corners. Reed pressed the button and heard a bell ring inside.

The man who came to the door was large; his face was broad with the high cheekbones and big nose of an Indian. He wore khaki pants with suspenders and a good dress shirt, collarless, the top buttons undone.

"Are you Mr. John Runnels? You work for the Dabney Oil Syndicate?"

The blunt face stayed blunt. "Yes."

Reed held out his hand. "My name is Albert Parker, Mr. Runnels. I'm with Mutual Assurance of Hartford. We're running an investigation of another employee of South Basin Oil and would like to ask you a few questions. Anything you say will be held strictly confidential, of course."

"Who are you investigating?"

"A Mr. Raymond Chandler."

Runnels's eyebrow flicked a fraction of an inch. "Come in," he said. He ushered Reed into the living room. They sat down. Reed got out his notebook, and Runnels looked him over—the kind of look Reed suspected was supposed to make employees stiffen and try to look dependable.

Runnels leaned forward. "Is this about any litigation he's started lately? I wouldn't want to talk about anything that's in court."

"No. This is entirely a matter between Mutual and Mr. Chandler. We are seeking information about his character. In your opinion, is Mr. Chandler a reliable man?"

"I don't consider him reliable," Runnels said, watching for Reed's reaction. Reed gave him nothing.

"We've got a hundred wells out on Signal Hill and I'm the field manager," Runnels continued. "I like working for Mr. Dabney. He's a good man." He paused and the silence stretched.

"Look, I don't know who told you to talk to me, but I'll tell you right now I don't like Chandler. He's a martinet and a hypocrite: he'll flatter Mr. Dabney on Tuesday morning and cuss him out for not backing one of his lawsuits on Tuesday afternoon. He runs that office like his little harem. If you'd watch him for a week you'd know."

"Yes."

Runnels got up and began pacing. "I've got no stomach for talking about a man behind his back," he said. "But Chandler is hurting the company and Mr. Dabney. He's dragged us into lawsuits just to prove how tough he is; he had us in court last year on a personal injury suit that the insurance company was ready to settle on, and then after he won—he did win—he turned around and cancelled the policy. That soured a lot of people on South Basin Oil.

"The only reason he was hired was because he had an in with Ralph Ives. He started in accounting. So he sucks up to Bartlett, the auditor, and gets the reputation for being some kind of fair-haired college boy. A year later Bartlett gets arrested for embezzling $30,000. Tried and convicted.

"Now it gets real interesting. Instead of promoting Chandler, Dabney goes out and hires a man named John Ballantine from a private accounting firm. This suits Chandler just fine because Ballantine's from Scotland, and Chandler impresses the hell out of him with his British upper-crust manners. Ballantine makes Chandler his assistant. A year later Ballantine drops dead in the office. Chandler helps the coroner, and the coroner decides it was a heart attack. Mr. Dabney gives up and makes Chandler the new auditor, and within another year he's office manager and vice president. Very neat, huh?"

Runnels had worked himself into a lather. Reed could have let him run on with just a few more neutral questions, but instead, as if someone else had taken over and was using his body like a ventriloquist's dummy, he said,

"You really hate him, don't you?"

Runnels froze. After a moment his big shoulders relaxed and his voice was back under control. "You've got to admit the story smells like a day-old mackerel."

"To hear you tell it."

"You don't have to believe me. Ask anyone on Olive Street. Check it with the coroner or the cops."

"If the cops thought there was anything to it I wouldn't have to check it with them. Chandler would be spending his weekends in the exercise yard instead of with those girls you tell me about."

Runnel's brow furrowed. He looked like a theologian trying to fathom Aimee Semple McPherson. "Cops aren't always too smart," he said.

"A startling revelation." I was getting to like Runnels. He

*reduced the moral complexities of this case. He reminded me
of a hand grenade ready to explode, and I was going to throw
my body at him to save Raymond Chandler. "Mostly they
aren't smart when someone pays them not to be," I said.
"Does the vice president of an oil company have that kind of
money?"*

"Don't overestimate a cop's integrity."

*"Who, me? I'm just an insurance investigator. You're the
one who knows what it costs to bribe cops."*

*The big shoulders were getting tense again, but the voice
was under control. "Look, I didn't start this talk about bribes.
You asked me my opinion. I gave it. Let's leave it at that."*

*He was right; I should have left it at that. Instead I pushed
on like a fighter who knows the fix is in and it's only a matter of
time before the other guy takes a dive.*

*"So Chandler killed Ballantine?" I said. "What about May
Peterson?"*

*"Peterson? Never heard of her. What kind of insurance man
are you, anyway?"*

*"I'm investigating an accident. Maybe you were out a little
late last night?"*

*Runnels took a step toward me. "Let's see your credentials,
pal."*

*I got up. "You wouldn't hit a man with glasses on, Runnels.
Let me turn my back."*

"Get the hell out of here."

*A woman wearing a gardening apron and gloves came into
the room. The house, which had seemed so cool when I had
entered, felt like an inferno. I slid the notebook into my pocket
and left. The porch swing hung steady as a candle flame in a
tomb; the sun on the sidewalk reawakened my headache.
Runnels stood in the doorway watching as I walked down to
the car. When I reached it he went back inside.*

Reed shuddered convulsively, loosened his tie, leaned
against the car. He focused on the street to keep the fear down:
he was a sick man. He'd totally lost control of himself in
Runnels's house. He wondered if that was what it felt like to
go crazy—to do and say things as if you were watching

yourself in a movie. He lifted his hand, looked at the backs of his knuckles. He touched his thumb to each of his fingertips. His hand did exactly what he told it to. He seemed able to do whatever he wanted; he could call Cissy Chandler and tell her to sweat out her marriage by herself. He could drive home and sleep for twelve hours and wake up alone and free. What was to stop him?

Reed was about to get into the car when he noticed a piece of wire lying on the pavement below his running board. Just a piece of wire. The freshly clipped end glinted in the sunlight. He bent over and tried to pick it up: it was attached to something beneath the car. Getting down on one knee, he saw the trailing wires where someone had cut each of his brake cables.

He rode the interurban east on Santa Monica Boulevard. Along the way he enjoyed what little breeze the streetcar's passage gave to the hot, syrupy air. He got off at Cahuenga and walked north toward his office at Ivar and Hollywood Boulevard, trying to piece together what had happened.

Runnels could have told his wife to take her pruning shears and cut the cables as soon as he recognized Reed on the porch. Runnels would have recognized him only if he was the one who had slugged Reed and gone on to murder May Peterson. He might have done it out of some misplaced desire to get back at Chandler.

But there was a problem with this theory. Why would Runnels go on to slander Chandler so badly? It would look better if he hid any hostility.

When Reed considered the picture of a middle-aged woman in gardening clothes crawling under a car on a residential street in broad daylight to cut brake cables, the whole card house collapsed. It couldn't be done, and not only that—Runnels simply had no reason to try such a stupid thing.

Then there was the question of why Reed had been slugged in the first place. Something about that had bothered him all day, and now he knew what it was: whoever killed May had no reason to knock out Reed. Reed had been on his way out and sapping him had only meant that he would be around to find her dead. It didn't make any sense.

Near the corner of Cahuenga and the boulevard he spotted a penny lying on the sidewalk. The bright copper shone in the late afternoon sun like a chip of heaven dropped at his feet. Normally he would have stopped to pick it up: one of the habits bred of a boyhood spent in Brooklyn where a penny meant your pick of candies on display at Applebaum's corner store. Instead he crossed the street.

But his mind, bemused by the puzzle of the cut brake cables and the senseless blow to the head, got stuck on this new mystery. If he'd paused to pick up the penny, he would have been a little later getting to the office. The whole sequence of events afterward would be subtly different; it was as if stopping or not stopping marked a fork in the chain of happenings that made his life.

This strange frame of mind refused to leave him. Normally he *would* have stopped, so by not stopping he had set himself down a track of possibilities he would not normally have followed. Why hadn't he stopped? What pushed him down this particular path? The incident expanded frighteningly in his mind until it swept away all other thoughts. Something had hold of him. It was just like the conversation with Runnels where he'd gone for the jugular—something was changing every decision he made, every emotion he felt. With a conviction that chilled him on this hottest of days, he knew that he was being manipulated and that there was nothing he could do about it. He wondered how long it had been happening without his knowing it. He should have picked up that penny.

After a moment the conviction went away. He was tired and he needed a drink. He could talk himself into all kinds of doubts if he let himself. He ought to take a good punch at the next passerby just to prove he could do whatever he wanted.

He didn't punch anybody.

Reed took the elevator up seven floors to his office.

Quintanella and Sanderson from homicide were in the waiting room.

"You don't keep your door locked," Sanderson said.

"I can't afford to turn away business."

Sanderson mashed his cigarette out in the standing ashtray and got up. "Let's have a talk."

Reed led them into the inner room. "What brings you two out to see me on a Sunday?"

"A lady got dead," Quintanella said. His face, pocked with acne scars, was stiff as a two-by-six.

Reed lit a cigarette, shook out the wooden match, broke it in half and dropped the pieces into an ashtray. They pinged as they hit the glass. The afternoon sun was shooting into the room at the same angle as when Cissy Chandler had come into this office.

I'd had about enough of them already.

"That's too bad," I said. "It's a rough business you boys are in. You going to try to solve this one?"

Sanderson belched. "We are. And you're gonna help us. You're gonna start by telling us where Raymond Chandler is."

"Don't know the man. Sure you've got the right Reed? There are a couple in the book."

"Will you tell this guy to cut the crap, Dutch?" Quintanella said to Sanderson. "He makes me sick."

"I didn't think they ran to delicate stomachs down at homicide," I said. "You have to swallow so many lies and keep your mouths shut."

"Tell him to shut up, Dutch."

"Calm down, Reed," Sanderson said.

"You tell me to talk, he tells me to shut up. Every time you guys get a burr in your paws, you make guys like me pull it out for you. Call me Androcles."

"We can do this downtown," Sanderson said. "It's a lot hotter there."

"You got a subpoena in that ugly suit?" The words were rolling out now and I was riding them. "If you don't," I said, "save the back room and the hose for some poor greaser. You

want any answers from me, you have to tell me what's going on. I'm not going to get bruised telling you things you've got no business knowing."

Quintanella mopped his brow, "C'mon, Dutch, let's take him in."

"Shut up, Tony." Sanderson looked pained. *"Don't try to kid us, Reed. We got a tip from the dreamers this afternoon. They said Mrs. Chandler hired you last week. We went back to her, and sure enough she said you knew about the murder of this call girl last night."*

Call girl. The words momentarily shook Reed out of it. That was what Cissy would say, and guys like Sanderson would figure that was the only kind of girl who got murdered.

"Cissy Chandler's not the most reliable source," Reed said.

"That's why we came to you. The neighbor lady at the Rosinante Apartments said she saw a man hanging around there last night. You fit the description. So why don't you tell us what's going on. Or should we let Tony take care of it?"

Reed watched them watch him. Quintanella was on the sofa near the door, flexing his hands. This case was getting beyond Reed fast. He had no reason to protect Chandler when for all he knew the man had killed May.

"Jesus," said Reed. "You're crazy if you think I need this kind of heat. I'm not in business to draw fire. I'll talk." He loosened his collar. "Will you let me get a drink out of the desk? No guns, just a little scotch."

Sanderson came over behind the desk; Quintanella tensed. "You let me get it," Sanderson said. "Which drawer?"

"Bottom right."

Do it. Do it now. Reed realized what was coming and tried to resist, but it was like his own blood talking to him. Like walking past the penny.

When Sanderson opened the drawer and reached for the bottle I punched him in the side of the throat. He fell back, hitting the corner of the desk. Quintanella, fumbling for his gun, leapt toward me. I slipped around the other side of the desk and out the door before the big man could get the heater out. I was down the stairs and out the exit to the alley before they hit the lobby; I zigzagged half a block between buildings that backed the alley, crossed the street and slipped into the rear of an apartment building on the opposite side of Ivar. I had just thrown away my investigator's license. I caught my breath and wondered what the hell I was going to do next.

Reed called Alice Ives from the lobby of the Bryson and she told him to come up. Although it was only early evening, she was in her robe. Her dark red hair shone like polished wood; her face was calm, with a trace of insouciance. She looked like Louise Brooks.

"I've got some trouble," Reed said. "Can I stay here for a while?"

"Yes."

She offered him coffee. They sat facing each other in the small living room. The two windows that fronted the street were open, and a hot, humid wind waved the curtains like a tired maid shaking out bed sheets. The air smelled like coming rain. Maybe the heat wave would be broken. Reed told her about his talk with Runnels.

"You don't believe what he said." There was an urgency in Alice's voice that Reed supposed came from her love for Chandler. He didn't understand why she would still care for a man years after he'd abandoned her. He didn't understand her very well at all, and he suddenly realized that he wanted to very much.

"I don't know what to believe," Reed said. "Did Runnels lie to me?"

"Bartlett was convicted of embezzling. Ballantine died of a heart attack. Raymond had nothing to do with either of those things."

"He was just lucky."

Alice exhaled cigarette smoke sharply. "I wouldn't use that word."

"I'm not trying to be sarcastic," Reed said. He hadn't had to try at all lately. "But you have to admit that it all has worked out nicely for him. He meets the right people, makes the right impression, and events break just the way you'd expect them to break if he was in the business of planning embezzlements and heart attacks. I can't blame a guy like Runnels for taking it the wrong way."

"Things don't always work out for Raymond. I know him better than you do. Look at his marriage."

"Okay, let's. Why did he marry her?"

Her brow knit. "He loves her, I guess."

"Why did he wait until his mother died?"

"She didn't approve."

"I'm not surprised. Age difference. But he was pretty old to still be listening to mom."

Alice took a last pull of her cigarette, then snuffed it out. Her dark eyes watched him. "I don't know. I don't know if I care anymore."

Reed wanted not to care about the whole case. But he had been hired to watch a man and he had lost that man. In the process a woman had been killed, and he couldn't bring himself to think she deserved it. *It was a matter of professional ethics.*

Ethics? Jesus. He wasn't some white knight on a horse. The idea of ethics in his business was ludicrous; it made him mad that such an idea had worked its way into his head. Only a schoolboy would expect ethics from a private eye. Only a schoolboy would avoid May Peterson because she had slept with Chandler. Only a schoolboy would have turned Alice down the previous night.

"I was surprised you asked me here last night," he said.

"That sounds sarcastic too."

"Not necessarily."

The wind strengthened, and it was blissfully cool. With a sound of distant thunder, the rain started. Alice got up to close the windows. She drew her robe tighter around her as she stood in the breeze; Reed watched her slender shoulders and hips as she pulled the windows shut. When she came back she folded her legs under her on the sofa. The line of her neck and shoulders against the darkness of the next room was as pure as the sweep of a child's sparkler through a Fourth of July night. She spoke somberly.

"I used to be a good girl. Being in love with a married man made me think that over. I'm not a good or bad girl anymore: I'm not any kind of girl." She paused. "You don't look to me like you're really the kind of man you're supposed to be."

Reed felt free of the compulsion for the first time in the last three days.

"I'm not," he said. "I feel like I've been playing some kind of game—or dreaming someone else's dream. I feel like I'm just about to wake up."

Alice simply watched him.

"I'd like to stay with you tonight," Reed said.

She smiled. "Not a very romantic pickup line. Raymond would do it funnier, or more poetic."

"He would?"

"Certainly. He's very poetic. He even wrote poetry—still does, as far as I know. You didn't know that?"

"I haven't been on this case very long. Is it any good?"

"When I was nineteen I loved it. Now I think it would be too sentimental for me."

"That's too bad."

Alice came to Reed, sat on the arm of his chair, kissed him. She pulled away, a little out of breath.

"No, it isn't."

All during their lovemaking he felt something trying to make him pull away, like a voice whispering over and over: *get up and leave. Go now. She will push you, absorb you. Doesn't she smell bad? She's an animal.*

It wasn't conscience. It was something outside him, alien, the same thing that had pulled him away from May Peterson. But Reed had finally picked up that penny, and he felt better, as he lay on the border of sleep, than he had in as long as he could remember. He felt that he and Alice were breaking a pattern merely by lying together, tired, the curve of her spine warm against his belly. Reed listened to the rain. Someone far away was laughing, and as he fell asleep the thought came to him, absurdly, that his father's name was Harry.

Reed dreamt there had been a shipwreck and that he and the other passengers were floundering among the debris, trying to keep afloat. There was no sound. He knew the others in the water: Alice was there, and Cissy, and Runnels and May Peterson and some others he could not make out—and Chandler. Chandler could not swim and he clutched at them, one after another, as if they were pieces of wreckage he could climb up on to keep afloat. They might have made it by themselves but they were all being shoved beneath the waves by the desperate man, and they would drown trying to save him. But Chandler never would drown, and would never understand the people dying around him. He could not even see them. He fumbled for Reed's head, his fingers in Reed's eyes, and Reed found that he did not have the strength to push him away. Reed coughed and sputtered and struggled toward the surface. Fighting against him in the salt sea, Reed saw that for Chandler, he was little more than a broken spar, an inanimate thing to be used without compunction because it was never alive. Drowning, Reed saw that Chandler had forced him under without even realizing what he had done.

He woke. It was still dark. Alice still slept; some noise from the other room had stirred him. The rain had stopped and the streetlights threw a pale wedge of light against the ceiling. Through the doorway, Reed saw something move. Two men slipped quietly into the room.

In the faint light Reed saw that they wore sailors' uniforms and that the smaller of the two had a sap in his hand. Reed snatched up the bedside clock and threw it at him.

The man ducked and it glanced off his shoulder. Reed leapt out of bed, dragging the bedclothes after him. He heard Alice gasp behind him as he hit the smaller sailor full in the chest. They slammed into the wall and the man hit his head against the doorjamb. He slumped to the floor. Reed struggled to his feet, still tangled in the sheets, and turned to see that the big man had Alice by the arm, a hand the size of a baseball mitt smothering her cries. He dragged her out of bed.

"Quiet now, buddy," the big sailor said in a soft voice. "Else I wring the little girl's neck."

The man on the floor moaned.

"What's the deal?" Reed asked. Alice's frightened eyes glittered in the dark.

"No deal. We just got some business to take care of."

Reed stood there, naked, helpless. He was no Houdini. All he had to keep them alive was words.

"You killed May Peterson," he said. "Why?"

"We had to. To get at that bastard Chandler. He makes a good impression. We wanna see the kind of impression he makes on the cops."

Reed shifted his feet and stepped on something hard. The sap.

"What have you got against him?"

The big man seemed content to stand there all night with his arm around Alice. He gasped, almost a chuckle. "Personal injury is what. Ten thousand bucks he cheated us outa. We hadda accident with one of his oil trucks. We had it as good as won until he made 'em go to court."

The man at Reed's feet rolled over, started to get up. "Be quiet, Lou," he said.

"What difference's it make?" the big sailor said. "They're dead already."

"Be quiet and let's do it. There's other people in this place."

Reed's thoughts raced. "It makes no sense to kill us. I'm no friend of Chandler's. I've been tailing him."

"You was there last night," the small sailor said, poking around the floor in the dark for the sap. "That's good enough. We got to get rid of you."

"Who says?"

Neither of them answered.

"What the hell are you looking for?" Reed asked.

"You'll know soon enough," the short one said.

"Damn, you guys are stupid. This doesn't make any sense. How do you expect to get away with this?"

Big Lou jerked back on his arm and Alice struggled ineffectually. "It was you two that got caught in bed together, right? Like a coupla animals? You don't deserve to live." He spoke with a wounded innocence, as if he had explained everything. As if, Reed realized, he were hearing the same voice that had whispered to Reed. Reed trembled, furious, holding himself back, feeling himself ready to fight and afraid of what might happen if he did. Don't move, he thought.
Move.

The runt was still obsessed with finding his weapon, shuffling through the sheets on the floor, picking up Alice's discarded camisole with two fingers as if it were a dead carp.

"Let me help," I said; I snatched the sap from beneath my foot and laid him out with a blow across the temple. He hit the floor like a loser in a prelim. At the same time I heard Lou yell. Alice had bitten his hand. Lou threw her aside, shook the pain away and catlike, quickly for such a big man, moved toward me.

Lou wasn't too big. Tunney could have taken him in twelve. I tried to dance out of his way but he cut me off and worked me toward the corner of the room. I swung the sap at his head; Lou caught the blow on his forearm and I tried to knee him in the groin. He danced back a half step. I stumbled forward like a rodeo clown who missed the bull. As I tried to get up I got hit in the ear with a fist that felt like a bowling ball. Just to show there were no hard feelings, Lou kicked me in the ribs.

"Stop!" Alice cried. "I've got a gun."

Lou turned slowly. Alice was kneeling on the bed, shaking. She had a small automatic pointed at him.

Lou charged her. Two shots, painfully loud in the small room, sounded before he got there. He knocked the gun away, grabbed Alice's head in one hand and smashed it against the brass bedstead: once, twice and she was still. I was on him, then. Oh yes, I was real quick. Lou shook me off his back and onto the floor, grunting now with the effort and the realization that he was shot. He shook his head as if dazed and stumbled toward me again. When he hit me I stood and heaved him over my shoulder. There was a crash and a rush of air into the room: Lou had gone through the window. Six stories to the street.

Reed shuddered with pain and rage—not at what Lou had done, but at himself. The smaller sailor was still out. Alice lay half off the bed, her head hanging, mouth open. Her straight, short hair brushed the floor. Reed lifted her onto the bed. He listened for a heartbeat and heard nothing. He touched her throat and felt no pulse. He lay his cheek against her lips and felt no wisp of breath.

A great anger, an anger close to despair, was building in him. He knew who had killed Alice, and why, and it was not the sailors.

No one had yet responded to the shots or the dead man in the street. Reed pulled on his clothes and left.

Reed didn't know how much time he would have. He burned with rage and impatience—and fear. Alice was dead. He shouldn't have moved. He was not a hero. Somebody had made him. Somebody had made him walk by that penny on the sidewalk, too, and as damp night gave way to dawn his confusion gave way to cold certainty: Chandler was his man. And, Reed realized, laughing aloud, he was Chandler's.

He took a streetcar downtown, past the construction site of the new civic center. He got off at Seventh and Hill and walked a block to South Olive. He was hungry but would not eat; he wondered if it was Chandler who decided when he became hungry. He watched the office workers come in for the beginning of the new week and wondered who was trapped in Chandler's web and who was not. In the men's room of the Bank of Italy Building he washed the crusted trickle of blood from his ear, combed his hair, straightened his clothes.

Nothing that had happened in the last three days made sense. Cissy hiring Reed, Chandler running off the road, Reed getting knocked out at May's apartment, the sailors killing May and then Alice, the cutting of Reed's brake cables, Sanderson and Quintanella letting him get away so easily—

and the crazy way things fit together, coincidence born from a novelist's desperation. All of these things ought not to have happened in any sensible world. The only way they could have was if he were being pulled from his own life into a nightmare. Chandler's nightmare.

Somehow, probably without his even knowing it, whatever Chandler wanted to happen, happened. Lives got jerked into new patterns and a gin-soaked businessman's fantasies came true. Maybe it went back to Bartlett's embezzlement and Ballantine's heart attack; maybe it went back to Chandler's childhood. Whatever, the things that had been happening to Cissy and May and Alice and even Big Lou and his partner, even the things that Reed could not imagine any man consciously wanting to come true—were all what Chandler wanted to happen. Alice and May were dead. There was no place in Chandler's world for women who liked sex and weren't afraid to go out and get it. There was no place in Chandler's world for a detective who failed to see each case as a moral crusade. He had to find the man before the next disaster occured.

He waited until Bradenton arrived for work at South Basin Oil and followed him up to the fourth floor. Most of the staff were already there and talking about May Peterson. They stared at Reed as if he were an apparition—he felt like one— and Bradenton turned to face him.

"May I help you?"

"Let's talk in your office, Mr. Bradenton."

The man eyed him darkly, then motioned toward the corner room. They shut the door. Reed refused to sit down.

"Where's Raymond Chandler?" he asked.

"I talked to the police yesterday. You're no policeman."

"That's right. Where is he?"

"I have no idea," Bradenton said. "And I'm not going—"

The phone rang. Bradenton looked irritated, then picked it up. "Yes?" he said. There was a silence and Bradenton looked as if he had swallowed a stone. "Put him on."

Reed smiled grimly: yet another improbable coincidence.

He had known the moment the phone rang who was calling. Bradenton listened; he looked distressed. After a moment Reed took the receiver from his unresisting hand.

The man on the phone spoke in a voice choked with emotion and slurred by alcohol, with a trace of a British accent.

". . . swear to God I'll do it this time, Phil, I can't bear to think what a rat I am and what I'm doing to Cissy—"

"Where are you?" Reed said softly.

"Phil?"

"This isn't Phil. This is Shaun Reed. I'm the man who helped you the other night when you ran off the road. Where are you?"

There was a pause and Chandler's voice came back, more sober. "I want to talk to Phil."

"He doesn't want to talk to you anymore, Raymond. He's sick of you. He wants me to help you out instead."

Another silence.

"Well, you can tell that bastard that I'm at the Mayfair Hotel and if he wants to help me he can identify my body when they pull it off the sidewalk because I'm going to do it this time."

"No, you won't. I'll be there in ten minutes." Reed gave the phone back to Bradenton, who looked ashen. "He says he's going to kill himself."

"He's threatened before. I could tell you stories—"

"Just talk to him."

Reed ignored the elevator and ran down to the lobby. He flagged a cab that took him speeding down Seventh Street. He didn't know what he was going to do when he got there, but he knew he had to reach Chandler. The ride seemed maddeningly slow. He peered out the window at the buildings and pedestrians, the sunlight flashing on storefronts and cars, searching for a sign that something had changed. Nothing happened. When Chandler died, would any of them who were controlled by him feel the difference? Would Reed collapse in the back seat of the taxi like a discarded puppet, leaving the driver with a ticking meter and a comatose man to pay the fare? Or would Chandler's death instead set Reed free? If Reed could only be sure of that, he would kill Chandler himself. Maybe he would kill him anyway. He needed to stay mad to keep from thinking about whether he could have saved Alice. If Reed had walked out of her apartment instead of asking to stay, if she had kicked him out, then she would probably still be alive. She'd be a good girl and he'd be a strong man. If May had slammed the door in his face—

They reached the Mayfair and Reed threw a couple of dollars at the driver. The desk clerk had a Mr. Chandler in room 712.

The door was not locked. The room stank of tobacco and sweat and booze. Chandler had to have his own private bootlegger to keep drunk so consistently. The man was sitting in an opened window wearing rumpled trousers, shoes without socks and a sleeveless T-shirt. An almost empty bottle stood on the sill in the crook of his knee. The phone lay on its side on the bedside table with the receiver dangling and a voice sounding tinnily from it. A book was opened facedown on the bed, which looked as if it hadn't been made in a couple of days. Beside the book lay a pulp magazine. *Black Mask*. Above a lurid picture of a man pointing a gun at another man who held a blonde in front of him as a shield was the slogan, "Smashing Detective Stories."

Chandler did not notice him enter. Reed crossed to the phone, stood it up and quietly hung up the receiver. The silencing of the voice seemed to rouse Chandler. He lifted his head.

"Who are you?"

Reed's weariness suddenly caught up with him. He sat down on the edge of the bed. He had felt some sympathy for Chandler even up to that moment, but seeing the man and remembering Alice's startled dead face, he now knew only disgust. Everyone who loved Chandler defended him, and he remained oblivious to it all, self-pitying and innocent when he ought to feel guilty as hell.

"You're the guy—" Chandler started.

"I'm the guy who pulled you out of the wreck. I'm the private detective hired by Cissy to keep you from hurting yourself. She didn't say anything about keeping you from hurting anyone else, and I was too stupid to catch on. Before Friday I had a life of my own, but now I'm the man you want me to be. I get beat up for twenty bucks a day and say please and thank you. I'm a regular guy and a strange one. I talk sex with the ladies and never follow through. I crack wise to the cops. I'm the best man in your world and good enough for any world. I go down these mean streets and don't get tarnished, and I'm not afraid. I'm the hero."

"What are you talking about?"

"You're mystified, huh? Before Friday I could touch a woman and not worry about her getting killed for it. Now I'm busy taking care of a sleazy momma's boy."

Chandler pointed a shaking finger at him. "Don't you mock me," he said. "I know what I've done. I know—"

Reed was raging inside. "What have you done?" he said grimly. "You sound like you've got a big conscience. So tell me."

Chandler's weeping turned to anger. "I've betrayed my wife. I'm not surprised she put you onto me—I would have told her to do it myself, in her situation. I've—" his voice became choked "—I've consorted with women who aren't any good. Women with death in their eyes who reek of cheap perfume."

"Are you serious?" Reed wanted to laugh but couldn't. "Where do you get all this malarkey? You don't know the first thing about women." As he spoke Reed realized bitterly that it was true of him, too, and the laughter was even harder to suppress. "May and Alice are dead. Really dead—not perfume dead."

Chandler jerked as if he had touched a live wire. He knocked his bottle out the open window and seconds later came the crash. His expression turned sour. "I'm not surprised about May. She led a fast life." He paused, and his voice became philosophical. "Even Alice. It doesn't surprise me. I finally figured out that she wasn't the innocent she pretended to be."

Reed's rage grew. He got up from the bed; the book beside him fell off. He could see the cover: *The Great Gatsby*.

"May and Alice were killed by those sailors you fought in the insurance suit. They said they were out to get revenge against you."

Chandler was shaken again. "That makes no sense," he said. "May and Alice had nothing to do with that. Anyone out to get me should come for me. There must have been some other reason they were killed."

Reed grabbed Chandler by the arm. He wanted to push him out of the window. Nobody would know: Bradenton would talk and the cops would call it suicide. It was a perfect setup. For the first time Chandler looked him in the eye. Reed saw desperation there and something more frightening: Chandler seemed to know what he was thinking, was granting him permission, was making an appeal. He did not struggle in Reed's grasp. Reed fought the desire to give the one quick shove that would end it—because that was exactly what Chandler wanted. He knew that if he killed the man now he would never be free. He pulled Chandler into the room.

"Quit the suicide act. What have you been doing since you left May?"

If Chandler had felt anything of the communication that had passed between them he did not show it. "I couldn't stay with her. When I first met her I thought she was innocent, defenseless, but I learned the kind she was quick. I couldn't go home and face Cissy, so I came here." He looked toward the window. "If I had any guts it wouldn't be an act."

"Those sailors had no reason to kill except you. They did it in the stupidest way possible. Not for revenge. Just so things could work out the way you want them to."

Chandler pushed by him and went into the bathroom; Reed heard the sound of running water. He was getting ready to shave. He seemed to be sobering fast.

"What are you saying—that the world is some kind of nightmare that I'm having? You're crazy." Chandler lathered his face. "Look, I feel like the bastard I am, but what did I have to do with any of this? Am I supposed to stop defending my company when we've got a good case? I've got to try to do the right thing, don't I?"

Reed said nothing. After a few minutes, Chandler came out of the bathroom. Hair combed, freshly shaven, he seemed already on the way to becoming vice president of South Basin Oil again. The news of the deaths, the moment on the windowsill, had knocked the booze out of him. Knocked the guilt out of him, too. He put on his shirt and began to button it.

Reed felt as if he were going to be sick.

"You know, that credo you spouted—you were just joking, I realize—but there's something to it," Chandler said seriously. "'Down these mean streets.' I'd like to believe in that. I'd like to be able to live up to that code—if we could only get all the other bastards to."

Reed rushed into the bathroom and vomited into the toilet.

Chandler stuck his head into the room. "Are you all right?"

Reed gasped for breath. He wet a towel and rubbed his face.

Chandler had his tie knotted and put on the jacket of his rumpled summer suit. "You should take better care of yourself," he said. "You look awful. What's your name?"

"Shaun Reed."

"Irish, huh?"

"On my father's side."

"I'll bet being a private investigator is interesting work. There's a kind of honor to it. You ought to write up your experiences some day."

Alice was dead, lying upside down with her hair brushing the dusty floor. Her mouth was open. "Most of them I'd rather forget."

Chandler took the copy of *Black Mask* from the bed. Reed felt hollow, but the way Chandler held the magazine, so reverently, sparked his anger again.

"You actually read that junk?"

The man ignored him. He bent over, a little unsteadiness the only evidence of his bender and the fact that he'd been ready to launch himself out the window a half an hour earlier. He picked up the copy of *Gatsby*.

"I've always wanted to be a writer," he said. "I used to write essays—even some poetry."

"Alice told me that."

Chandler looked only momentarily uncomfortable. He motioned with the book in his hand. "So you don't like detective stories. Have you tried Fitzgerald?"

"No."

"Best damn writer in America. Best damn book. About a man chasing his dream."

"Does he catch it?"

Sadly, Chandler replied, "No, he doesn't."

"He ought to quit dreaming then."

Chandler put his hand on Reed's shoulder. "We can't do that. We've got nothing else."

Reed wanted to tell him what a load of crap that was, but Chandler had turned his back and walked out of the room.

Escapist

The lock clicked as Chandler shut the door behind him, and something clicked in Shaun's head as well. He knew that the copy of *Black Mask* and the unmade bed would disappear, that room 712 and indeed the entire Mayfair Hotel would flick out of existence and he would wake up in his bed at Freedom Beach.

Except that he was someplace else; surf did not pound against the shag rug in his bedroom. He was dazzled by intense sunlight and could smell the sea on the warm breeze. He squinted against the brightness; he was sitting at a table under a red-and-white awning on the esplanade, facing the beach. The same table at which he and Myrna had sat watching the volleyball game that first day at Freedom Beach. Vic sat beside him now.

Vic stared out at the islands. Shaun imagined superimposing Chandler's sallow drunkard's face on Vic. It was easy.

Chandler had stared down from the hotel window to the sidewalk below in exactly the same way. Vic was wearing tennis whites and running shoes. He turned to Shaun. His face was as blank as the face of the sphinx.

"A day for daydreaming," he said.

Shaun felt as if he were on a choke chain. He wanted to throw himself at Vic, beat that face bloody. Yet he knew he could not do it. He could hardly breathe he was so frustrated. Finally he jerked himself out of the beach chair and headed for the pool.

There were only a couple of others there; everybody else was in the clubhouse playing raquetball. Shaun stripped and swam slow laps until the rhythms of his body overcame the mad jangle of his thoughts. If the dreamers were trying to drive him to desperation, they were doing a first class job.

After that, he spent every day at the pool. He would swim laps to slow the thoughts that would not stop.

The longer Shaun stayed at Freedom Beach, the more isolated he became. It was hard knowing about the others when they seemed to know so little about him. No one wanted to hear what he remembered. Ever since he had arrived there he had fought to regain his memory. Yet each time he was made to relive his past—and to go through the strange dreams that inevitably followed—he lost more of himself to the dreamers. Chandler's rumpled bed at the Mayfair Hotel was more real to him now than his memory of the bed he had shared with Myrna in the dorm at Columbia. Sometimes he would wake in the middle of the night to catch himself speaking strange names aloud. He would peer across the room in the darkness, and the mirrored closet doors would show only a man sitting up in a waterbed in a blue room. He was alone. His only chance was to escape.

Shaun tucked just short of the wall and turned without touching. Eighty laps. Eighty times fifty meters was four kilometers. Which in miles was two point four eight six—he had long since worked out the conversions. He scissored his legs harder now, reached a little farther on each stroke. He had resumed his regular sessions in the pool and kept reducing his intake of communion until most evenings he was openly offering his wafer to any takers. It was so easy that he began to suspect that the guests had been lied to about communion's addictive qualities. And if that were a lie, might not the boundaries be a lie as well? Ready to yield if pushed hard enough? Shaun kept expecting the dreamers to make him stop training, but nothing happened.

He guessed that the islands were between five and ten miles offshore. It would be a tremendous risk but—as far as he could remember—he had never been in better shape. He was peaking; if he were going to make the attempt he thought it would have to be soon. Yet he waited. And he was not quite sure why.

A man with no memory, looking at the water in the Poseidon fountain, would never know that it had run pink with Myrna's blood. Poseidon's trident, however, remained bent a couple of inches out of true. Evidence that Shaun could indeed change things. Still, it was not much comfort. Every afternoon, on returning from the pool, he would sit exhausted on the edge of the fountain.

"I'm thinking of swimming for the islands," he said one day.

"We would be sad to lose you, Shaun," the statue said. "Your case is very promising."

"Great." He was too tired to get angry. "Who says I need any more of your stinking therapy?"

"You certainly won't need it once you drown."

"I'm not going to drown. I'm going to make it to the islands." His calf muscles were beginning to stiffen up; he bent to massage them. "Just like Myrna did," he muttered.

"Myrna is dead, Shaun."

He straightened up. "Look, I'm leaving no matter what you say. Since you're so sure I'm going to drown, why not tell me what this is all about before I go? I promise not to say anything to the others."

Silence.

"All right, maybe you can't come straight out and tell me. We can weasel around that. I'll tell *you* why I think I'm here. All you have to do is nod yes or no."

"Statues can't nod, Shaun."

"Can't talk either!" Shaun's mockery tore at himself more than at the statue—as if a statue could be mocked. "How about this: you can say whether you would nod if you could." Although Poseidon made no reply, Shaun pushed on. "Okay, here's what I think. This therapy has to do with my becoming a writer. You've dredged my memory to find my favorite writers and now you're showing me that they had lots of problems— the same kinds of problems that were keeping me from writing. You can tell, by psychological testing or some other method, that I was meant to become a great writer. Or maybe you can see the future. Maybe you know that I've got at least six hundred kilowords in me and some day I'm going to end up as a BOB in the Empire State Building. One of the greats." He chuckled, then fell silent for a moment. "Anyway," he continued, "I've been pissing my talent away. You brought me here, along with the people from my past life, so I could straighten myself out. Such a great writer might do great things, maybe change the world. Which is exactly what the dreamers want. So it's worth your time and expense to cure me. Am I right?"

The statue was silent. The jets of water coming from the trident sputtered, as if there were an air bubble in the line, then resumed.

"Was that your impression of a nod?" said Shaun.

No reply.

"Okay, so I'm wrong. Joke's on me; I can take a joke. The real reason that I'm here is so that I'll give up the idea of writing. You determined that I have no talent for it, which is pretty clear from my history, and you want to break me of the delusion once and for all by showing me how all my favorites got messed up. Writing is useless for a man like me. Time for me to grow up and get a real job. Like maybe as a dreamer.

That's what Junior thought anyway. Do you know Junior? No, never mind. Just tell them to make me an offer. I'll listen. Anything to get out of here."

Shaun thought that Poseidon was going to ignore him again, but after a moment the statue said, "What about Myrna?"

The question frightened him. "What about her? She's dead."

"If you return without her, she will be missed."

"So? What about all these other people? Aren't they missed back home too?"

"How old is Murray?"

Shaun frowned. Who cared how old Murray was? As he thought about it he started to sweat. "You killed Myrna. No matter what you say, you were responsible."

"It's clear that your therapy is not yet completed."

"Damn it! I want out! I know I would never have agreed to anything like this. Or if I did it was because you lied. You have no right to continue this against my will."

The statue did not respond. Shaun was tempted to splash into the fountain and bend the trident a few more inches. He thought better of it. Now was the time to go, he realized; he ought to save his strength for swimming. Shaun crossed the atrium to his suite. They might keep him for months, years, before they let him leave. He would go crazy. Myrna had found the only way out; that was why every dream they gave him ended with her gone, and now Shaun realized what she meant when she said she would see him on the islands. They would be together whether he made it or not. He *had* to swim; whatever happened would be better than staying at Freedom Beach.

He ate dinner that evening with Akira and Jihan. They seemed relieved that he concentrated more on the meal than on haranguing them about his dreams. Jihan even made a joke about his coming to terms with his term at Freedom Beach. Coming to terms. He smiled and scooped up the gravy from his chicken paprika with a chunk of French bread.

After that the three of them began to trade old jokes, some dating back to grammar school days. Although none were particularly funny, a silly mood prevailed and soon they were almost helpless with laughter. Murray came by, attracted by the merriment, and tried to join in, but his puns and insult jokes were too freighted with pain to suit Shaun's fey mood. Shaun told him he had no heart.

"Get real, Shaun," Murray said. "Who cares anyway? Here's the latest theory: Freedom Beach, and all of us, too, are figments of the dreamers' imaginations. As soon as they get their wake-up call—poof!—out like a light."

"Is that so, professor?" said Akira. "Well here's my theory:

> I know a professor who swallowed a fly—
> I don't know why
> He swallowed a fly—
> Perhaps he'll die . . ."

Jihan and Shaun burst out laughing; Akira went on, Murray went away. Just before communion, Jihan asked Shaun if he wanted to join them for a threesome that night. Shaun almost choked on his cherry strudel. "Sorry," he said, giggling, "but coach says no sex the night before the big meet."

The commons fell silent as the trashcans shuttled around distributing communion; the guests were waiting to see what Shaun would do with his wafer. That this pause had become a nightly ritual at once gratified and annoyed Shaun. It was a sign of his preeminence in the community of guests; it was a reminder that he was alone.

"Friends and fellow loonies," he said, holding the communion wafer aloft for all to see. "This is our last night together." The silence was complete. "Tomorrow I leave you for parts unknown." There was a nervous stirring, but no one raised a voice to object. The pause stretched; someone at a back table coughed. Suddenly Shaun was embarrassed. He had prepared a grand farewell speech, had tossed and turned in bed for many a sleepless night, honing his rhetorical points to a razor edge. Points he would never drive home now, in a speech it would be too cruel to give. "It's . . . what I have to do," he said lamely.

He crossed the room to where Vic slouched in a wicker chair. Vic glanced up, eyes glazed with communal euphoria, as Shaun offered him the wafer. "Yours," said Shaun.

Vic took it in the palm of his hand and then clenched his fist, working his fingers back and forth to crush it. "I have enough," he said in a thick voice. "Don't need more." He threw the crumbs in Shaun's face.

Shaun nodded. For the first time he felt pity for Vic. As he turned to go, Akira called out, "Good luck!" Several others chimed in. Shaun waved over his shoulder as he walked away from them.

He could not sleep. Well after midnight, long after the others had retired for the night, Shaun went down to the beach. There was no wind; a few wavelets licked at his jogging shoes. The moonlight gleamed on the still water. The islands were shadows at the world's edge.

Shaun pulled off his shirt and dropped it on the wet sand. He waded in until he was up to his neck and then pushed off and began to swim. At first it was easy, so easy that he almost laughed as he propelled himself through the warm water. He began to lose himself in the sensations of his body at work. Stroke-stroke-breathe, stroke-stroke-breathe, kick, work those legs! The salt water stung his eyes but he did not have too much difficulty navigating. The moon was full and its reflection on the bay was like an arrow pointing at the islands. He followed it. In no time at all he reached the reef. He congratulated himself then for deciding to swim at night; even if the dreamers decided to release the sharks from their psychic menagerie, he would not be able to see them. And he refused to let himself be afraid of things he could not see.

The nausea started as he was wading across the reef. Maybe the trashcans had poisoned his last meal. He gritted his teeth and tried to ignore it. At the far side he kicked off his jogging shoes and began to swim again. The sea was choppier beyond the reef. It was harder to settle into a rhythm. The nausea faded and the cramps started, slowly overpowering him. He felt as if someone were slowly sewing up his lungs. He fought down his instinctive panic. To save energy he floated on his back, staring up at the bright stars. As he lay there, taking shallow breaths to ease the pain, he heard the distant chop of a helicopter. He thought the dreamers might be after him, that they might come to fetch him back to Freedom Beach. He picked out the copter's marker beacon low on the horizon, bearing toward him. A spotlight played over the water. As it closed on him, Shaun dove, holding his breath until he thought he would explode.

When he finally came up for air the helicopter was gone, but he was sure that the dreamers had spotted him—because something had triggered another memory. All he could think about was a helicopter like a huge dragonfly circling behind a line of skyscrapers to land in a park. Not Freedom Beach—Central Park, the Great Lawn, a muggy August afternoon when he and Myrna had stood among a crowd of people watching the arrival of the first of the dreamers to visit New York. Vendors sold snow cones and T-shirts, and a knot of hecklers gathered around a born-again Christian denouncing the dreamers as servants of the Antichrist.

The shadow of the white helicopter passed over them. The rotors flung dust into their faces and the roar of the turbines drowned out the testimony of the Christian. It settled on its hydraulic struts like an old man easing into a lawn chair. The rotors stopped turning, the noise died. The crowd, even the Jesus freak, waited. The white door slid open and out stepped three dreamers.

"Dei ex machina," Myrna had whispered, as if to herself.

Such was the power of this new memory that, floating on his back in the sea, suspended in the middle of his attempt to escape, Shaun could still see them. A black man with conked red hair, wearing a sleeveless red shirt, torn jeans, blue Nikes. Mirrored sunglasses hid his eyes. An elderly woman in a green calico dress who was lowered to the ground in a wheelchair. A square, brown Arab in a blue blazer, a long white caftan and a blue headcloth. He raised a hand to the crowd, a politician's gesture. "*Bismallah*." It was eerie the way his voice carried. "In God's name."

Then all three of them spoke in unison. "You begin today a new era." There were no loudspeakers, no microphones. Later, people all over Manhattan claimed to have heard the speech. "Together we will all work. The world will change." Shaun heard the woman's soft voice, a voice that soothed. He had wanted to stay but after a minute of watching the three dreamers with apparent indifference Myrna had turned away.

"What's the matter?"

"I can't stand this," Myrna had said. "I'm leaving."

He realized now that she had been afraid of them. It was funny; Shaun had always believed that she was the stronger of the two of them. She had always seemed to be ahead of him, impatient, waiting for him to catch up. He had tried so hard to keep up with her, by writing mostly, but Shaun could remember now that as the years passed the distance between them had widened instead of closing. He had had so many illusions about Myrna. He had never thought she might be unfaithful to him up until the moment he caught her at the motel. Even afterward he had refused to believe it. He was easily as deluded about women as Chandler had been.

As suddenly as it had come, the memory was gone. The water had turned much colder. His lungs were raw; his body felt numb. He lifted his head high, scanning the horizon for the helicopter. The effort was excruciating, but there was no sign of the dreamers. The moon still rode high enough to light his way to the islands. Miles away. He rolled off his back and swam on.

As the hours passed, Shaun recognized that his chances of making the islands were not particularly good. It was difficult keeping his direction. He was in the grip of a current that was trying to sweep him south toward the channel out to sea. A wind had picked up from the north, pushing waves at him. The cold made the cramps seem slightly more bearable, but now he worried about hypothermia. He tried to concentrate on swimming, but even as he forced his leaden arms and legs to move he knew it was no use. He was not going to make it without help. He was like a man hanging by a rope over the edge of a cliff—with no way to pull himself up. Sooner or later he would have to let go.

He could feel the helicopter before he could hear it: a steady throb in the water like the pounding of blood. He no longer had the strength to dive and try to hide. Instead he rolled over onto his back and waited for it, resigned to being recaptured. He would have to train harder next time.

The pilot must have picked him out right away; soon the helicopter hovered directly overhead. Waves danced around and over him in the backwash of the rotors. The spotlight was blinding. Shaun could barely keep his head above water.

"You all right down there?" He thought he recognized Junior's voice, amplified by a bullhorn.

He waved feebly. "H-Help!" The word seemed to stick in his throat.

"Almost there!" called one of the women. She sounded like a cheerleader.

"Can't . . ." A wave washed into his mouth and he choked.

"Keep up the good work." The pitch of the rotors changed abruptly as the spotlight snapped out. The helicopter lifted rapidly away from him and shot out of sight, heading toward the islands.

"Wait!" cried Shaun. But it was no use. They were gone. Another, larger wave broke over his head, driving him beneath the surface. His scream drowned in dark water. For an awful moment he was lost, pummeling the sea blindly. He could not find the surface, *he was drowning!* The calm acceptance with which he had pushed himself into the sea had been an illusion: he did not want to die.

He broke through to air, trying to cough and breathe and shout a curse at the dreamers all at the same time. Still another

FREEDOM BEACH 173

wave pushed him under the cold water. He floundered weakly, weightless, lost. The bastards. How could they let him get so far, and then leave him to die? Thinking what a cliché it was to have his life pass before him as he drowned, Shaun felt the pressure of the frigid water around him recede as his memory loomed.

February 12, 1986

The doorman at Gateway Towers was dressed like a pallbearer, which struck Shaun as appropriate once he entered the building. With its dim indirect lighting and walls and floor of onyx, the lobby looked like a crypt filled with tropical plants. Ancient Egypt on the East River. The doorman stopped in front of a bank of television monitors and punched in Myrna's apartment number. With a polite but cold smile he pointed up at the wall-mounted television camera. Abruptly the screen nearest it was filled with Myrna's face.

"Shaun?" The microphone gave her voice a metallic edge.

He shrugged. "I came."

"I'm glad, Shaun. Patrick will show you to the elevator."

He could not tell much about her from a black-and-white TV picture. She had cropped her hair; she looked tired. The screen went blank.

Shaun brushed the melting snow from his parka and pulled

off his woolen cap. He touched the top of his head; his hair was matted and tangled.

"Is there a bathroom?" he said to the doorman. He wanted to make an impression, to conceal all the signs of how disheveled his life had become.

"Of course, sir. This way."

After all, he had not seen her in three years.

The view alone was worth a quarter of a million dollars. The blizzard swirled around the lights of the Brooklyn Bridge. East River Drive was fast disappearing under the snow. The plows had so far managed to keep the right lane open but it was starting to look like a wagon trail: a pair of black ruts on white. Shaun had always found magic in the sight of New York filling up with snow.

This is fantastic!" he said.

Myrna hung Reed's parka in the closet and slid the door shut. "Thank you."

"You must be doing well. You look good."

She nodded absently, as if she were listening in on another conversation. "Can I get you anything? Scotch, wine, beer?"

"Whatever you're having."

"I'm trying to cut down." She gave a nervous little laugh as the silence stretched. "Not to worry. We'll open a bottle of Beaujolais and see what happens."

As he followed her into the kitchen Shaun inspected her twenty-fifth floor co-op. When she had described it as minimalist, she had not been joking. All the interior walls had been ripped out so that you could see the modular couch from the bathroom sink, the dining table from the bed. A folding screen concealed the toilet and tub. The exterior walls were beige, as was the carpet. The few pieces of spartan furniture were bright primary colors: the thinly padded couch was lipstick red, the table and chairs had been painted with yellow enamel, the bed was electric blue. Everything was very boxy: only the scattering of plants and Myrna were permitted to curve. There was no art, no books. The place reminded Shaun of a prison cell done by Mondrian. Who the hell wanted to live in the Museum of Modern Art?

She offered him a glass of wine. "Well, what do you think?" She had been watching him look at the apartment.

"Must be easy to keep clean."

She smiled as they touched glasses. "You hate it."

"I don't *hate* it." Shaun sipped the wine cautiously. He thought he detected a twinkle in her eye. "Who did the design, the Department of Correction?"

She laughed. Shaun relaxed; it had been a long time since he had heard that laugh. He had the sense that this evening was going to be all right after all.

"Actually," she said, slipping her arm around his and steering him toward the couch, "the idea was to keep everything in here simple to focus attention on the view. The city is all the decoration I need." They sat on the couch, facing the window wall. "I love to sit here and watch. New York seems to make so much more sense when you look down on it from a height."

Shaun put his empty glass on the yellow cube which served as coffee table. Myrna refilled it and topped hers off as well. "Tell me about yourself," she said. "What are you doing these days? How is the writing going?"

"It isn't." This was the moment that Shaun had feared; it was what had almost kept him from coming. He had spent several sleepless nights trying to think what he would say. He could be noncommittal, tell her that he had a few projects working, dance around the subject. He could lie, say things were fine, that he had a couple of manuscripts making the rounds, hoped to hear any day now. Or he could tell her the truth. The truth was that he had burned all his old stories, had not written a word in a year, was working part time at an A&P and part time reading the slush pile at minimum wage for a publisher of paperback gothics. The truth was that he was lost.

"It's funny," he said, "when you come to think about it. I mean, here I am a guy who has written hardly anything and sold nothing. How can I be blocked? I was never a writer to begin with!"

"You wrote lots of things for Electrotech and for the computer magazines."

He shook his head. "That wasn't writing. Besides, I can't even do that anymore." He refilled both their glasses; they had almost emptied the bottle already. "But it isn't all bad. After all, I have a job in publishing, so I'm keeping my hand in. I read a lot. I think it will come back—I know it will—someday when I have something to write. That's the problem, I think. Always has been. There's nothing I *have* to write about."

He was not sure whether he believed this or not, but Myrna had seemed so concerned that he did not want her to think that he was despairing. Sometimes he was surprised to hear himself say such things. It was as if another person were speaking, someone who knew him better than he knew himself. "Don't worry about me," he said, clenching his fist and striking a muscle man pose. "I may be a loser but I'm tough."

"Not a loser." She reached over and, with a tipsy giggle, patted his biceps. "But you are tough."

If they had been married then, and still in love, he would have kissed her. But theirs was an amicable divorce—best to keep it that way.

At that moment a bell began to ring in the kitchen. "Dinner," said Myrna. "Are you hungry?" Of course, she had made all of his favorites: stuffed mushrooms, garlic bread, fettuccine carbonara . . .

"Asparagus!" said Reed, lifting the lid of a Dansk serving dish. "Myrna, asparagus aren't in season yet—they're $3.29 a pound!"

She frowned as she opened a bottle of Chardonnay. "Do you think they'll be tough?"

"No, no. It's not that. I'm sure they'll be fine. They smell wonderful!" He told himself to stop sounding like a six-year-old at Disneyland. If this was the way she could afford to live . . . well, it was rude to gawk. "Would you pass the mushrooms? So tell me about yourself. How's Julian?"

"Julian had a stroke." Myrna broke a slice of garlic bread

from the loaf. "About a year ago; he's slowed down quite a bit. He made me a partner."

She spent the dinner talking about work, the new accounts, the wars between the art director and account managers, the problems of managing twenty-three people, twenty of whom were only marginally sane. She had a funny story to tell about a dachshund that had thrown up in a celebrity's lap while they were making a dog food commercial and another about the eccentricities of a famous potato chip mogul. Shaun ate a lot and said little. He was surprised that she would be so garrulous about the agency; she had not told him this much about her work the entire two years they were married. He had the sense that she was telling some of these stories for the first time. Maybe now that she was a partner at work and a single in private, there was no one she *could* tell them to.

Myrna had even bought Häagen-Dazs pistachio ice cream for dessert. Afterward they drank Courvoisier and then Myrna produced a joint of sensimilla. Shaun tried to beg off—he was afraid he would pass out—but she lit it up anyway.

There was an irony here. "When we were married," he said, taking the joint from her, "I thought I was the drinker and smoker in the family." He took a light drag; it seemed to balloon in his lungs and lift him out of his chair. It had been a long time since he had been able to afford pot this good. "At this point . . . my dear . . . what was I—oh, yes . . . at this point I confess that you're about to put me under the table."

She frowned. He realized he had made a false step somewhere. Bringing up their abortive marriage? Pointing out her prodigious capacity for substance abuse? He could not think.

She took the joint from him. "Let's move to the couch. No table there to worry about."

"Good idea." Reed tried to stand; he was not sure his feet were touching the floor. "Maybe put some coffee on?"

He flopped onto the couch and stared out the window while she worked in the kitchen. The storm had swallowed most of Brooklyn; the bridges were a blur. He looked at his watch.

Ten-thirty. Time to think about going home. He wondered if she intended him to go home. He wondered what his own muddled intentions were.

She brought coffee. The joint was still working—or maybe it was a new one. The combination of tetrahydrocannabinol and caffeine had a curious effect on him. The vestiges of his natural caution were sheared away and he felt a dangerous cockiness come over him. He knew he was higher than the Dog Star and he did not care.

Myrna was still rambling on about work, as if she were intoxicated by the sound of her own voice. ". . . so he took the account over to Childs and Birling and sales dropped eight percent. Then he has the nerve to call me up the other day to ask me to 'take a lunch' with him. I told him to take his lunch and shove it, the ungrateful bastard."

"How about Vic Slesar? You still handling his account?"

"No." She took a very deliberate sip of coffee, then said, "and 'no' to your implied question, too. I haven't seen Vic in two years."

"Are you seeing anyone?"

Her smile was distant. "My, my, we are getting personal, aren't we?"

Reed shrugged. "Just wondering what you do for fun around here when you get tired of looking out the window."

She reached down to the yellow cube in front of the couch, opened a hidden door and pulled out a remote control. A screen slid over the window and, on the opposite wall, a hatch slid away from a television projector. "There's a satellite dish on the roof. I can get two hundred stations, TV from all over the world." She handed him the controller. "Actually, I don't use it that often. I spend a lot of time at work. Maybe too much."

He looked at the controller as if it were a summons to appear in court, the honorable Myrna Rosny presiding. His self-confidence started to slip away. He put the controller back into the yellow cube and the screen rolled up from the window.

"I suppose I might as well tell you, Shaun. Maybe that's why I asked you over here in the first place. I don't have that many people I can talk to." She leaned her head against the back of the couch and gazed up at the ceiling. "I'm celibate." She did not look at him to see his reaction. He sensed that she did not care. "People think that's a hard way to live but they're wrong. It's the easiest thing in the world.

"Vic and I split a couple of months after the divorce became final. I don't know whose fault it was. Maybe it was just my year for losing men. It was a hard time; I even had a few sessions with a psychiatrist. Me, who never needed anyone's help. Ever. Well, that didn't last long. I saw what the answer was. Simplify, simplify. All I had to do was make my life less complex. Most people have to scramble to meet all the demands put on them. They just muddle through the day doing a little of everything and nothing well. But if you can simplify your life, channel all your energies into the one thing you're best at . . . well . . ." She looked at him and then gestured at the window, "they give you an apartment with a river view."

"But does it make you happy?"

She shook her head wearily. "But then," she said, after a moment's consideration, "the way I used to live didn't make me very happy either."

"That was partly my fault."

"Maybe." She shrugged. "And maybe there was nothing you could have done." She tapped him on the shoulder. "Hey, let's not get into one of our funks. All that is behind us, understand? The books are closed."

He nodded. She seemed so strong, so clearly in control of her life. Shaun was prepared to accept the proposition that there was nothing at all strange about the new life Myrna had made for herself. He felt very comfortable, parked on her couch, his brain idling in neutral. What did it matter if he was happy or not? He was at rest.

She interrupted his reverie. "And you?"

"Me?"

"Are you seeing anyone?"

"Oh." He sat up. "I have a lot of friends." He hesitated, trying to find the truth of his life. "Acquaintances, really. I see

Akira occasionally. He's always fixing me up with his idea of exciting women." He tilted his coffee cup to see if there was any left: it was empty. "I don't know. There's no passion; it's all very lukewarm. You spend the night with someone and then you don't hear from them for a couple of days or a week. And the hell of it is that it doesn't matter if you get together again or not."

They sat quietly, heads resting against the back of the couch. He did not look at her; he was content to share her solitude in silence.

After a while, Myrna said, "Do I seem all right to you?"

"You seem fine." He patted her hand. "You know, they don't sell this kind of real estate to self-doubters."

Myrna's chuckle was dry. "I told you that after the divorce I saw a psychiatrist? He got me to say some things—I'm not sure whether I meant them or not. But you know, once you tie words around your feelings, you're bound to them whether you like it or not." She sighed. "One day I actually heard myself talking about suicide. I was calm, he was calm—we might have been discussing a vacation on St. Croix. But afterward I was so scared. I stopped seeing him. But the damned word won't go away." Noting his look of alarm, she smiled. "Don't worry, I'm not about to hurl myself out the window. Not before April, anyway. You should see my appointment calendar. I can't die: I'm booked!"

The attempt at a joke made the hair on the back of Shaun's neck prickle. "Myrna, I . . ."

"There are not many people who know me as well as you, Shaun. No one, as a matter of fact. I just wondered if you'd give me a little friendly advice."

He was shaken. "Myrna, I don't know." At that moment he knew why he had accepted her invitation. He had come to confess and be comforted. How could he help Myrna when he himself was helpless? He stared at her, unsure of what he was supposed to look for. What he saw was a calm, tired face. The green eyes had a boozy, stoned glaze. There were wrinkles that he had not noticed before. Staring at that face, he realized how much he had missed seeing it—and how when he had lived with her, he had stopped seeing it because he had not taken the time to look. He wanted to kiss her. He shivered. "It's not my place to say. You seem all right to me. But what do I know? Maybe you ought to see another—"

"No," she said, and it was like a door closing. "No." Not only on this conversation, but on him. It was time to go. "It's not that big a thing, really." She looked at her watch. "God, look at the time. I've kept you so late, especially in this weather. You want to stay here tonight? I can make up the couch."

"No, thanks. I can still catch the late train and I've got to be at work at seven tomorrow morning."

The good-bye was as brisk as if he had been making a sales call. She handed him his coat, he thanked her. "I owe you one," he said. "Can you come over to my place some time?"

"I'm pretty busy the next couple of weeks."

"That's okay. If I start tonight, it'll take me at least two weeks to clean the place up."

She laughed. "Sure. I'd be glad to."

He did kiss her then: a polite peck on the cheek, as formal as a business handshake.

"Call me," she said as she closed the door.

He nodded at Patrick the doorman as he passed through the funereal lobby. Shaun paused at the door, watching the snow swirl. He could already feel its chill deep within him. The street was deserted. He pushed out into the storm.

The Empty World

Reed awoke in a drift of snow. Huge flakes dropped from the twilit sky like spiders on invisible webs. He sat up and shook himself. His head was pounding; when he touched his brow his fingers came away bloody. He had no idea where he was, but he knew that if he did not move soon the storm would bury him.

He brushed the snow from his clothing. He was wearing a blue frock coat over a waistcoat of gray wool. His knee breeches were tucked into polished black boots. Reed might have been appropriately dressed for tea in a country parlor but was woefully underdressed for winter, lacking greatcoat, hat and gloves. He stood and waded to what seemed to be a road. The snow was already ankle-deep and was rapidly filling a track left by hooves and carriage wheels. There were footprints as well but they were too blurred by the storm to tell much of a story. He assumed that he had met some sort of misadventure. A robbery, perhaps, or an accident; he could not remember. He was Shaun Reed of New York: this was the year 1858. The last thing he remembered was boarding a train in London for a holiday up-country. Beyond that his memory was as blank as the white landscape around him. He set out to find shelter from night and the storm.

Darkness was coming rapidly, and he was shivering and near despair when he saw the light. On a knoll well back from the road sprawled the shadow of a great house. All the windows but one were dark, but that single beacon promised Reed's salvation. He left the road and climbed toward it.

The immediate grounds of the house were surrounded by a forbidding stone wall, eight feet high. Reed followed along the outside, searching for a gate. The drifts were already up to the tops of his boots. His spirits flagged once again; he could no longer see the light or anything but dark rock and gray snow. He cursed the builder for a fool who had constructed a wall fit for a Norman castellan, not a country squire. As he slogged onward the cold dulled all thought.

He came to himself with a start when he saw footprints in *front* of him. He had gone completely around the wall. Reed could not imagine how he could have missed the gate. He was too weary to make another circuit. He decided he must scale the wall. The inhabitants of the house would surely understand his desperation. With numb fingers he grasped the stone and scrambled up and over like a thief.

Although there was no light on this side, he could make out a few details. The house stood three stories tall and was built of granite blocks, with some lighter stone used for quoining and coping. Clearly the owner was a gentleman of substance. Reed picked his way through an espalier garden and peered through one of the arched windows. The glass was filthy. He thought he could see a few white shapes in the room, suggesting furniture covered with sheets against the dust, but it was too dark to be sure.

He walked around to the front portico with its imposing eight-panel door. The knocker was unusual, a huge brass pen which struck against a plate in the shape of an open book. He knocked and waited, stamping his boots to keep the blood circulating. Reed's theory was that this was the country seat of a declining peer or of some financially embarrassed London merchant. He did not expect to be greeted by the owner—a caretaker was more likely. He knocked again. His toes ached: he was worried about frostbite. Was the poor wretch deaf? Reed was perishing from the cold. With a curse he decided to walk around the house to the window where he had seen the light. At the edge of the portico, however, he was brought up short in astonishment. Even in the driving snow, the front walk was clearly outlined by two low boxwood hedges. He gazed through the storm in disbelief.

The walk ran to a dead end at the wall. There was no gate.

She was a small woman, as hard and as plain as a stone barn. She had the pale skin of an invalid. He guessed that she was in her early thirties. She wore a cheap, factory-made dress of mourning black and a gray hand-knitted shawl. A smile would have softened the grimness which seemed etched on her face, but Reed suspected that this woman did not often indulge in smiling.

"Why have you come here?" She stood in the doorway of the servants' annex, blocking his entrance. "Who are you to disturb my peace?"

Reed was startled by her gruffness. He was without hat and coat and the snow was swirling around him. There was a clot of dried blood on his temple. "I beg your pardon, ma'am. I've had an accident, and I was lost in the storm when I saw your light. I wondered if I might stay here until it passes—a chair by the hearth would suffice."

She frowned. Her green eyes betrayed her suspicion.

"Of course, I'm willing to pay for your hospitality."

"Come in if you must."

She lit his way with an oil lamp through the wooden annex which contained a washhouse, coal bin, pump and empty pigeon cote, arriving at last in the kitchen. A fire was dying in a brick hearth. Beside it lay a huge brown mastiff, a dog that certainly outweighed its mistress. It raised its head and growled at Reed. "Down, Keeper," she said. There was gray on its muzzle and its eyes were cloudy with age. It settled down immediately as she threw two small logs and a lump of coal onto the fire.

"Tea?"

"It would save my life. Please." A country spinster, he thought to himself. As suspicious as a mouse and with just about as much conversation in her.

She poured water from a pitcher into a cast-iron kettle which hung over the fire. "What kind of accident?"

Reed stood with his back to the hearth. "I'm not quite sure. I'm an American, newly arrived in your country. I remember leaving London; I thought I might spend my first holiday traveling up-country. I must have gotten off the train but I can't really say why. All I can remember now is waking up in a drift of snow. I started walking and here I am."

"A holiday in Yorkshire? In the winter?"

Reed moved closer to the fire.

"The nearest station is ten miles away."

He shrugged. "I suppose there must have been a carriage at some point. . . ."

"You were on the train and suddenly you find yourself wandering across the moor miles from the nearest track. That is hardly a credible story, sir."

"No." Reed shook his head and smiled. "I'll try to think of a better one. By the way, my name is Shaun Reed." He waited for an introduction which did not come. "And whom do I have the pleasure of addressing?"

"You may call me what you will, Mr. Reed, for all the pleasure it gives you!" Her look was fierce, as if challenging him to pursue the subject. He said nothing. "You've a nasty cut on your head. It needs cleaning." She went out to the pump house.

He glanced about him. Cast-iron cooking utensils hung from hooks on the wall beside the hearth. There was a round wooden table with six loop-back Windsor chairs. On the table was a portable rosewood desk which had on it three steel pen nibs, a quill nib, a silver pen holder, a bottle of ink and a sheaf of papers. He had interrupted her in the midst of writing. Love letters? He was not embarrassed to peek at the topmost sheet.

> So hopeless is the world without,
> The world within I deeply prize;
> Thy world where guile and hate and doubt
> And cold suspicion never rise . . .

He pulled one of the chairs over to the hearth and stretched his feet toward the fire. A country poet.

She returned with a washcloth and a bowl full of cold water which she set on Reed's lap. "Stay still now while I wash away the blood." She daubed at his forehead with the washcloth.

"Do you live here by yourself, ma'am?"

"There's the dog."

Reed smiled again; he was determined to find her truculence amusing. He imagined that she was testing him. "And the master of the house? Where is he?"

She gazed at him with disdain. "This is my house, sir."

"Yours?" It hurt when he raised his eyebrow. "I see. Well, it is an *interesting* old place. A bit odd, but you English seem to prefer things that way, if you don't mind my saying so. Do you know that I walked completely around your property without seeing the gate?"

"And yet here you are, Mr. Reed."

"I confess that I was forced to scale the wall. Then there is the matter of your front walk. It doesn't seem to go anywhere."

"I see no point in encouraging visitors." She rinsed the washcloth out and took the bowl away.

"Do you mean to say that there is no gate?"

"I shouldn't think you'll need to see a doctor, Mr. Reed. It's not a large wound and the bleeding has stopped." She brought tea in a delft cup.

"You amaze me, ma'am." He shivered. Even though he had escaped the storm, he seemed to be getting colder. Snow had melted on his coat and soaked through. The niggardly fire cast little heat. Even the tea was tepid. "Do you mind if I remove my coat? I'm afraid it's soaked."

"My advice would be to change out of those wet clothes immediately. You should retire. I'll show you to your room."

"You needn't bother. I'll be fine right here by the fire, thank you."

She put her papers into the rosewood desk and picked it up. "I do not want a strange man sleeping in my kitchen or prowling about my house in the night, Mr. Reed. I must insist that you go now to your room and remain there until morning."

Reed felt sorry for her. He was sure that she did not realize how rude she was: the curse of a solitary life. "As you wish, ma'am."

She lit the way to a great stair hall which was so cold that he could see his breath. He paused to admire the wallpaper, decorated with grisaille views of English gentry strolling through Roman ruins.

"Why, this is magnificent!" There were picnics beside crumbling walls. Lazy shepherds watched their flocks. Well-dressed children played beside headless statues. "It must have been hand painted."

She nodded. "In the studio of M. Dufour, in Paris. This way please."

His second-story room was large but sparsely furnished with a walnut highboy, an armchair with a threadbare seat, and a canopied bed. The wallpaper with its crossed goose quill pattern was waterstained; the heavy curtains smelled of mildew. There were three logs in the fireplace.

"You may start a fire to dry your clothing." His hostess lit the candles which stood on either end of the mantelshelf. "There's a feather comforter under the counterpane; you should be warm enough." She glanced around the room as if to assure herself that he had everything he needed. "This is an old house, Mr. Reed, and it's full of stories. The wind will fill the cracks tonight and the house may speak. Do not be alarmed. You'll be quite safe as long as you remain in the room. Good evening to you, sir." She bowed and closed the door behind her.

Reed chuckled. He had heard about the English and their ghosts. This dotty woman had a few things to learn about New Yorkers if she thought that she could frighten him so easily. He used a candle to light the kindling in the fireplace. It blazed up quickly but, as with the kitchen fire, seemed to radiate little heat. Reed pulled off his coat and waistcoat and draped them over the chair in front of the fireplace. He did not scruple to search the highboy for a change of clothing. All the drawers were empty but one. In it were a set of twelve wooden soldiers and a remarkable collection of miniature books, each the size of a gold quarter-eagle piece. They were hand printed. The light was too poor and the lettering too small for Reed to be able to make out anything but the title pages. A number of them were copies of something called Branwell's Blackwood's Magazine. He picked up another:

YOUNG MEN'S
MAGAZINE NO.
THIRD
FOR OCTOBER 1830
Edited by Charlotte Brontë

Someone started to batter at the door.

"Who's in there?" It was a drunkard's voice, thick and angry. "Open up at once!" The old door bucked on its hinges.

"I'm coming." Reed tried the knob but it turned uselessly in his hand. "I can't get it open," he called.

"Emily! Damn your eyes, Emily; where are you?" The man outside did not seem to have heard him. "Emily, there's someone in my room." He began to weep.

Reed peered through the keyhole but all he could see were shadows and the flickering of light. Presently he heard a light step and the voice of his hostess.

"Branwell, whatever are you doing?" Her whisper was harsh. "Thank God Father is not here to see you like this. You promised him! You promised all of us!"

"Hello!" called Reed. "Ma'am? The door seems to be stuck, ma'am."

Branwell's voice went from a mumble to a wail. "It's all over with me, Emily. I'm a failure; we're all failures. All the stories we told each other, the magical lives we would lead when we grew up. Lies, Emily. Lies, all of them. We're nothing but a lot of Yorkshire bumpkins."

"Get up, Branwell. You're no brother of mine." Something scraped against the door. "Go back to your whiskey and your fashionable opium. You are a hopeless being and I will not have you in my house."

The man outside grunted. "You've found him then?" There came a single tap on the door. "Is this the lover you've been hoping for all these years?" It sounded like a taunt. Reed no longer tried to make his presence known. He eavesdropped in embarrassed silence.

"I'm not waiting for anyone, Branwell. I don't need anyone. My world is complete, I'm content to be alone in it. Now, would you please go?"

They passed from his door, still bickering. Reed strained to hear long after the voices had faded. Then he realized what he was doing and shivered. He was ashamed of his ungentlemanly behavior and yet . . . For all the inexplicable gaps in his memory, he remembered reading Mrs. Gaskell's *Life of Charlotte Brontë*: he knew all about the famous sisters. His hostess had called the fellow Branwell. There had been a Brontë brother named Branwell who had debauched himself into the grave. And he had called her . . . Emily. No, it was unthinkable. Emily Brontë had been dead for ten years. He tried the door again and pulled the knob right out of its escutcheon. It felt like a lump of ice in his hand; there was no escape, nothing to do but wait out the night.

Reed was chilled; he returned to the fire. The incident had left him with a queasy feeling. He worried that he was having a delayed reaction to his head wound. He stripped the feather comforter from the bed, wrapped himself in it and stood by the fire, stamping his feet and blowing into his hands. Damn the woman anyway! He could not believe how cold the house was.

He went to the window and parted the dusty curtains to see if it was still snowing.

"Dear God!" For a moment, Reed doubted his sanity. The window did not overlook snow-covered Yorkshire moors. The sky was clear and the light of a full moon gleamed above the Great Pyramid and Sphinx at Giza. Beyond them the level plain stretched to the horizon, broken only by a few date palms and the huddled mud huts of a distant village. Dust lifted by the khamsin winds swirled around two men in dirty white robes leading a camel by a short rope. The battered head of the Sphinx gazed at him with sightless eyes.

He rushed to the room's other window, tore back the curtains. He felt his legs going out from under him and sank to his knees. He peered over the sill, certain now that he had taken leave of his senses. Sunlight filtered dimly through the canopy of a wooded park. A stone footbridge crossed a muddy brook. Wildflowers poked through the deep layer of humus on the forest floor: violets and trilliums and jack-in-the-pulpits. Not six feet from the window, the leaf buds had burst along the branches of a gnarled ash.

He knelt there for several minutes, staring down at the park, willing it to vanish. A squirrel climbed down the ash and sat on a branch just outside the window, tail flicking. On an impulse Reed tried to raise the inner sash, but it was painted shut. He gave it a sharp blow with the heel of his hand, and the squirrel leapt away. With a grunt Reed forced the window open.

"Hullo! Is anyone there?" He could hear the brook gurgling, feel the sweet spring breeze. No one answered. "Ma'am? Miss Emily?" The hair on the back of Reed's neck prickled. He had to find out. He crawled onto the sill, stretched for the nearby branch and swung onto it.

He stooped at the foot of the ash and picked up a handful of dirt. It was cold and wet and it smelled like the mud pies he had made as a boy. He could no sooner doubt its reality than he could doubt his own. He stepped up to the house and touched the stone foundation. Flakes of gray-green lichen clung to it; a living patina that could only have grown over the course of decades.

Reed's instincts told him to climb back to his room, shut the window and pull the covers over his head, lest his reason be overthrown by the terrible impossibility of what he was witnessing. And yet he could not imagine himself cowering in his room like a child afraid of the dark. He convinced himself that he must probe this mystery to its source. Cautiously he circled around the house.

On the southern side the ground pitched steeply away from the foundation. The windows above him were open but they were too high for him to see into the house. Reed paused, looking up. A woman was speaking in the room above him.

". . . a trap. You receive no visitors; you never leave this house. Perhaps you deceive yourself that tomorrow you'll go back out into the world. But each day that you spend here makes it less likely that you will *ever* escape. You're burying yourself here."

"I'm content, Charlotte." He recognized his hostess's voice. "I cannot change what I am. The world has no claim on me. Would you have me lose my soul for the sake of pleasing fools?"

"It pains me to hear you talk like this. You have a great talent, Emily, far greater than mine. Do not deny it. What of your poems, your novel? Do you call your readers fools?"

Emily chuckled bitterly. "I should never have let you talk me into publishing the poems. They were messages to myself. Two copies sold—two! And the novel was scarcely better received. I love you and Anne and Father and yes, even poor Branwell—but that is all. As long as I have you, and this place, I shall not complain."

Reed leapt up and curled fingers around the sill. He scratched for a foothold in the joints between the stone blocks.

"I love you too, Emily. You are my sister. I want to help you overcome this unnatural shyness."

"Would that it were only shyness!" At that moment Reed pulled himself up and gained a view of the room. "You should know me better than that! You must!"

He looked through red damask curtains into a parlor which, unlike the other room he had seen, showed every evidence of daily use. Three Chinese Chippendale chairs were arranged around a marble fireplace. The walls were hung with family portraits. There were two women in the room. One, a stranger, sat on a carved mahogany sofa facing the window. Could this be Charlotte Brontë? But she was three years dead. The woman was wearing an old-fashioned dress of a dark, rusty green. She was smaller than her sister but her features seemed disproportionately large; her lip jutted and her nose had a slight hook.

Emily stood with her back to him. She must have noticed the look of horror on her sister's face because she turned and gazed out at Reed. A smile tugged at the corners of her mouth, as if his presence confirmed her arguments. When she spoke it was as much to him as to her sister.

> "No coward soul is mine,
> No trembler in the world's storm-troubled sphere
> I see Heaven's glories shine,
> And Faith shines equal arming me from Fear."

Emily sighed, and the image of her sister on the sofa shimmered and disappeared. Suddenly the furniture was covered with sheets; the portraits vanished. Emily waved her hand as if dismissing a servant and Reed lost his grip.

He lay where he had fallen for some time, eyes clamped shut. The colloquy of the two dead sisters whirled through his fevered imagination again and again; Charlotte's futile concern, the fierce pride with which Emily had claimed her solitude. He was terrified at the thought of how easily Emily had manipulated what he had perceived as reality. Might she not on a whim consign him to nothingness as well?

Reed sensed that he was not alone. He rolled onto hands and knees and saw a squad of twelve wooden redcoats, tiny bayonets at the ready. One of them gestured for him to stand. With a shriek, Reed leapt away from them and ran around the house. He bounded up the steps of the front portico and battered on the door. It swung open. Stumbling into the great entrance hall, he crossed the boundary between dream and nightmare. Darkness closed around him; the air was as cold as a tomb. He scrabbled up the stairs, whimpering like a frightened dog. The door to his room was ajar. The candles on the mantelshelf flickered in the icy wind that gusted through the open window. He slammed the sash, blew out the candles and hurled himself into the bed. There were no sounds of pursuit, only the hiss of the dying fire and the rattle of the windowpanes as the storm swirled around the house. He tried to imagine where she was in the house, what she might be doing at that moment while he shivered beneath the feather comforter. Did she lie in her bed, alone, imagining the universe? He thought he heard distant laughter, and then a voice—her voice—in the wind's moaning. "Sleep," it urged. "Sleep." He could not resist it.

"It's half past ten, Mr. Reed. Is it your intention to sleep all day?"

Reed awoke with a shiver. His hostess was standing in the doorway.

"If you're going to reach town before sunset you'd best get started soon." She went to the windows and parted the curtains. Sunlight reflecting from the snow-covered moors dazzled him. He sat up, blinking. "I'm afraid you'll have to walk. I keep neither horse nor carriage."

She took his coat from the chair by the fireplace and brushed the wrinkles out with her hand. "Your coat has dried nicely." She brought it over and laid it across the foot of the bed.

Reed was confused. He waited in vain to be rebuked for leaving his room and violating the conditions of her hospitality. He would not have been surprised had she announced that she was a devil's pawn and that his soul was forfeit. Yet she acted as if nothing had happened. He reexamined his memory in the clear morning light. Might not his terror have been the stuff of nightmares? He pushed the covers aside and swung his feet out of the bed. "I have had the strangest dream!" he said.

"I don't doubt it, Mr. Reed. There are fresh eggs and bread for your breakfast. Would you care for tea?"

He pulled on his boots. "I beg your pardon, ma'am, but did you have any visitors last night?"

"Visitors?" She smiled. He remembered how she had smiled when she had seen him at the window—but, of course, that must have been a dream. "I seem to remember an unfortunate gentleman who appeared on my doorstep begging for shelter."

He frowned and reached for his frock coat. It was still slightly damp, her assurances to the contrary.

"You needn't bother with the bedclothes. Come down now and eat."

Reed followed her down the stairs to the entrance hall. He had the eerie feeling that the people painted on the wallpaper had changed places. His hostess turned toward the kitchen wing. Reed hesitated. A doorway in the opposite direction opened onto the parlor where he had seen the two sisters.

"This way, please."

He did not move. "You have a remarkable house, ma'am." Every detail of the room was as he remembered it. There was a stack of birch logs in the dusty marble fireplace. Sheets covered the sofa and the chairs. There were even shadows on the wall where portraits had once protected the paint from fading in the sun. "I can't believe that you live here alone."

She shrugged wordlessly and once again gestured for him to follow. Instead, Reed gazed about him, as if admiring the magnificence of the grand stair hall. On the wallpaper in front of him was painted a scene of a ruined seaside village. A gentleman and lady were strolling its outskirts along a dirt road. A shepherd sat with his back to an oak, watching his flock graze. Reed gathered his courage. "Pardon me, ma'am, but do you have a sister named Charlotte?"

"Oh, Mr. Reed!" She stamped her foot in impatience. "What is the purpose of this interrogation? Clearly you have some question which you are burning to ask me. Come to it, man!"

Reed stiffened. "I did not mean to be impertinent."

"Yet you're succeeding admirably." She sighed. "I had hoped to keep you in ignorance. For your own good. However, if you insist . . ." She waved her hand.

The painted lady twirled her lace parasol. The sheep looked up as the shepherd lifted his pipes and began to blow a mournful tune. The gentleman pointed at Reed and laughed.

"Dear God, ma'am! Dear God."

There was a rumble behind him. A volcano belched gray smoke. Picnickers looked up in alarm and then hurriedly stuffed their supplies into a basket. The leaves in the trees shivered in the wind.

Emily Brontë was frowning at him. "Will you come to breakfast *now*, Mr. Reed?"

She set a plate of fried eggs in front of him. He tasted them gingerly. They were bland, like the dry toast; more an appearance of food than the thing itself. Reed wanted desperately to believe that he was still dreaming. Perhaps he was dozing on the train; he tried to convince himself that the blood pounding in his ears was actually the sound of wheels crossing rough track. "I simply can't believe it," he said. "I can't believe that you're . . ." The word seemed to swell in his throat; he felt as if he might choke on it.

She sat down across from him. She seemed to study the table top as she said,

> "There is not room for Death
> Nor atom that his might could render void:
> Since thou art Being and Breath,
> And what thou art may never be destroyed."

Reed sipped lukewarm tea. He was stunned to silence by the prosaic manner of this—ghost? Spirit? He would have expected Byronic misery, howls of anger against the unjust fates, but not this. Not a bit of mid-morning melancholy over eggs and toast. Certainly this was not the Emily Brontë he would have expected.

"We buried my brother, Branwell, in the graveyard of my father's church in Haworth. Branwell died of consumption, brought on by his shameless dissipation. It was cold in the church; I took a chill that grew in me. My sisters feared I too would succumb to consumption. For myself, I had no fear. It was a lesser part of me that ailed; my spirit, the cold fire within me, grew ever stronger. And then I seemed to step out of time, to this place. It's what I had hoped for. This is where I belong."

"But that's . . . preposterous!"

She bowed her head slightly. "As you say."

He dared not believe her. Although in his soul he now glimpsed a level of existence transcending reality, Reed clung to the notion that this was all an illusion. To do otherwise was to accept the fact that he, too, was forever locked out of time. That he, too, was dead.

"And your family. They can visit you?"

"They are creatures of my memory. The past is like a great poem, Mr. Reed. *Paradise Lost* never changes, yet one returns to the same unforgettable lines again and again."

"Then you are alone?"

"You value your company too lightly, Mr. Reed." Her eyebrows arched; Reed laughed nervously. "From time to time I receive visitors like yourself. I can't say why they come; I don't know what happens to them when they go. And even when I'm alone in this house, I watch from my windows and worlds rise up before my eyes. I see men and women as real as you passing before me. They laugh and die and fall in love. I've made my choice and I'm content."

"And you never go out?"

"No." She looked away from him. "It's an experiment I have not seen fit to try. You see, none of my visitors has ever returned."

Reed pushed his chair back from the table. He did not envy this woman; he could not find it within himself to pity her. There was something profoundly distrubing about Miss Emily Brontë. The quiet power of her solitude terrified him, yet at the same time he was fascinated by it. He realized, however, that he was not willing to barter his life—however mundane—for spiritual transcendence. Reed knew he must try to escape. "But you say I can go?"

"You are your own man, Mr. Reed. You may do as you wish."

"Then I must take my leave." He stood. "How far is the next town?"

"Follow the road east. You should reach Haworth by sunset. From there you may hire a carriage to take you to the railway station at Keighley."

She led him to the stair hall. The people on the wall went about their business, indifferent to his passage. Emily opened the door. There was a wooden gate now at the end of the walk. Reed stepped through and buttoned his frock coat against the cold. The winds had died and the snow glistened in the midday sun. He hesitated.

"Won't you come with me?" He was surprised to hear himself say it. "I-I cannot believe that you will be happy in this house. By yourself, I mean." He felt like a fool.

Her anger came suddenly, like a winter squall sweeping across the cold sea. "Why is it, Mr. Reed, that people like you always ask the same questions? Do you imagine that I am made of stone, that I am immune to regret and temptation, even here?" Her hands curled into fists as if she meant to strike him—or herself. "If I suffer in this place it is because I *choose* to remain, not because I'm helpless! Your cruelty is thoughtless, Mr. Reed; I suppose I must make an allowance for that. But go now; I can no longer abide the sight of you." She propelled him from her house. "I watch, Mr. Reed. It is enough because it has to be." She slammed the door.

He trudged through the gate and down to the road. There were fresh tracks in the snow and he followed them to the east. Halfway up a hill Reed paused to look back. He expected she was watching him. It was then that he noticed the farm cart following him at a distance. He waited for it, heart pounding. Snow crunched beneath the crude wheels as it approached.

Reed plastered a smile on his face and waved. The driver was an old man in a dirty homespun greatcoat. He muttered to the horse as he reined in. "Mim! Mim! Mim! Did ever Christian body see aught like it?"

"Excuse me, sir, but I've had an accident. Can you give me a ride to the village?"

The old man looked doubtful. "Is't Haworth ye want?"

"Haworth would be fine, thank you."

"Come along then."

Reed climbed up beside him. "I can't thank you enough. I'm a stranger here, an American, and I wasn't at all sure that I was heading in the right direction."

The old man tapped the reins and said nothing.

"I wonder if you can tell me, good fellow, who lives in the house back there." Reed pointed. "I stopped there earlier but no one seemed to be home."

The driver turned for a brief look backward. "House?" He stared at Reed. "And they call *me* daft. I see nought but a ruin what's been since the time yer grandfather was a King's man. It's empty; ye may have it all to yerself, if such be yer pleasure." He laughed.

Even as Reed watched, the roof seemed to disappear. The stone wall crumbled; the windows gaped like the empty sockets of a skull.

They reached the top of the hill and the old man grunted. "There be Haworth."

Across the valley Reed saw a village of small dark stone houses. The roofs were covered with sooty snow. There were a few hulking mills with stacks vomiting smoke into the blue sky. He imagined that the people who scuttled down its narrow streets would be like the old man, crass and shabby, mired in the hurly-burly of the material world. These were his people; he felt a tingle of horror at the prospect of passing among them. It reminded him of lines from one of Emily's poems, lines he had studied at Columbia—in another time and place.

> Once drinking deep of that divinest anguish,
> How could I seek the empty world again?

The cart trundled down the steep slope. This world, that other world—both empty. He shivered, preparing himself for the transition he now knew to be coming, and looked back one last time at the ruin, gray and alone in the snow.

The Best of All Possible Worlds

Something brushed against the top of his head. In desperation Shaun flailed and struck a chunk of Styrofoam flotsam. Part of a wrecked dock, it had been in the water long enough to collect a coating of black slime. He clawed at it, held on. As he broke the surface, he drew a huge, shuddering breath. His dream of Yorkshire had shattered like an icicle; only the chill remained.

Daylight now stung his eyes. His throat felt like sandpaper from all the water he had swallowed. But he had not drowned. Yet. The dreamers had abandoned him when he was in trouble and then forced another dream on him, and still he had survived. He lifted his head, treading water, to find the islands. Through a salt blur he could make out a mottled beach and a haze of green that stretched behind it. He was going to make it. They had all been wrong. Vic. The sphinx. The dreamers. *He was going to make it.*

He let go of the Styrofoam, put his head down again and forced himself to swim the last few strokes. He heard shouts. He stopped swimming, stretched for the bottom and touched the sand. He was about thirty yards from the beach. The mottles had resolved themselves into men and women and children, beach umbrellas and folding chairs and brightly colored towels. Shaun was too weary to muster much astonishment. He staggered through the scattering of swimmers, past two cool teenage boys throwing a Frisbee and a gang of kids having a splash fight. A lifeguard on a white tower glared, blew his whistle and waved for him to get out. Weeping, Reed stumbled at the water's edge. Akira O'Connor helped him up.

"You okay, Shaun? There are easier ways to get to Europe, you know."

A dark woman was at his other side. "What were you doing out there?" said Jihan. "The lifeguard was ready to go after you."

Shaun looked from one to the other. They led him up the beach and sat him in a folding chair. Jihan toweled him off. Akira popped him a Schaefer from the ice chest. He sat between them for ten minutes without saying anything. He watched the swimmers. Joggers skirted the waves. Boys and girls tried to bodysurf. From behind him on the boardwalk came a steady stream of people carrying Cokes and hot dogs and greasy fries in cardboard trays. The water was green, the sky clear, the horizon as mathematical a line as any a draftsman might draw. He could not see Freedom Beach.

"Jones Beach," he said at last. "I'm home."

Akira smiled his easy smile. "You ain't home yet, pal. The traffic copter on the radio says they're bumper to bumper on the Meadowbrook Parkway."

"Who cares?" said Jihan. "We'll wait them out. We've got plenty of beer and we haven't even touched the potato salad yet. Let's not talk about going home."

"Why not?" Akira tickled the palm of her hand. "There are some things you can do at home you can't do here."

"Don't be so sure." Jihan grinned. "Why don't you come in the water with me and we'll find out just how much you can do here."

Shaun wanted to laugh or cry—do something—but was too exhausted. "Something happened to me," he said. "I don't know what it was. . . ." He shook his head.

Jihan touched his arm. "You sure you're all right, Shaun?"

"Just happy," he said. "It's good to be back."

Akira shrugged. "Right."

"Is Myrna here too?" Shaun asked.

Akira and Jihan exchanged a glance. "No, she's not," said Jihan.

"Look, Shaun—" Akira grabbed a handful of sand and let it sift through his fingers "—maybe this is out of line, but why don't you just put it behind you? You were divorced, there was nothing you could have done. Forget her."

Jihan shot him a dirty look.

"Forget?" said Shaun. "Why?"

"She's dead," said Akira. "The sooner you accept that, the better."

"*Akira.*" Jihan shook her head.

On the way home they treated him like a lunatic with a gun, as if by his silent estrangement he had kidnapped their Sunday outing. At first he did not care; he was too busy trying to work his way back into reality using nothing but his senses and reason. He stared through the twilight at the line of red taillights crawling down the parkway and filled his nostrils with the familiar stink of exhaust. But this traffic jam in Nassau County seemed no more substantial than the snowstorm on the bleak Yorkshire moors. When at last they broke free of the tie-up, the hot breeze that came through the car windows felt the same on his moist skin as the Santa Ana blowing the hot breath of the Mojave through the window of a seedy office on the corner of Ivar and Hollywood Boulevard.

He could not figure out what had happened by himself. He needed help.

When he finally began to ask questions, Jihan and Akira responded with an eagerness that made him certain they thought he was crazy. Maybe they were right; he was willing to consider the possibility.

They told Shaun that Myrna had killed herself two months before. He forced them to tell how she had slashed her wrists as she lay in the bathtub, moved the screen away so she could lie there and watch the river as her blood mingled with the warm water. An anonymous caller had tipped the police; he had never been found. They told Shaun that he had disappeared for a week after he had heard the news, that he had refused to answer the phone or come to the door of his apartment. They said that he had finally come out again in order to keep his job editing textbooks at St. Martin's for the Project. The more they told him, the more confused Shaun became. It was not that he thought they were lying, but rather that he thought they must be wrong. What job at St. Martin's? There was a strained silence while he considered these things. Then Akira filled it by pushing a cassette into the tape player. A saxophone honked like an enraged goose; at the same time someone banged seemingly random chords at the piano. It took a while before Shaun recognized the melody underneath all the noise. A bebop trio was attacking Stephen Foster's "Beautiful Dreamer."

Shaun was suddenly afraid. He leaned forward and looked at the other tapes. Ornette Coleman, Thelonius Monk, Charlie Parker. Where was the Irish music? "How long have you been a jazz fan, Akira?"

"How long?" His friend's laugh was nervous. "It started in college, I guess. My roommate was a Coltrane fan. What's the matter, too esoteric? I'm really into modal improvisation these days, atonality, you know."

"Frankly," said Jihan, "it makes my molars ache."

"Here, let's put something more structured on."

"Stop it! Can't you see what they . . . don't you realize who . . . ?" Shaun sank back against the seat and covered his face with his hands. "I'm sorry. I have to think.

FREEDOM BEACH

* * *

That night Shaun had the nightmare for the first time. He was back in the Empire State Building, walking down a hallway with one of the BOBs, except this time it was Akira instead of Aristophanes. They were on the twenty-fifth floor, on their way to Fantastic's room. "Hurry, Akira," Shaun said. "She's waiting."

"For you." Akira stopped. "This is as far as I go."

Shaun realized that Akira was afraid, and was suddenly afraid himself. He continued down the hallway, and with every step he took the fear grew, like a bubble caught in his throat. The floor was marble, hard and cold. Potted plants lined the walls, their leaves withered and gray with dust. He came to a black door. Shaun reached for the knob, let his hand drop. She was waiting for him, waiting. As he hesitated, terrified yet not sure why, the door began to open on its own. It was Myrna's apartment on the East River. The bubble of fear expanded, choked him. He wanted to turn and run but something was pulling him through the doorway. It took a tremendous effort to tear himself away. And then he woke up, sweating, in his own apartment.

The bedside clock read seven-fifteen. He stumbled out of bed. He showered, shaved, and got dressed for work. Everything seemed to be more or less in its place: nothing had been disturbed—except him. According to his check register his NOW account held a balance of three thousand, one hundred and twenty dollars and thirty-nine cents. That, at least, was an improvement. The checkbook showed regular deposits every two weeks: five hundred and two dollars and twenty one cents. It all came back to him now, like the plot of a favorite novel he was rereading. He looked up St. Martin's address in the phone book just to be sure, although he knew it was going to be 175 Fifth Avenue.

He hit the subway early and found that things had changed beneath the city as well. The cars were immaculate; all the graffiti had been scrubbed away. Even the ad panels were spotless and there were two mint-condition subway maps in each car. Shaun ate a quick breakfast at Chico's on Broadway.

Just outside the Flatiron Building a man in a brush cut and a severe black suit was shouting at the passersby. A cap with a few coins in it lay on the sidewalk at his feet.

"They do not merely speak for God, brothers and sisters—they are God incarnate! They travel in threes because they are manifestations of His Holy Trinity. And it is not ours to question Their Will. The Bible says, Book of Job 33:12, 'For God is greater than man. Why then do you make complaint against him that he gives no account of his doings . . .'"

Shaun dropped a subway token into the man's hat and entered the building. The office was familiar, and his cubicle more familiar still. There was an interoffice envelope on his desk which contained a manuscript on a floppy disk and a note from Beckwith saying they needed a copyedited version by Wednesday for the Project. Shaun got to work. Akira called at ten to ask how he was doing and offered to buy him lunch. They met at eleven-thirty at the Bandbox.

"After we dropped you off last night, Jihan and I had a little talk about you," Akira said.

"Did you manage to fit all the pieces together again?"

Akira looked embarrassed. "I'm sorry if I was too blunt yesterday. But you know I'm a friend. I really think you've been brooding too much about Myrna, even before she—even before this last business—"

"Last business. You said it."

"You've got to give yourself a chance to get over her. There's this therapist that helped Jihan once that we want you to go see. I'll—"

Therapy. Shaun glared at Akira. "You remember. You were there." His voice was flat and hard.

"Where? What are you talking about?"

He searched Akira's face. The man was either a great actor or utterly sincere. Either way, Shaun was in trouble. He looked around the restaurant and his courage failed him. He was afraid that they would book him into a rubber room at Bellevue if he started raving about Freedom Beach. He crumpled his napkin into a ball and put it on the table. "I don't need this, Akira." He pushed his chair back.

"Yes, you do. You need someone to talk to."

"Am I boring you?"

"Someone who's not involved. Jihan thinks this woman would be good for you. I do too."

"I can't afford it."

"St. Martin's has a health plan, don't they? And if you're not covered yet, Jihan and I will pay."

It was Shaun's turn to be embarrassed. "Look, I can't do this. It would be too hard . . ."

"Go once. A favor for me, friend Reed. If you don't like her you can forget it and we'll get off your case. Okay?"

"Forget?" Shaun laughed bitterly. "I'm beginning to wish I could."

Shaun did not know quite what to expect when he started seeing Dr. Pendergast. All during their first session he kept waiting for a trio of dreamers to drop through trap doors in the ceiling or float by the window in a hot air balloon. He was ready for them—ready to grill them, denounce them, even throttle them if he got the chance. Above all, he was determined not to let them go until he had an explanation. But the dreamers never showed up and there were no explanations forthcoming from the cool and elegant Dr. Rose Pendergast. Although Shaun knew all too well how deceiving appearances could be, she appeared to be unconnected with the dreamers' conspiracy.

Shaun eventually came to appreciate the monied blandness of her reception room. Whistler would have called it *Fantasia in Maroon and Green*. The flocked wallpaper was the color of dried blood; the Mondrian print was framed in dark chrome. There were enough ferns and bromeliads to decorate a rain forest. The receptionist, Charles, was young and blonde and manicured. He treated Shaun like a patient and not a friend, which Shaun appreciated. Shaun would show up for his appointment ten minutes early, and Charles would simply say hello and let him be. Shaun would sit on the sofa and page through the doctor's quirky subscriptions: *Gourmet* and *Print* and *Yankee* and, of course, the ubiquitous *Progress*, official magazine of the Project.

Dr. Pendergast was a slender, distinguished-looking woman. Her hair was the silver color so fashionable with television news anchors, her eyes were gray, her dresses dark. In contrast to her body, her face was round and open; she wore little makeup, and the lines at the corners of her eyes and mouth suggested a person who smiled a lot—when she was not working. When he walked in to see her, she would shake his hand and offer him either of two chairs opposite her, on the other side of a chrome and glass coffee table. On one side of him was a schefflera that was almost big enough to picnic under; on the other, between the chairs, was a small table with a rattan box of Kleenex and a heavy chrome ashtray. The view through the window was typical Manhattan, Upper West Side: rooftops and the windows of taller buildings, a sliver of the Hudson and a peek at Jersey.

When he first started seeing Dr. Pendergast, her couchside manner was to let him do most of the talking while she sat, impassive as a sphinx, taking notes with a felt-tipped pen that made a scratching sound when she wrote too fast. Shaun was never sure he felt good going to see her, but he never exactly felt bad, and for that respite he was grateful. She kept asking him why he came. Given his suspicions at the mere suggestion of the word therapy, it was a good question. He ran through several answers in ensuing sessions. First it was because his friends had suggested that he come. Next it was because he was having trouble doing his work for the Project. Next it was because his ex-wife had killed herself. To some extent all of these were the same answer. After several of these guarded and unsatisfactory sessions, he decided to take a chance. He told her about Freedom Beach and his escape and how the world he had returned to seemed different from the one he remembered.

"Different how?" Dr. Pendergast asked.

"Lots of ways. None of them make sense. I have a job that I didn't remember having, except that when I go into my back files there, I find memos that I know I wrote. I have a close friend whose tastes in music have completely changed." The litany started to embarrass Shaun; still he plunged on. "I've been keeping a journal, writing down all the discrepancies I notice. It's so bad that sometimes I'm not even sure that I remember the Project or the dreamers."

"You're not the only one who has suffered from dissociation related to the Project. After all, there are changes being made."

"I know, I know." Shaun considered for a moment, then decided to tell her. "Look, they told me I was at Freedom Beach for something called dream therapy. You ever hear of anything like that?"

"They?"

"The statues claimed to speak for the dreamers. We were told that the dreamers ran Freedom Beach." As soon as he said it Shaun felt as if he had given something away. What it was, and why he should not reveal it to his therapist, he did not understand.

Dr. Pendergast seized the opportunity. "So the dreamers took time out from their work on the Project just to persecute you?"

Shaun was taken aback. Of course the dreamers of Freedom Beach had to connect with the dreamers who ran the Project. Yet he was certain that he had known nothing about any Project when he had waded ashore at Jones Beach. And aside from an odd memory of a helicopter in Central Park, he had been totally unprepared to find the dreamers in charge of New York—the world!

"I don't know—yes!" He imagined she was writing the word "paranoid" in her notes—probably double-underlining it. The thought made him uncomfortable; time to change the subject. "Why do they call themselves the dreamers anyway?"

She seemed annoyed at the question, but after a moment's hesitation she said, "In their magazine they claim it's because they're visionaries. I suppose a little PR doesn't hurt when you're groping your way toward what you hope will be utopia."

"Do you think they're really just people?"

"So they say." Her felt-tip was scratching now. "But you don't think they are?"

"I don't believe everything they say." The dreamers did not need the truth; they could make up their own. Here they were, tampering with the very fabric of reality with the claim that they were executing God's plan for humanity, and people accepted it without hesitation. He knew that they had edited his memories of the world—inserting some things, deleting others. But they had bungled the job because he could still remember a world without them.

It was a memory he must protect at all costs. Not something to discuss with this woman who had yet to earn his complete trust. He refused to talk about it any more and they ended that session early.

Another time she asked him about Freedom Beach and he began to tell her about the dream therapy.

"Dream therapy." Dr. Pendergast flipped the pages of her notebook. "Yes, you mentioned that before. Some kind of Freudian analysis?"

"No. I mean experiencing things that never happened, that couldn't possibly happen. When I first arrived, the dreams came only while I was asleep. Later they were able to zap me whenever they damn well pleased. And the guests at Freedom Beach turned up in the dreams."

"For example?"

"One of the dreams was like a Marx Brothers movie. Myrna and Murray were in it too."

"You recognized it as a dream at the time?"

Shaun clapped his hands together in his lap. "No. That's why it was so insidious; I thought it was really happening. It followed the story of Doctor Faustus only it was Groucho Marx playing Faustus and Myrna was Helen of Troy."

"Who were you?"

"I was Faustus's student. I spent most of the time chasing Helen, and I almost had her but then she was gone."

"Sounds familiar, no?"

He sighed. "You're saying it was just a delusion, that it reflects what happened to us later, in our marriage. Okay. My point is that when I examine my memory it seems as real as my childhood, my marriage, my last visit here. I can find no difference, and that frightens me."

She flipped a page of her notebook. "All right, Shaun. For now we won't worry about whether this really happened or not. Let's just talk about it. You say this experience reflected what happened later. Why later? When did it happen to you?"

"I don't know exactly. When this happened to me, we were much younger—college age. In fact, Faustus was a younger version of Murray Gross, a professor we had at Columbia in the class where I first met Myrna. I didn't like him much."

"Why?"

"Because he gave me an *F* on the best paper I ever wrote in college."

"You disliked him because of his bad judgment?"

Shaun grimaced. "I disliked him because he was a smartass and a phony and I knew it but nobody else saw through him. I gave him back exactly what he was putting out in that class, and he flunked me for it."

"You objected to his hypocrisy."

"Yes. And that he took himself so seriously."

"And this serious man was Groucho in your movie?"

"Well—he wasn't that serious. He was like Groucho in the classroom. Always a smart remark for everything, but you knew he really thought he was as good a scholar as anyone. He was a fraud, but he was the most popular professor in the department."

"You objected to his popularity."

Shaun felt defensive. Dr. Pendergast watched him calmly. He wondered what she would look like if someone put an ice cube down her blouse.

"I disliked him because he was sleeping with Myrna."

"I see. The *F* didn't matter."

"You're not listening! Of course the *F* mattered. That was

the whole point. He gave me an *F* because he knew Myrna was attracted to me. And he was nothing, he had no heart to him! Still, I think she slept with him. It made me mad."

"Why did it make you mad?"

Shaun paused. "Because I wanted her myself."

Dr. Pendergast poured herself a glass of water. She took a sip. Shaun's collar felt tight. "I take it that Myrna eventually broke it off with Professor Gross," she said. "Why do you think she did that?"

"I guess she fell in love with me."

Dr. Pendergast sighed. "You should hear the tone of your voice, Shaun. You sound as if you were confessing a crime."

Shaun's face was hot. "I guess I feel a little guilty."

"Because Myrna left Professor Gross for you? Or because you're attractive to women?"

Shaun said nothing. He could not deny the truth of her analysis, but he wondered why she kept missing the point.

Soon after Shaun began his sessions with Dr. Pendergast, the dreamers, meeting in Geneva, announced God's plan to improve the lot of American poets. Every sports publication in the United States, from *Archery World* to *Wrestling Guide*, was required to carry a poetry supplement, that supplement to represent not less than ten percent of the total editorial copy and to have no connection whatsoever to sports. Newspapers were to carry a page of poetry next to their regular standing and scoreboard listings. Every pack of bubblegum cards was to have at least one card with a picture of a famous poet on one side and a short poem on the other.

It was no surprise then, that by the time Shaun had gotten around to discussing his visions with Dr. Pendergast, the first in an avalanche of textbooks explaining modern poetry to a population almost totally ignorant of its existence began to spill across his desk. Nor was Shaun particularly surprised when he opened an interoffice envelope to find a manuscript disk labelled: *The Light Fantastic: Contemporary Science Fiction and Fantasy Poets*. *The Light Fantastic* was a book of essays patched together by a ambitious Rutgers professor with the timing of a commodities broker. Shaun was stunned, however, when he booted the disk and scanned the contents page. One of the essays was called "Pop Lit Goes Legit," by Murray Gross, Associate Professor of English, Columbia University. This was just a few days after Shaun had told Dr. Pendergast about his former teacher.

The coincidence troubled Shaun all morning. He thought about calling Dr. Pendergast and throwing it in her face. Let her scoff now about his persecution complex. The dreamers had taken an interest in him—he was certain of it.

Gross's essay was, of course, the first thing he looked at in the book. Its thesis was that almost all of the noteworthy work done in the last twenty years had been done by poets associated in some way with the pulp fantasy and science fiction tradition. Poets who, like Gross, had as often as not been sneered at by the literary establishment.

Shaun was gratified to discover that Gross was without a doubt one of the worst writers he had ever had to edit. With cursor flashing he savaged Gross's sloppy, pun-laden prose. He knew full well that if Gross and his Rutgers friend wanted this to be a Project-approved book, they would have little choice but to accept his copyediting.

Just before lunch break Shaun was working up a truly wretched section mentioning all the promising new poets of the eighties who had broken into print in the mass-market pulps. Shaun had never heard of any of them; he doubted if anyone else had, either. The thought stuck with him. He paused, fingers curled over the keyboard, chilled with inspiration.

Ever since he had stumbled ashore at Jones Beach, he had been casting about for an appropriate act of rebellion. Yes, this was completely unprofessional, but still, but still . . . It was the perfect way to serve notice that he would not accept a world run by the dreamers. That he knew his escape from Freedom Beach was not yet complete.

It was easy enough to do. He inserted a short paragraph into Gross's essay:

One of the most interesting new poets of the eighties was Myrna Rosny, whose best work deals with a passionate quest for escape from the artificiality of the modern world. Her work has been seen by some as a dissent from the announced program of the Project. Unfortunately, her career was cut short by her mysterious death in 1986.

He saved this addition to disk and went to lunch; he felt the same sense of wicked exhilaration he had felt the first time he had made love to Myrna. He had done something! Maybe he could not bring the dreamers down single-handedly, but at least he could spit in their faces. As he was wolfing down a chiliburger at Chico's, Shaun thought about how much fun it would be to call Gross and gloat. By the time he finished his coffee he decided against it. Better if the old man never knew who had tampered with his essay. Besides, Shaun's quarrel was not really with Gross.

As he brought the check to the register, he hit upon a new tactic for his underground rebellion. He dashed up Broadway until he found a newsstand that carried pulp science fiction magazines. He bought one of each. Sure enough, several of them published poetry. Back at the office he typed from memory the poem Myrna had written him at Freedom Beach. He called it "Sea Change" and mailed it to the editor of the first magazine on the stack: *Amazing Science Fiction Stories*.

Shaun was so pleased with himself that it was hard to get back to work. When he brought Gross's essay back to the screen to finish it, he could not help but reread the paragraph about Myrna. Several times. Suddenly he realized that there was still another change he could make. He deleted the word "death" in the last sentence. In its place he inserted "disappearance." And shivered.

Two days later he sent the copyedited manuscript on to Beckwith for final approval. Three weeks after that he pasted into his journal a Xerox of a check from *Amazing* for thirty-five dollars.

* * *

Getting the check reopened old wounds. One of them was Shaun's tattered ambition to write. He remembered the first time he had had a free-lance article accepted by one of the computer magazines. A triumph, but how quickly the exhilaration had faded! It was not enough. Maybe if he had finished his novel—but it was too late now. He had kept the dead-ended manuscript in the back of his desk drawer until the day he moved out of the apartment after the divorce. He had brought it with him to his new apartment, his new life, but when he had gotten around to unpacking his papers, the mere sight of it disgusted him. Just another symbol of his failure. He had thrown the manuscript away.

And now Myrna had succeeded where he had failed. Once again she was ahead of him. He had always resented her for seeming to be the stronger of the two of them. But he had never told her. He realized that his sense of frustration at the world included some anger at her for abandoning it without a fight, the way she had abandoned sex. His attitude toward Myrna was evolving; he understood things about her that he had never understood before. Too bad the change had to come as a result of the dreamers' alleged therapy. Seeing her as Emily Brontë, as Alice Ives, as Fantastic—a vulnerable and manipulated person—had shown him that she *might* indeed have had her own reasons for killing herself. He was ashamed now to remember how he had demanded that she understand him when he had never understood her.

In the evenings, after coming home from work at St. Martin's, he would sit thinking. Like coral, by slow accretion, some conclusions grew in him. Despite all the clean subway cars, tax rollbacks, and disarmament talks, the dreamers were either incompetent or malicious. If they were working out God's plan, then God had screwed up. The road to utopia was not paved with corpses and burnt-out cases. For all her troubles, it had to have been the dreamers who had pushed Myrna over the edge. All she had really wanted was control of her own life. It was not an unreasonable goal—except in a world where the dreamers seemed intent on changing everything.

Something that Poseidon had asked came back to him: "How old is Murray?" Knowing that Murray had been Professor Gross, older than he and Myrna when they had been undergrads fifteen years earlier, how could he be so young at Freedom Beach? Shaun supposed he could look up the Dr. Gross who wrote the article for the poetry textbook and see whether he had been miraculously rejuvenated, but he was ready to bet he had not. So the Murray at Freedom Beach had not been the real Murray Gross. The dreamers had made a mistake, probably were continuing to make mistakes.

The longer he considered the dreamers' fallibility, the more sense it seemed to make. And from that proposition arose a plan of action. He had to fight them. He would start small, choose his battles carefully. A guerrilla war. The only problem with being an underground man, however, was that it was lonely work. His journal was not enough. He needed a co-conspirator, or at the very least, someone willing to listen. That ruled out Dr. Pendergast. She would listen, all right, but what she heard was not what he was telling her. She would sit there writing in her notebook, filtering his story through Freudian analysis, searching for Jungian archetypes. Every so often she would offer up an educated and elegant interpretation that was absolutely beside the point. Until she accepted the fact that the dreamers had intervened in his life, sent him to Freedom Beach and changed him as well as the world, she would never be able to help him.

When he could not bring himself to tell her that he had revised Gross's essay, he considered breaking off therapy. Two things prevented him. The first was that he had not yet given up the hope that she might someday help him understand what was happening. The other was that, despite everything, he liked her. Eighty dollars an hour seemed a rather steep price to pay for companionship, but he had so few people he could talk to. Besides, St. Martin's was picking up the tab.

Still the question remained: whom could he trust? The more he thought it over, the clearer the answer became.

* * *

They sat in the parking lot arguing for ten minutes before Shaun could persuade him to go in.

"This was a stupid idea, friend Reed," said Akira. They stood in the doorway as their eyes adjusted to the gloom. "Just plain dumb." Still, he threaded his way through the tightly packed tables to his favorite spot near the tiny stage.

Nothing had changed at the Limerick and everything had changed. The sign over the door was still there. The big tables had a few more dents. Shaun could feel cracks in the leather on the benches. The menu still hung on the wall; the smell was the same.

"Look, there's your picture," said Shaun, pointing to the gallery of honor. "Right next to Brendan Behan."

Akira rolled his eyes toward heaven. "Are you going to keep this up all night? If so, I'm leaving now."

It was the faces, though; none of the faces were the same. It used to be that at Thursday happy hour Shaun would recognize at least half the house. The crowd gathered around the bar had the look of regulars, but they were all strangers to Shaun.

A gum-chewing waitress came up to take their order. "You want a Guinness, Akira?" said Shaun.

"Hell, no! Swill tastes like used motor oil. You have Schaefer on draft?"

The waitress nodded.

"I'll have a Guinness," said Shaun. "I was wondering, does Nell still work here?"

"She left." The waitress turned toward the bar.

"Excuse me," said Shaun. "We were friends of hers—regulars, anyway. We were wondering if you could tell us where she went?"

"Friends, eh?" The waitress snapped her gum to show her opinion of friendship. "She got divorced and moved to New Mexico. We heard she had cancer. That's a Schaefer and a stout."

Akira and Shaun looked at each other. "When was the last time you were here?" said Shaun.

"I don't know," Akira sighed. "Four, maybe five years. You?"

"I don't think I've been here since the night I got into that brawl. You remember?"

"Sure." The beers came and each of them took a long pull.

"Myrna didn't want me to come," said Shaun. "She was always on my case about that night."

There was a long silence in gloomy tribute to the shades of Myrna and Nell. "Isn't nostalgia fun?" said Akira as he finished his beer. "Are we staying or what?" He waved at the waitress.

"I'd like to give it a try. Please."

"Sure. Whatever you want." He gave the waitress his best smile. Its dazzle seemed to thaw her coolness; at least she stopped frowning at them. "In that case, my dear, save yourself some walking and bring me a pitcher this time. And the special is bacon and cabbage, is it? Please."

During dinner they talked about the Mets and the weather and work. They complained to each other about traffic and getting old. The same conversation was going on all over the bar: the exchange of the commonplace, transactions in currency of friendship. Shaun studied his friend's face, the perfect white teeth, the strong lines at the corners of his mouth. His hair was almost totally gray now, still thick, and he was as lean as he had been ten years earlier. Shaun worked hard to resurrect the spirit of those times. He thought that if he could reinforce the groundwork of trust that they had built up over the years, their friendship might withstand the test he had planned for it.

The alcohol helped. People are always so frank, Shaun thought, when they get a bellyful. Maybe too frank.

They had been in the Limerick for about two hours and three pitchers when Akira leaned his chair back and stared at Shaun. His eyes were shiny. He shook his head.

"This is all well and good, laddie, but still . . . Why do I have the impression that there is something more you want from me than pub chat?"

"You're right, Akira." Shaun drained his glass and poured himself a refill from Akira's pitcher. "Let's talk about the dreamers."

"The dreamers? High-tech saviors. Geniuses of the New Managerial Revolution. I read it in *Time*."

"Ever wonder how they work?"

"That was in *Time*, too. Some kind of breakthrough in artificial intelligence. Vastly efficient economic modeling. Plus brilliant teams of publicists, the shock troops of the information revolution. Political cadres dedicated to networking a consensus on resolving East-West tensions. Their approval rating is off the scale, and they're kind to animals to boot. How am I doing so far?"

Shaun smiled grimly through the litany of slogans. "All right then, let's talk about you. Why did you stop coming here? What did you do with all your Clancy Brothers tapes? Why did you give up singing?"

"Ah, much better, much better." Akira gave him a lopsided smile. "Not much to tell, really. I woke up one morning and realized that it was all a pose. The Irish bard with a hankering for immortality. Nuts. None of those songs had anything to do with me. I'm not an immigrant; I've lived in Queens my whole life. And all the silly mooning over the green fields of Ireland. Well, I went to Ireland. You know what I found in the green fields? Stinging nettles and sheep shit. I was living in a fantasy world, Shaun. A dream. One morning I woke up, that's all."

"Overnight, you mean." Shaun leaned toward him.

"What?"

"This waking up, as you call it. It happened suddenly. It wasn't something you thought about for a long time?"

Akira touched a bead of sweat on his forehead. "Yeah. Sure, I guess you're right."

"And the records? The tapes? You had everything the Chieftains ever recorded."

"The records, well, let's see. I guess I must have sold most of them. Recorded over the tapes."

"Sure, Akira. And with the money from the Irish records you went out and bought swing, bebop, synthesizer music for Christ's sake: all the stuff you used to tell me you hated. Except now you claim you were a jazz fan in college. It's news to me, Akira. You must have been listening in your closet all these years we've been buddies. When did it start? When did they change you?"

The sweat started to dribble down Akira's temple. "Somebody must have given them . . ." His voice fell to a whisper. "I don't remember."

Although this was what Shaun had been waiting to hear, Akira's admission left him more depressed than elated. How could he fight something as big as this? He swirled the beer in his glass. His friend's distress only made things harder. "Don't you see, Akira? That's how it happens. They tamper with your memories, with your life. They do it with a kind of structured dreaming. While you sleep. Then they boast about it in their damn magazine. 'Changing the world.' They don't mention that to change the world you have to change people."

"They can't possibly change everyone."

"They don't have to. Most people are so wrapped up in their own little lives that they don't realize what's happening. How many people in this bar do you think would notice if tomorrow the dreamers decided to do away with the Seventeenth Amendment? What the hell is the Seventeenth Amendment, anyway? I'm telling you, Joe Sixpack doesn't care what they do, as long as he gets fed and laid often enough."

"You mean me." Akira looked hurt. "Well I don't buy it. And even assuming they do tamper with people's memories, which I don't concede for a minute . . ."

"You don't concede? You don't concede? For Christ's sake, what about those records, Akira? There's a hole in your memory big enough to roll a keg through." A pitcher of beer had made Shaun reckless. "Listen, doesn't what's happening ever worry you? Who the hell are these dreamers? I can remember when they didn't even exist, and now they run the world like a cross between Mussolini and the pope. Don't you wonder where they came from; don't you remember what it was like before?"

"Before? That's like asking what it was like before there was a sky. What are you talking about? There was no before."

The anger and fear that Shaun had repressed since he had returned welled up in him. "I finally know why you're such a rotten driver. You don't care what's going on around you. You're part of the problem. They could flatten Long Island and you wouldn't care as long as you were in Manhattan when it happened."

"You're fucking crazy. A runaway bedbug." Akira watched his beer for a moment as if he were reading a message in the bubbles. "You're not even drunk enough to use that as an excuse, Shaun." He got up and took his glass to the bar without looking back.

Shaun watched him for a while. The waitress cruised by with a heavily laden tray and gave Shaun an odd glance. Shaun tapped his glass on the table for another round. Maybe the thing to do was to keep drinking until he stopped remembering. But when he tried to chug the refill, the room tilted. His stomach churned and he set the glass in front of him. He was content to watch the dregs go flat. It was getting late. When Akira started talking to a woman at the bar, Shaun thought he should probably leave. He did not blame Akira for not wanting to know. Hell, he thought, there were times when he wished he didn't know himself. Like now.

"Akira? Is that you? Christ, if it isn't Akira O'Connor!" MacSweeney pushed through the crowd near the door and pumped Akira's hand as if he had just won the Sweepstakes. "Beer for me and my pal here, the best damn singer ever walked into this crummy joint." His voice boomed across the bar. The bartender hesitated as if wondering whether to serve him; MacSweeney had obviously had more than his share. "Hell, man! Where the hell have you been all these years?"

Shaun could not hear the reply. Akira pointed Shaun out across the room; MacSweeney squinted, waved and then forgot about him. The woman Akira had been talking to picked up her purse and walked toward the bathroom.

"Who wants to hear this man sing?" MacSweeney shouted the question and the room fell silent. "Man has the sweetest voice you'll hear this side of the grave."

"Let him sing," said a man next to Shaun in a low voice. "Then maybe the asshole will shut up."

"Sing, sing!" someone called. Soon it was a chant that could not be ignored. Shaun watched Akira intently as he walked to the stage. He seemed to be taking the challenge with a drunken good humor, but he would not look Shaun's way. "I can't sing well when I'm drunk," Akira started.

"We can't listen when we're not!" someone shouted, to a chorus of laughter and boos.

"And I haven't done this in a long time. Nevertheless—" Akira drew a deep breath "—nevertheless, I *will* sing you a song. I'll sing you 'Maggie.'"

More boos. "Boring, *bor*ing!" someone cried.

"Shut up, there!" MacSweeney yelled, to little effect.

Akira began to sing. His tenor had lost a little of the sweetness it had once held and a little of the range, but there seemed to be more emotion in it than Shaun remembered. Though the talk in the bar continued, it was considerably subdued.

> "The violets were scenting the woods, Maggie,
> displaying their charms to the breeze,
> when I first said I loved only you, Maggie,
> And you said you loved only me—"

Akira swayed a little, eyes closed, as he sang. Shaun looked down at his glass. How could Akira pretend that the old songs meant nothing to him? He had a way with sad lyrics that could bring tears to a statue. Where was the improvement in tampering with a talent like that? The dreamers could not possibly make such a change if they really wanted to improve the world.

> "Our dreams, they have never come true, Maggie,
> Our hopes, they never were to be,
> When I first said I loved only you, Maggie,
> And you said you loved only me."

Akira finished, and the crowd applauded raucously. They called for another song. Akira held up his hands to beg off, eyes glistening. Finally he met Shaun's gaze. He brushed past MacSweeney as if he were not there and came straight over to Shaun's table.

"Maybe you're right," he said. His expression was unreadable.

Shaun was embarrassed. "I'm sorry, Akira. I thought that if I could make you understand . . ."

"Maybe you're right," Akira repeated, as if he had not heard, "but even if you are, so what? You can't change what's happening to us, you bastard. Do you know what it felt like to do what I just did? It felt . . . it felt like sliding down a razor blade. Try to stop, catch yourself, and something slices into your guts."

Akira sat down heavily. "Maybe I'm not as strong as you," he said with eyes closed. Then he glared at Shaun. "Or maybe it's already made you so crazy that you can't feel anymore. In either case, leave me out of it. Do you hear? Leave me alone!"

"Cognitive dissonance," said Dr. Pendergast.

More jargon. Shaun stifled a groan. "And what's that?"

"When what you think, your *cognitions*, are inconsistent with your environment, you experience tension, dissonance. Your psyche acts in specific and predictable ways to reduce the tension. For example, when dissonance is high, people tend to seek information which reduces dissonance and reject information which increases dissonance."

"Which is why no one will listen to me about the dreamers."

"I listen."

"You'd listen to any looney with eighty bucks and an hour to kill."

"Looney is an unscientific term, Mr. Reed," she said with a smile. "We in the profession like to refer to clients as the whackos."

The thaw had begun with Dr. Pendergast when she asked

him if she could see his journal. He gave her an evasive reply and she told him that she had sensed that he was not giving their sessions his fullest effort. When he denied this she asked him to call her by her first name.

At first he could not decide whether this was a new therapeutic strategy or a sign of personal affection. Or an order from Geneva. The sessions became less formal, more like conversations in which Rose Pendergast took a full part. She struck a much more tolerant pose with regard to his beliefs about Freedom Beach and the visions. There were other changes, too. Charles, the receptionist, no longer wore suits; sometimes he even came without a tie. Rose had the office redecorated: the plants disappeared and the walls were stripped and repainted with a lemon semi-gloss. She kept asking to see the journal and Shaun kept putting her off, especially now that more and more of the entries concerned her.

"What makes you so sure that Freedom Beach had anything to do with your writing?"

"The sign on the monument said 'Don't write.'" Shaun was in a contrary mood. "If it had said 'Don't rollerskate,' there wouldn't have been any problem."

"Why do you think you were sent there?"

More circular questions. "You sound like Murray," he said.

"Do I sound like Murray, or Professor Gross, or Groucho?" She twinkled at him. It was at times like this that he wished she still had her nose buried in her notebook.

"I'm not paying you to make jokes."

Rose sat straighter in her chair. "Fine. What do you want to talk about, then?"

"I want to talk about Myrna."

Rose said nothing. Shaun got crankier. "Stop looking at me like that! It's not your job to criticize me."

"How am I criticizing you?"

"Your whole attitude. The way you raise one eyebrow. The way you cross your legs. Your tone of voice."

"Why are you so angry, Shaun?"

"Goddamn it, stop asking questions! Can't you make a

statement now and then so I know you're not a computer program?"

For the first time in the therapy sessions, Rose looked hurt. It surprised him. He had been trying to rouse an emotional response in her for weeks, and now that he had one he did not much like it.

"Okay," she said. "Here're several statements: Everyone at Freedom Beach was forbidden to write. Akira was at Freedom Beach. Therefore Akira had a writing problem. What did he write?"

Reed was confused. "Well, he isn't exactly a writer. More like a performer."

"You want to talk about Myrna?" said Rose. "Myrna was at Freedom Beach. Therefore, Myrna had a writing problem. What did she write?"

Silence.

"Your turn, Shaun."

"She wrote me a poem, once." He wanted to change the subject.

"Where was it published?" When Shaun did not reply, she nodded. He thought she was enjoying this; it was a kind of revenge for his crack about the computer program. "Statements," she said. "Everyone at Freedom Beach had a writing problem. Shaun Reed was at Freedom Beach. Therefore Shaun Reed . . ."

"What did I write?" said Shaun. "I'm sorry I lost my temper, Rose."

"Apology accepted. Answer the question."

"Well, shit!" He stared at the rug for a few seconds. "I never wrote a thing."

"You were the only writer there!"

"I never wrote anything successful."

"But you *published*. Somebody paid you to line words up into sentences, stack sentences into paragraphs."

"Public relations and software reviews are not writing."

"No." She stood up and walked around the room as she spoke. She had never done that before. "Of course it's not writing. Writing is holy work; only shamans can do it when the gods shoot them full of divine juice. A lousy PR flack could never write a novel or a play or even a literate press release. It's unthinkable. Because he doesn't realize that writing isn't a job, it's a vocation." She stopped her pacing and faced him. "Does that about sum up your attitude?" She smiled and he thought she looked a little sheepish.

"Just." He smiled back at her. "Maybe you should be the patient for a while. You're pretty good at it."

"I've had practice, believe me." She sat down again. "I wanted to be a writer once. A pretty common fantasy, after all. Then I began to analyze it."

She leaned back in the chair and stared at the ceiling as if she were counting the holes in the acoustical tile. "When I was in school I began to work up notes for an experiment about the motivations of the writer. Got some writing classes to take the MMPI, got a sample from published writers on the faculty, ran some correlations—I was trying to see if I could work up a typical personality profile. Problem was, I was always more interested in clinical psychology." She was silent for a few moments. "Did you know that the goal of the Project's psychology division is to eliminate the need for clinical practitioners?"

"No." said Shaun. "I didn't."

"I suppose it's a hell of a thing to want to go on making a living from other people's troubles."

"But you help them."

"Some of them." Rose tried to smooth the wrinkles out of her gray cotton skirt. "Some of the time."

"You feel bad about that? You wish you could do better."

Her nod was almost imperceptible. Then she shivered and gazed at him, her expression full of wonder. "How did that happen? I thought I was supposed to be the therapist."

"I wasn't complaining." Shaun smiled. "You'll get my bill at the end of the month."

"And I'll have you arrested for practicing without a license. I don't believe that just happened." Rose pulled back her silver hair and lifted it away from the nape of her neck. "What were we talking about?"

"Your experiment with writers."

"Right." She seemed nettled. "It fell through. No profile emerged. Control group, student writers, professionals—everyone thinks she can be a writer, that her life experience is at least as interesting as the stuff on the best-seller lists. You've heard it yourself: 'Everybody has at least one good book in them.' Naturally, most people underestimate the difficulties in translating their memories into print because the brain stores memories of what they've read side by side with memories of what they've actually done and memories of what they've fantasized doing. Some have a hard time keeping it all straight."

"Some." Shaun grinned.

She grinned back at him.

The letter had not said much. It was a formal notification from the law firm of Morris and Morris of Southampton, New York: Shaun had been mentioned in Myrna's will. He made an appointment to see LaMarr Morris the next day.

"Glad you could come, Mr. Reed." Morris was a big man with a handshake strong enough to crack walnuts. The wall behind his desk was covered with gymnastics medals and law degrees. Shaun placed Morris as soon as he saw him: Myrna's lawyer at the divorce.

They sat. "Let's see, I have the will here somewhere." Morris shuffled through the papers of his In box.

"It's been nearly four months since she died," said Shaun. "Why haven't I heard of this before now?"

"Why indeed?" Morris pulled a manila envelope from the stack. "We only received it ourselves two weeks ago. It was posted from Manhattan. No return address. No cover letter. Just the document." He passed the will over to Shaun. "Normally this would be a good reason to suspect its authenticity. However, it has been properly witnessed and notarized. All parties confirm that the testator signed it in their presence."

It was dated the day she was supposed to have died. Shaun picked out his name right away.

> My intent is to create a trust by requesting that any rights or interests that I may hold in the publication, sale or other transfer of written materials including short stories, novels, plays, poetry or other created material including all proceeds from the same, shall be distributed as follows:
>
> One half of the proceeds to my former spouse, Shaun K. Reed of Queens, New York.
>
> The other half to my good friend, Victor H. Slesar of Palo Alto, California.
>
> I further request that said Shaun K. Reed be appointed to administer the trust as trustee and that he give periodic accountings of his doings to my estate. In the administration of this trust I place complete confidence in Shaun K. Reed that he will act in a responsible manner to insure that my interests will best be met.

Shaun looked up, puzzled. "Am I correct in assuming," said Morris, "that you have the literary properties to which she refers in your possession?"

All he knew about was the poem he had sold to *Amazing Science Fiction Stories*. The poem she had written at Freedom Beach, that no one could know about except someone who had been there—or who had sent them there. Shaun shook his head. "This is news to me."

"The police assure me that they found no manuscripts in her apartment."

"She wrote a poem once."

"Come now, Mr. Reed. I hardly think she would have gone to all the trouble of setting up this trust for one poem. Maybe someone else is holding the manuscripts?"

"Vic?" Shaun handed the will back.

"Mr. Slesar has so far refused to return my calls. I sent him a registered letter last Wednesday. I'll certainly ask him when I get the chance."

"Well, how am I supposed to know what she meant? Didn't you write the will? What did she tell you?"

"No." Morris stood a pencil on its point and let it fall to his desk. "No, we had nothing to do with it. It appears that Ms. Rosny wrote this document herself and had it witnessed at a notary public. Personally, it is my belief that if there were interested parties willing to contest this will, it might well be set aside. On the surface, there would seem to be a lack of testamentary capacity."

"Lack of capacity?"

Morris ticked off points on his fingers. "The will is drawn up on the day of the testator's suicide. It provides for literary properties which do not seem to exist. And the bulk of the considerable estate is put into a trust to build a monument which is, to put it mildly, rather bizarre."

"Monument?" Shaun was suddenly chilled.

"She orders that an estate estimated at two and a half million dollars be used to build a sphinx in Central Park."

That night Shaun had the nightmare again. This time he was talking to Rose Pendergast in her office. Rose's hair was red instead of silver. "We're not getting anywhere," she said. "Come with me."

He did not want to go but she led him out of her office anyway. They walked down the same hallway, past the spot where Akira had balked. The marble floor was the same, so cold he could almost feel it through his shoes. The plants were still dying. He followed her, his fear ballooning with every step, to the same black door. "Next Tuesday at four then," said Rose. She opened the door. When he hesitated, she pushed him in.

Once again he was in Myrna's apartment. It was late. The only light came from behind the screen around the bath. Through the floor-to-ceiling windows he could see lights along the river. The moon was rising.

Shaun wanted to escape. He passed through the living room in a trance. No one there. He glanced at the kitchen: empty. He was trembling. He did not want to look behind the bathroom screen, but the amber light drew him with quiet insistence. He could not stop himself. He stepped forward, and as he did, saw the corner of the bathtub. Her foot was resting on the ledge.

He felt as if he were choking. He spun away, staggered back into the living room. The TV screen had descended to cover the windows and on it was a Marx Brothers movie. The room rang with harsh laughter. On the yellow coffee table was a red typewriter, the same typewriter that had sat on his desk all the time he had lived with Myrna. Wound around the platen was a sheet of paper, and on the paper were three words: *"waiting for you."* Shaun began to scream. And woke up.

"Sometimes," said Shaun, "sometimes I feel like Dorothy in *The Wizard of Oz*. Remember when she woke up back in gray old Kansas at the end? The actors playing the farmhands were the same as the Scarecrow and Tin Woodman."

"Bert Lahr," said Rose. "Ray Bolger and Jack Somebody."

"Right." Shaun filled his glass from the pitcher of water on the chrome table between them. "I have that problem with Akira. Sometimes I forget that he doesn't remember Freedom Beach."

"And he doesn't think he's Aristophanes? Shaun, the fact that the man won't acknowledge that he's a character from one of your dreams is not exactly grounds for committing him."

"Go ahead, make jokes. I'm trying to tell you that I'm losing my best friend. I don't know who he is anymore. He won't take responsibility for his own actions, he won't *do* anything."

"It's a common problem."

Shaun saw what she was getting at. "You mean me?" He fell silent for a time. "I want to see Vic Slesar. I want to ask him about the will."

"And Freedom Beach."

Shaun shifted in his chair. "Maybe."

"Ask him if he reads Raymond Chandler every night?"

Shaun felt light-headed, as if he had nothing to lose. "Are you a dreamer?"

"What?"

"You've changed, you know. When I first came in you were a cold fish, but now you act as if you're my friend. I want to know why."

Rose did not reply at first. She looked angry, started to speak, stopped, then seemed to calm herself.

"I'd like to think I'm your friend," she said.

"And the dreamers?"

"Are just as much a mystery to me as they are to you. No, I'm not working for them. If it were up to them there wouldn't be any psychiatrists. Soon there may not be. Everyone will be healthy. Except maybe you, if you keep running away from things."

Shaun wondered whether she might still be lying. But he did not care anymore. "I've stopped running away," he said. "I'm going to make things go my way." He told her about Myrna's poem and its publication. He told her she could read his journal whenever she wanted. He told her about the nightmare he had had about Myrna's apartment, about the note and the typewriter. Rose sat thoughtfully for a while after he finished.

"Your rebellion is to publish Myrna's poem?"

"That's a beginning. I'm not going to accept what they did to her and what they're doing to me."

Rose looked guarded. "Shaun, I'm not working for the dreamers, believe me. But why do you assume that everything that happens is their responsibility?"

He started to answer, then remained silent.

"You know," said Rose, "this nightmare about Myrna's apartment reminds me of an idea I had the other day about your dreams. The nightmare didn't end until you saw the typewriter. Yet the person in the bathtub had to be Myrna, dead, a much more violent image. Why didn't you wake up as soon as you found her?"

Shaun tried to anticipate her. "Maybe because I saw it before at Freedom Beach. Though it was more horrible in my dream. But the typewriter was still worse."

"Doesn't that seem strange to you—the typewriter was worse? Why do you keep dreaming about writers?"

He felt like he did in the nightmare when she was pushing him through the doorway. "Groucho wasn't a writer."

"He was the ideal writer. He had ultimate understanding of people and he had the power to change the world through magic words." She pointed a finger at him and said firmly, "*All* your dreams involve writers."

Shaun took a sip of water and nodded for her to continue.

"You say you want to be a writer. What do you expect it will get you? According to the dreams you will never find the meaning of life by writing—life is absurd. You will never achieve literary immortality—it's impossible. Writing will not make you a better person; it will just tempt you to pretend your faults are virtues. And it won't be glamorous; it's lonely work that can cut you off from the world until you're trapped in your own creative solitude. Maybe the dreams were designed only to discourage you from being a writer, and you just filled in the blanks in them with Myrna."

Shaun considered. "And Akira. And Vic. And Murray." He paused, rubbing his chin. "I thought about that already. But what does it mean?"

"Either you give up the fantasy of being a writer or figure out a better reason for doing it. Or else give up entirely, like Myrna."

It made Shawn mad sometimes. She was so quick with explanations. Rat-a-tat-tat: your problems are solved. Next? "How do you know Myrna gave up?"

Rose sighed. "Look at who she was, Shaun, not who you wanted her to be."

"You didn't know her."

"No, I didn't. Maybe I'm wrong. I know I'm not doing her justice. But think about it."

Shaun stretched back against the chair. "Damn it! If I wasn't thinking about it, I wouldn't be here now."

Victor H. Slesar of Palo Alto, California, was a difficult man to reach. Morris called back at the end of the month to say that Vic disclaimed any interest in the inheritance. He also denied any knowledge of Myrna's writing.

Shaun might have let it go at that; he could not see the value of flying out to California to harass Vic in person. At least, not until he understood more of what was happening. But as he was browsing through a copy of *InfoWorld* at the newsstand one day he saw a familiar face in the People section. The picture had either been taken very late at night or when its subject was very drunk. Vic—indefatigable Vic!—looked weary. The story beneath it said that Vic's company, Reality Engineering, was introducing a new game. $uccess was being touted as the most complex and realistic simulation ever made available for home computers; it would only run on one of the new thirty-two bit machines with a hard disk and at least a megabyte of memory. Vic was going to appear at Madison Square Garden at the fall ComCon, the computer users show, to promote his new masterpiece.

Back at the office, Shaun called Akira. "Guess who's going to be in town in two weeks," he said.

"Buddy Holly."

"Nope."

"Amelia Earhart."

"Vic Slesar."

There was a pause. "Still chasing that?"

"Look, Akira, by now you must think I'm a certified nut case. But I'm functioning, man, and this is what helps keep me going. All I need is for you to help me get to see him."

"Christ!" He heard a rattling on the other end of the line and thought for a moment that his friend was going to hang up on him. Akira's voice came back. "Sorry. I dropped the phone. Look, I'll see what I can do. No promises."

The author of $uccess was not on display on the floor of the convention, where sweaty crowds swirled among the booths in search of new laser disk games and paperback-sized computers that could sort sixty-five thousand records in three minutes. The dreamers' economy had been booming, and the prices of VLSI chips had been falling. Anyone who wanted a computer now could afford one. At the Reality Engineering booth they stood ten deep watching a wall-sized monitor as a programming loop ran the game through its most spectacular paces. Those interested enough to push their way to the booth itself were rewarded with a glossy brochure studded with four-color screen shots and a heavily airbrushed photograph of Vic sitting at a keyboard.

Akira soon discovered that Reality Engineering had taken a suite of rooms at the New York Penta, a block away. He and Shaun were admitted by a flack in gray suit. There was a wet bar on one side of the living room, stocked with top-shelf alcohol and cold hors d'oeuvres. On the other side a beta-test version of $uccess was up and running on an IBM and an Apple. The group around the IBM wore sincere ties and were quiet as golf fans. The Apple lovers were a tanned lot; whenever the game did something spectacular they whooped and clapped each other on the back. Akira went over to join them; Shaun poked around the fringes of the crowd near the bar.

He peeked through a half-opened bedroom door and saw Vic. He was sitting at a window, staring down at Penn Station and the Garden. There was a pitcher of martinis within reach; a young woman in a dark blue pin-striped suit was talking to him. Vic was not listening. Shaun stepped into the room. Both glanced up, but only the woman seemed to notice him.

"Vic?" he said.

The woman stood, looking nervous. She carried herself like a flack, as if she thought she might fall into a hole at any moment. She reminded Shaun of himself, ten years ago. "Mr. Slesar is not feeling well," she said. "An attack of hay fever."

"New York doesn't agree with me," Vic said. "I don't agree with it."

"He's taking medication," said the flack, inviting Shaun to pretend that there were no martinis at ten-thirty in the morning. "The interviews have been postponed. If you're on a deadline, maybe I can help."

"Hello, Vic. Remember me?"

Vic squinted. "No."

"I really must insist—"

"My name is Reed. We first met when Private Eye came out."

"Reed?" He tilted his head as if all the gin had pooled to one side. "John Reed." Vic tapped the chair next to him. "Shaun."

"Get out of here, Levine. This is my old pal, John Reed. Have a drink, John? Levine, get John a clean glass from the bar."

Levine was backing through the door. "Mr. Slesar, remember that you have to be on a panel at one—"

"Panel? Fuck the panel! Bunch of fucking strangers. This is an old friend, see? Tell them to play the game and leave me out of it. All right." Levine was already gone but Vic kept talking. "There'll never be another game like it. Not in this world. The best, you understand?" Levine returned with Shaun's glass, gave him a disapproving stare and retreated again, closing the door behind her.

'So tell me, John. Where the hell do I know you from?"

"My name is Shaun," he said as he filled his glass. "Shaun Reed. You slept with my wife, Myrna Rosny."

Either Vic was too drunk to care or not drunk enough and still cautious. He nodded gravely as if they were discussing a business deal. "That so?"

"You heard about Myrna?"

"My lawyer told me."

"They say she's dead. Killed herself."

Vic drank. "They should know." He drank again. "You waiting for me to say I'm sorry? Is that what you want?"

"No." Shaun loosened his tie. "You seem to be doing pretty well for yourself. Working on the Project?"

"Me? Hell, no. The money is nowhere near good enough. And even if it were, the dreamers want too much input. I'm my own boss, sport. That's the way it has to be."

"I envy you."

Vic nodded, as if this were not the first time he had heard someone say it. "I brought $uccess to some people connected with the Project and all they could talk about was how God would do it." Vic stood. "Those assholes would meddle with chess, if you'd let 'em." He shuffled to the bathroom. When he closed the door, Shaun scanned the room, half expecting to spot a copy of *The Big Sleep* or *Farewell, My Lovely*. He got up and poked through the stacks of fanfold paper scattered across the credenza. Drafts of the rules for $uccess. He heard a toilet flush.

"Want the scoop?" Vic came up behind him. "To start, you have to build your character."

Shaun looked at the pitcher and thought about alcohol as character builder. Vic followed his glance.

"Not like that, sport. For the game. You take a kind of a test, a personality inventory, custom designed by some guys at the psych department at Stanford. Rates you on scales for intelligence, charisma, cooperation, ambition. See, it's not just a character playing, it's *you*. Once you boot this up, you'll be hooked, believe me. I squeezed the whole world into 800K of the tightest code you'll ever see. Over a hundred major characters, all of them with their own motivations and goals. Three hundred different locales, complete with streets, houses, rooms, *furniture*. A hundred high-res screens on the data disk, another two hundred in medium resolution."

"Sounds like a lot of work."

"Was." He sat heavily, facing the window again.

"How do you win?"

"People will try to do it by running for office, becoming generals and CEO's. They'll come close, they'll be tantalized, and then it'll all come crashing down. Social entropy. Programmed into the game."

"You can't win?"

Vic laughed. It was a quiet, reflective sound, as if the joke were going stale. "Of course, that's not for attribution. You still write for the computer magazines?"

"No." Reed sat next to him. "I wanted to ask you about Myrna. Whether you had any idea why she put you in her will."

"I hadn't seen her in three years. We broke up pretty soon after you got divorced."

"She told me."

"Then you know more than I do. I run through a lot of women, sport. None of 'em seem to stick." Vic paused. "Myrna was better than most. Not that I ever knew what she wanted."

"The last time I saw her she was living alone," Shaun said. "She told me she was celibate."

"Surprise," said Vic. Shaun wondered if Vic had ever really been surprised. "I had the impression that Myrna had been with plenty of men. And enjoyed the hell out of every one of them."

Shaun closed his eyes. When he opened them, Vic was watching. "I never had . . . that impression." He took a deep breath. "One of the things I still wonder is whether her death might connect with a bad affair."

"Give her more credit than that, sport. Maybe in books people kill themselves for love. We're talking real life; whatever killed Myrna was more important than that." He drew a line through the condensation on his glass. "She'd get crazy sometimes over things out of her control. I could never figure out why. But I'm sure it wasn't because of what some man did or didn't do. I know I never made much of a difference to her; she was one self-contained lady, that one. You must have seen it when you were married, if you paid any attention at all."

"Sure."

"Well, then, we constitute a little club, don't we?" Vic nodded at his reflection in the window. "The Men Mystified by Myrna. The good old triple-M. There must be more of us. We should hold meetings."

Shaun's fists clenched.

"So you're not working for the computer magazines anymore." Vic yawned. "What are you doing?"

"I'm a copy editor at St. Martin's. Working on textbooks for the Project."

"Ah, the Project." Vic raised his glass to his reflection and drank.

Shaun was irked by the man's condescension. "You think you can escape the dreamers just by ignoring them?" The ice clinked at the bottom of Shaun's glass as he drained it. He knew he was going to make a fool of himself. "Listen, can you remember how it was before they came? I can, but when I tell people they think I'm crazy. You do remember, don't you, Vic?"

"Remember?" Vic continued to gaze out the window. "I was a nobody, sport. A junior-high-school phys-ed teacher. Then I bought an Aristotle and taught myself to program in BASIC." Vic gave the room an airy wave. "And here I am."

"Have you ever heard of a place called Freedom Beach? A kind of resort for people who can't write?"

Vic's laugh was brittle. "I just spent three weeks in Santa Cruz working on the manual for $uccess with some consultants. One hundred and eighty-five unreadable pages. I left all the people who can't write working for me back there."

"Freedom Beach."

"What are you talking about?"

"You remember it?"

"Memory is a funny thing, John." Vic sighed. "Suppose you have this recurring dream. Vivid. Have it every night, say, for several months. After a while you remember it; you have to. You think about it when you're awake. Maybe you tell someone about it. It seems real, part of your life."

"The statues," said Shaun. "Communion, the boundaries."

Vic's hand trembled as he reached for his drink. "Still, it's only a dream." His hand closed around the glass and he smiled. "A game. You don't take it seriously: if you do you lose. So you wake up in your own bed every morning and you go out into the real world. Another game."

"You're just like Akira, you know that? You're both making it easy for the dreamers: you do it to yourselves. They trash your minds and you clean up after them. Pretend that all the gaping holes aren't really there at all."

"Is this Akira animal, vegetable or mineral?"

"We were all at Freedom Beach together!"

"No, we weren't." Vic faced Shaun. "Sounds to me like

we've got different dreams, John, old buddy. You should just forget it." He held up a hand to quiet him. "Want to know how? One—" he ticked off points on his fingers "—you work. You find something that's so hard to do right that you lose yourself while you're at it. Two: you screw. Actually, that's sort of the same as one. Three: when you're done working and screwing, you drink. Tried and true, sport. Written on the walls of the pyramids and all that."

"But it's not a dream, Vic. It really happened and you know it! Myrna killed herself."

Vic's look was full of pity. "Right. In a fancy co-op apartment on the Lower East Side. At least, that's what I hear." He glanced at his watch. "Got to go, sport. Poor Levine will be working on her second ulcer." He stood, wobbled.

Shaun grabbed Vic's arm and spun him around. "You're not leaving here until you admit it."

Vic's expression hardened. "Seems like we've done this part before." He pulled away. They stood for a few moments, glowering at each other. Then a smile played at the corners of Vic's mouth. He patted Shaun on the shoulder.

"Lighten up. God helps those who help themselves." He opened the bedroom door.

"Wait a minute," said Shaun. Vic sighed. Shaun pulled a check for seventeen dollars and fifty cents out of his wallet. "This is for you. Royalties on a poem that Myrna wrote."

For some reason the check seemed to sober him. He folded it and put it into his pocket. "Thanks," he said, and turned to the living room. The people fell silent as he made his entrance. Someone at the bar applauded. None of the players around the computers looked up from their games.

He found her sitting on one of the bench seats in the foyer. She was watching bleary tourists trudge out of the Museum of Modern Art. As Shaun approached, he saw that she held a half-eaten apple.

"I'm late." He settled next to her, facing the Miro sculpture that dominated the foyer. "For our first date." He shrugged in disgust. "Beckwith decided to be a son-of-a-bitch today. Anyway, sorry."

"That's okay, I just got here myself. Want some?" Rose offered him the apple.

"Thanks." He took a bite. "Had to work through lunch."

"This isn't a date, by the way. I told you that."

"Okay. Just so long as the meter isn't running. Busy day?" He took another bite of apple.

"Dead. Another patient cured—at least that's what she claimed when she called to cancel. I'm down to two now: you and Tytla. I don't know what I'm going to do."

"Open an apple stand?" The joke fell flat. He took her hand. "Sorry."

"The world thinks it's happy. Who am I to disagree?" She wore a summer dress printed with purple irises, and a broad-brimmed straw hat with a wide purple band. Her hair hung to her shoulders. In this light it seemed more white than silver. She pushed the apple core through the swinging door of a trash can. "Let's get on with it, then."

He rushed her through the Post-Impressionist and Cubist and Abstract galleries until he came to an odd little statue in the Picasso room. A portly bronze monkey stood upright holding its offspring to its breast. The head of the monkey was a toy car. Its bumper grin seemed to mock them.

"*Baboon and Young*, 1951." Rose read the plate. "Kind of cute."

"This was in a gazebo at the top of the hill overlooking the beach. An exact copy, except that it had a microphone in its mouth and could talk."

She met Shaun's gaze for a moment and then glanced quickly back at the statue. She said nothing.

"Until a couple of months ago," said Shaun, "you couldn't have paid me enough to come to this museum. Hated modern art. I swear I never knew this statue existed before I saw it at Freedom Beach."

"You could have seen pictures and not remembered."

"No."

"How about Myrna? She could have seen it and then told you."

"But she never . . . I don't know. I'm not sure what I know about Myrna anymore." Shaun's expression was grim. "Come on."

They went back through the galleries and down the escalator and out into the sculpture garden. About half of it had been torn up, tilled and planted with pumpkins: the Project's latest innovation was vegetable gardening in public spaces. The thriving vines had sent runners across the slate paving; Shaun and Rose had to step carefully to keep from tripping. They found empty wire garden chairs at the east end of the patch and sat in front of the statue of Balzac. Wrapped in a bronze bathrobe, he stared down at them over his belly like a supercilious god.

"The original plaster is in the Rodin Museum in Paris," said Shaun. "I did some research. There have been seven castings made from it; this one was done in 1954. All the others seem to be accounted for. At Freedom Beach, Balzac stood in the commons. Sort of the ringmaster. All of the statues there had faceted electronic eyes. Creepy. And they could talk, too. Some kind of speaker implant, but with better fidelity and power than I've ever heard before."

"And this one isn't like that?"

Her skepticism infuriated him. "Look for yourself, damn it." He strode up to the pedestal. His eyes were at the level of Balzac's feet. He glared up at the sightless face the color of an old hammer. A fat museum worker in a green Notre Dame T-shirt turned to stare. "This is a statue. That thing at Freedom Beach was one of the dreamers' tools."

She tugged on his sleeve. "Come on, Shaun. You're upset."

He turned reluctantly. "You'd be mad too, if . . ." He made a sudden decision. "Look, I want you to sit down and listen to some things."

She searched his face. "Sure." They went back to the chairs. "Go ahead."

Shaun had another moment of doubt. She might be working

for the dreamers—certainly he had no guarantee that she was not. But he had no guarantee of anything, and he felt the need to confide in someone before trying what he had planned for that evening. "I want you to listen to this without making a judgment. I think I've figured some things out."

Rose nodded.

"I saw Vic recently. Something he's working on connected up with my memories of Freedom Beach. He's worked out an interactive computer game that reproduces life. It's just a matter of words and pictures on a screen, but it reminded me of Fantastic's interactive novels and something the dreamers on the carousel said. Look at all the things you've pointed out about Freedom Beach that don't make sense. Like these statues I don't remember having seen before going there. And the fact that none of the other people who were there will admit it."

"So?"

"I think the whole Freedom Beach experience," Shaun continued, "was an interactive program run by the dreamers. They created the Freedom Beach scenario and let me react to it in whatever way I could within the limits they set. They simulated Vic, Akira and the rest; that's why none of them remember the place. That's why Murray at Freedom Beach was young instead of old. They programmed in a few props like the villas and the foliage and the statues, and let me go from there."

Rose looked skeptical. "But you said you swam away from Freedom Beach and ended up on Jones Beach."

"How could I have? Obviously Freedom Beach isn't in the Atlantic Ocean; it has to be someplace else. Why not in silicon? The dreamers are supposed to be such computer whizzes." Shaun realized he sounded like her, critiquing his experience in one of their sessions. "I swam out from Jones Beach, they plucked me out of the water, gave me these experiences and put me back. I think they could do that. They've done stranger things."

"What about Akira? As far as he knows you were just out swimming?"

"That's right. The whole experience—Freedom Beach, my dreams, the escape—could not possibly have happened in real time, while I was gone from the beach."

"Why would they do such a thing?"

"I don't know. They claimed I was there voluntarily. If it happened the way I've told you, under Akira's nose in a single afternoon, maybe I did agree to it. I can't imagine why, but . . ."

Rose looked bemused. "I hate to contradict anything that could help you put this obsession to rest, Shaun, but your explanation explains nothing. You could explain anything that way." She waved a hand at the statue garden. "Even *this* could be another dream."

"It could."

Rose picked up her pocketbook. "We'd better go eat." She looked upset. "We'll be late to the park."

"But—"

She shook her head. "Save it. Please." She thrust her arm in his and towed him quickly out of the museum.

Rose said she knew a good Italian restaurant within walking distance. The tables had red-checked tablecloths and flickering candles in straw-wrapped Chianti bottles. On the front of Shaun's menu was a sketch of a gondolier; the back was spattered with tomato sauce. Speakers hidden behind bunches of plastic grapes piped mandolin music into every corner of the dark room. Still, for all the ersatz atmosphere the garlic bread was extra spicy and the pasta freshly made.

Though Rose's face was round and open in the shifting light, she seemed distant. Shaun had the feeling he had gone too far at the museum; he hesitated now to tell her what he was going to do when they got to the park. Instead he tried to change the mood by drawing her out. Rose's tone was ironic, slightly brittle, as she told him about her marriage and divorce, but she seemed willing to ignore his theories for a while.

"Stuart lives in Los Cruces now," she said. "He used to run a Reichian retreat and rebirthing center. That was before the dreamers, in their wisdom, banned neurosis. I haven't heard from him in a while."

"Do you miss him?"

"Not him, no." She brushed a wisp of silver hair away from her forehead. "I think what I miss is being married. Another body to warm up the bed in winter. Someone to talk to beside myself."

"I don't know if what I miss is Myrna or being young," said Shaun. "I used to think *I* would change the world someday."

"Shovelling dirt into your own grave?" Rose reached across the table to touch his hand. "You're in your prime, Shaun. Why, you're barely old enough to be president."

"How do you know? We'll probably pick up the *Times* tomorrow and read that the Constitution has been amended. Nobody but meter maids, third basemen and grocery baggers will be eligible."

Laughing, she held up her wine glass. "Changing the world!"

"To progress." They touched glasses. "Wherever the hell you find it." Shaun realized—too late—how their voices were carrying. The maitre d' rubbed his hands across his red vest as he argued with their waiter. A few moments later the bill arrived, unasked for. Rose started to laugh. Shaun would have joined her had he not realized just then how like Myrna's her laugh was.

For a moment, he could not tell what color Rose's eyes were. As he peered through the candlelight, he could almost make himself believe that they were green. Shaun felt dizzy, as if he were tipsy and seeing double: the sound and smell and sight of the restaurant and Rose overlaid with another reality—similar but distorted. His perceptions kept moving along the boundary between those two worlds. They had toasted with the last of the wine; Shaun reached out and brought his water glass to his lips. The cold helped him to focus.

"Are you all right, Shaun?"

He looked at her, wondering what she really thought of him. She was as much a mystery as Myrna. "You think I'm crazy, don't you."

"That's not fair, Shaun. I think—"

"Rose—listen now. When its my turn to speak at the

dedication, I'm going to blow the dreamers' cover. I'll tell how they're using the Freedom Beach treatment to meddle with the world. Social reality is ninety-nine percent perception; all they need to do is work over a relatively few people—the opinion makers. Maybe they send politicians to Campaign Beach and reporters to Scandal Beach, but once they get people on the tube spouting their line, cognitive dissonance goes to work. It's just like you said. As long as things seem good to most people, they don't want to listen to gripes."

"Except that you're not an opinion maker, Shaun."

"Well . . . yes." Shaun blushed. "Maybe I've underestimated how much the dreamers have done already. Maybe they've already netted all the big fish and are starting now to scoop up minnows."

"Then you're under their influence?"

"No! No, because I beat Freedom Beach. That's why I can still see what's going on. They're not improving anything. Are you any happier than you were? Was Myrna? Am I? The Project may be good for the world but it crushes individuals."

"Shaun—"

He didn't want to be argued out of it. He opened his wallet, pulled three twenties out of the billfold and tossed them onto the table. "Let's get out of here."

Rose said nothing as they walked out. He felt a little steadier by the time they reached the street. They started walking uptown toward Central Park. He felt guilty about taking out his anger on her. He could tell that she was bothered by his silence, but she let him go several blocks before she spoke.

"Want to talk about it?" It sounded like a professional question.

"I don't know." He reached for her hand. "I had this strange feeling . . . What color was your hair when you were in school?"

She stopped so abruptly that he almost spun into a streetlight to keep from dropping her hand. "Oh, no you don't, Shaun Reed! You want me to say red; I know you. You want to make me into one of your delusions, just another piece to be fitted neatly into some bizarre puzzle. Well, I've got something to show you, mister." She opened her pocketbook and took out her wallet. "Maybe reality is a little more complex than you imagined."

She thrust a snapshot at him: a man and a woman, standing on a beach. The woman's hair was black. Rose and her ex-husband. "The dreamers didn't take that picture; my cousin Betsy did. At Malibu in 1974. If you think I'm going to let you make me into what you want me to be, then you *are* crazy." She snatched the photograph out of his nerveless hand, shoved it and the wallet back into her purse. "And if you want to jump off a cliff, you can jump without me.

"You want an explanation for the dreamers, here's one: they're a secret society that's existed throughout history, that has influenced events by drugs and hypnosis and now computerized dreams—just like you say. They've only come out into the open because we're doing such a bad job of running things ourselves. I'm not Rose Pendergast from Dayton, Ohio; I'm Myrna Rosny come back from the dead. They've changed my hair and given me pictures of a husband I never had and a head full of phony memories. All for your benefit. How's that? Do you feel better now? Does the world make sense? God, this is what I get for going out with patients."

Shaun was nonplussed. "I'm sorry, Rose," he said finally. He scuffed at a gum spot on the sidewalk. "You're right; that was out of line."

She gave no sign of accepting his apology. Still, she did not turn away from him.

"I haven't convinced you. You haven't cured me. Stalemate." Shaun thought he would be noble. "You want me to flag a cab for you? I'll go on by myself."

"I'll flag my own damn cab. *When* I want one." She started walking uptown again. He followed.

"Thanks," he said. She did not reply. "I know I can't have everything my own way. That's what frustrates me." Still no answer. "Why do you bother with me anyway?"

"Because it's my job, what's left of it." She hitched her purse strap onto her shoulder. "Because you're not so different from anybody else." She was staring straight ahead. Without missing a stride, she grasped his hand. "Because—God help me—because what they're doing worries me, too."

They entered Central Park at 66th and walked uptown on East Drive, which had been closed to traffic. Several hundred New Yorkers joined them, joggers and roller skaters, lovers and people watchers; some out for a twilight stroll on an Indian summer night, others purposefully walking toward Cleopatra's Needle, where the unveiling was to take place. One of the dreamers' major accomplishments—even Shaun had to admit it—was that the park had at last been cleared of nocturnal predators. In fact, for all their whimsy, the dreamers had curtailed crime across the world. Employment was up, food supplies were more evenly distributed, people were optimistic. The dreamers' proposed utopia of peace and plenty might well turn out to be boring, but hungry people were more than willing to exchange the freedom to starve for their daily bread, no matter how tediously produced.

So why was Shaun filled with anger? Arguing with Rose had left him confused and upset. He tried to weigh the benefits of what some were calling the dreamers' Golden Age against the accusations he held in his heart against them. As he looked back over the things that had happened to him since he had come to himself in the middle of a conversation with a woman named Myrna at Freedom Beach, he saw a history of misunderstanding, of opportunities squandered, of promise unfulfilled, of people tearing at each other because they could not tear at the thing that was stunting their lives. What could that thing be but the dreamers who ran the world? If he could not blame them, who could he blame? He wanted to laugh when he realized that as recently as a couple of months earlier he had never heard of the dreamers. And now they were building sphinxes in Central Park, and Myrna was dead, and he did not know whether he could trust the earth he walked on not to evaporate in the next instant. He only knew he was determined to take control of his own life. He had to tell what he knew. For Myrna's sake, if not for his own.

The city had moved quickly to accept the terms of Myrna's will. On a vote of 25-0 the Council had waived the environmental impact statement; the same margin did away with the competitive bidding statute. That same afternoon the Mayor announced selection of a general contractor. The dreamers had long since tamed New York.

Construction had gone forward under tight security. The general contractor had built a temporary metal building over the site; it had only come down the week before. In that time the landscapers had done an excellent job of rearranging the trees and resodding east of the obelisk, across the pond from the Delacorte Theater; there was no sign at all that the fabric of the park had been altered.

No sign, that is, except a tarpaulin-swaddled figure, thirty feet long, eighteen high, crouching on a granite base within a pop foul's distance of the softball fields.

Shaun and Rose walked up to the wooden platform that had been constructed in front of the forepaws of the sphinx. They slipped among the city officials and the police around the steps that led to the podium.

The crowd was small by Central Park's standards: two or three thousand. The Commissioner of Parks and Recreation introduced the Central Park administrator, who gave a generic dedication speech. When she finished, an army band played Sousa marches. One of the commissioner's flunkies brought a warm Coke which Shaun and Rose shared. It was dark now; spotlights lit the sphinx. Shaun was getting nervous. He wondered what the thing looked like. There had been no pictures. Reports were that it was not a copy of the Great Sphinx at Giza, which was, after all, a portrait of the pharaoh Khafre. Its features would be feminine, most agreed, perhaps in the likeness of the generous donor.

Rose put an arm around Shaun's shoulder. "Whatever happens, you can handle this. I know you can."

A redheaded man from the Central Park Conservancy was at the podium. "And now the moment you've been waiting for!" he said, raising his hands to quiet the restless crowd. "To unveil this unique addition to the greatest urban park in the greatest city in the world, I would like to introduce to you the husband of the donor, Mr. Shaun Reed."

From where he stood Shaun could hear the ripple of polite applause but could not see the crowd. He froze. It was not until Rose gave him a push that he started up the stairs. Someone whispered to the man from the Conservancy and Shaun heard him reply, "What do you mean ex-husband? Never mind that now!"

When Shaun reached his side, the Conservancy man cupped his hand over the microphone and said, "If you're going to talk, keep it short."

Here was his chance. He felt a mass of conflicting emotions, a hundred impulses at once. Shaun looked out past the podium but the lights were blinding, and although he could hear the crowd, he still could not see it. His thoughts whirled. The dreamers are . . . Myrna was . . . I am . . . Something snapped in him, and he let out a huge breath.

He looked around for the man from the Conservancy. The man stepped forward, looked worried, put his hand over the microphone again. "What's up?" he asked Shaun.

"Nothing to say." Shaun rubbed his sweaty hands on his pants. "Let's just do it."

The man pointed at a yellow winch on which the words "Parks Department" were stencilled in blue. "Give it a couple of cranks, then. They say the tarps should slide off pretty easy once you get started." He took his hand off the microphone and smiled at the crowd. "Shaun Reed!"

So he had a part to play and he could play it. The joke was on him, on Myrna. Shaun felt more sad than bitter. He had to use two hands to turn the crank. At first he thought something was wrong, but then the crowd shouted. He straightened up and was blinded by flashes. He heard applause. He felt calm. He felt like he had let something go.

The Conservancy man's amplified voice said, "Thank you. Thank you, very much. That concludes our ceremonies for tonight. Please be sure to leave the park as clean as you found it. Thank you and good night."

The Central Park administrator looked at her watch. "That wasn't too bad," she said. "Not even eight, yet."

Shaun turned to look at the sphinx.

It was a muddy bronze. Darkness flattened much of the detailing so that Shaun could barely make out the shape of the paws. Still, anyone could recognize the tension in the figure; the sphinx seemed ready to spring into the crowd. Looking up at it from between its forelegs, Shaun felt like a mouse being toyed with before the kill. Most of the spotlights were aimed at the face so that he saw immediately that this was not a portrait of Myrna. The features were serene and bland—at odds with the gathered muscles of the body.

"Hello, Shaun," said the sphinx.

He staggered and almost fell off the podium. One of the administrator's flacks caught his arm.

"Sit him down," someone said.

They led him to a gray folding chair.

"Don't tell me you're surprised," said the sphinx. "You must have expected something like this. It's what you've known all along."

"Known?" Shaun said, dazed.

"What's that?" one of the politicians asked him.

The statue's mouth did not move. The empty eyes still stared across the park toward the theater. "We care about you."

Shaun was gathering his wits. "Who are you?" he said more loudly.

The politician grabbed his hand and gave it a single vigorous shake. "Hi, howyadoing? John Baravelli, I'm running for an at-large seat on the Board of Education. I hope I can count on your support in November. You're Mr. Reed, aren't you. Where are you from?"

"You don't have to shout," said the sphinx. "You don't have to talk at all. I'm right here. I can hear you."

"Are you all right? Mr. Reed?" Baravelli seemed anxious.

"Queens," Shaun said. "I live in Queens. Sorry, I'm feeling a little woozy. I'll be all right in a minute."

Baravelli went down the stairs.

"Myrna?" Shaun whispered. "Is it you?"

"Myrna is dead."

"Then you're not Myrna?"

"Myrna, not-Myrna; these are the wrong questions."

"What do you want from me? Are you responsible for Freedom Beach?"

"Yes."

"You killed her. You've changed everything."

Rose was beside him. "Shaun. What's the matter?"

"Myrna killed herself, Shaun," the sphinx said.

"At Freedom Beach."

"At Freedom Beach. In New York. In all these places she could not live with the things she could not control. We've changed things, but we are not the only source of change. You're not helpless."

"I don't understand."

The sphinx laughed. "Do you expect that, too? I'm sorry, Shaun, but we can't keep letting you blame us for everything. Even Myrna had sense enough not to do that."

He had been staring fixedly at the sphinx so long it was a blur. Suddenly a familiar face swam into his vision. "Shaun, what's the matter?" Rose shook him. "Shaun!"

"You sent me to Freedom Beach."

"We gave you the chance to deal with your problems. You were the one who found Myrna dead, who called the police. Remember, Shaun."

Even as the sphinx spoke, memory and nightmare merged. Central Park was not half so real. He was the one who had found her.

It was spring. He had thought about Myrna incessantly in the weeks after he had had dinner with her. He remembered how easy their intimacy had been after the initial awkwardness, how she had opened up to him more than she ever had. He took it as a sign, one he must not let pass. He would invite her to dinner. He would show her how he lived, hide nothing. They were too far along for him to hide from her anymore.

He rehearsed his invitation too many times before he found the nerve to call her. All he got was her answering machine.

He tried her office. They would tell him only that she was on vacation for two weeks. That bothered him. She had said she was overworked, booked solid for months. Maybe she had decided to take a break. Still, it felt wrong.

So he composed his message as carefully as a seventeen-year-old working out a prom invitation. He called Myrna's apartment and spoke to her machine: "You can't get free of me that easily, woman. You're on vacation—so come to dinner at my resort. Reed Beach, in sunny Queens. Friday night. 7:30."

He waited. He tried not to remember the way she had turned away from him at the end of that night, almost shoving him out the door when he tried to get too close. He worried. He tried to convince himself that she was out of town, at some Caribbean playground beneath the sun and the palms. He could tell she needed a break from her work. He would catch her when she got back.

On Friday evening, when he came home from work, there was a message on his own answering machine—an old machine that had been hers, that he had inherited when they split up. "It's too late for us to make dinner plans, Shaun. Come here. Tonight. 7:30. Waiting for you, lover." He remembered that voice.

It had been a long time since Shaun had been as thrilled. He arrived in Manhattan early, then thought better of going up too soon. So he stood across the street from the Gateway Towers until 7:30, staring at the building in the cold March night. Finally he screwed his courage to the sticking place. He crossed the street, getting there just as another resident, tall and young and right out of *GQ*, unlocked the door. The doorman was not in the lobby; probably in the men's room. Shaun waited. The young man got on the elevator and went up. When, after a few minutes, the doorman had still not shown up, Shaun punched the elevator button himself and rode up to the twenty-fifth floor.

He walked down the hall, past potted plants in need of water. His cheap shoes squeaked on the marble floor. Myrna's lacquered door was black as obsidian. He knocked upon his own dark reflection; no one answered. Feeling like a burglar, he tried the door and found it unlocked.

The room was dark. "Myrna?" he called. There was no answer and suddenly he was afraid.

He closed the door behind him. The only light came from behind the bathroom screen, a low amber light that draped shadows in the room's corners and softened the garish furniture. There was a sickly sweet odor to the air; he almost gagged on it. Not wanting to, as in a dream although he knew he was awake, he approached the screen. A foot rested on the ledge of the tub.

He pushed the screen aside. In the tub lay Myrna. She must have been there all day. The water was a ghastly red, with a crust of dried blood around the edges of the porcelain. Her skin was the color of Carraran marble—but a woman was not supposed to be made of marble, and this was no statue. Her body was twisted awkwardly to the side, her forearms wrist-up just beneath the surface of the water. Long slashes lay open along them, pale, puckered, washed clean. Dead, the emaciation Shaun had made himself ignore before was all too plain to see, the flesh of her arm so wasted that he could have encircled it with his thumb and forefinger. Her mouth was open and her eyes stared hollowly up at him. Her hair was cropped brutally short. She was a monster and she wanted him.

Shaun reeled, fighting the impulse to run. But he was supposed to love her, and if you loved somebody you did not run away. He knelt beside the tub and tried to make himself touch her face. He trembled. He could not do it. He could not breathe; his nose filled with the smell of her blood. It was wrong, so wrong; this could not be real—she had always known more than he but her face now held no knowledge, only death. He gripped the side of the tub, trying not to be sick.

In the soap dish was a note: "Don't be afraid, Shaun. I'm free now and waiting for you. There are lots of ways: wrists, neck, pills, heights, the water, gentle water. An end to my loneliness, an end to your failure. Don't be afraid. I love you."

He sat beside the tub, stared at her face. Waiting for you. If only he could kiss her she would sit up. It would be all right. But he could not. After a while he got up, feeling numb, and staggered out, closing the door behind him. He took the back stairs to the alley and wandered the streets for a long time. Late at night he called the police from a booth on Third Avenue.

"Shaun! Shaun, are you all right?" Rose shook him again.

Shaun saw her, saw the sphinx. Yet the image of Myrna, dead, no dream but a reality, stayed with him. The joke *was* on him, on Myrna. A joke no one could take. A useless death. The sadness welled up in him, overwhelming; he could see it all clearly and it was almost more than he could stand. He had not wanted her to be who she was and so had played the joke on himself. Myrna was the one who had needed help. Maybe if he had been able to break through his illusions about her to see the desperation she had felt, he could have done something—

"You felt responsible," the sphinx told him. "You decided to follow her. When you walked into the water that day at Jones Beach, you had no intention of coming out again. We spoke to you. Once you agreed to face these problems directly—writing, Myrna, your sense of failure—we made arrangements to bring them all together for you in one place. Freedom Beach."

Rose was still beside him, looking around for help. He did not want to worry her. He was not going to follow Myrna any more. He felt worn out but calm, like a man who had run a very long race he had not expected to finish. He felt mystified, wondering. "You took my memories, changed me with your dreams."

"Yes. They were educational, were they not? We strive for verisimilitude in all our work."

"Lie him down," said Rose. The others on the platform touched him gently, made him lie down.

"I can make things different," Shaun said, looking up at the sphinx.

He thought he saw the head nod slightly. Perhaps it was only the shadow of a cloud moving across the bright moon. "That is up to you."

"I don't understand."

"You escaped from Freedom Beach. You published a poem. You've involved yourself in the world again. You've taken what we gave and made what you would of it. And now you've accepted her death. The testing is over. From now on you're going to have to live life on your own, with whatever help you can find. You're not alone. There are many like you, many dreamers."

"Who are you? Where did you come from?"

"You dislike our new world, Shaun? Good." The voice of the sphinx had faded to a whisper. "Help us change it."

"Change," Shaun said. Rose cradled his head on her arms. "It's okay, Shaun," she said.

He could feel things passing him by: a breeze whispering across his face, the rustle of the dying leaves in the trees, a horn honking in the distance and the rumble of traffic accelerating away from lights on Fifth Avenue. Then he felt a tear fall on him. Rose was crying.

"Someone call an ambulance," a man's voice said. "This guy is sick."

"No," said Shaun. He struggled up. Reluctantly, Rose let him. "No, I'm fine now."

Rose refused to let go of him as he stood. He shook himself and stared at her shadowed face in the darkness. Across the park the lights of the city were waiting.

Shaun K. Reed

Oct. 22. Rain. Finished vol. 2 of *The Dreamers' Anthology of English Literature*, Abridged and Revised (I'll say!). Nothing on my desk for tomorrow. B. says not to work so fast.

Office feels like a hospital waiting room. Tense. Will the patient survive? Nothing from the dreamers in almost two weeks. Front office says stop buying poetry books—market glutted. Rumors of layoffs.

Oct. 23. Still raining. Bought new umbrella. Vappi's birthday today, gooey cake at coffee break. Spent morning straightening files: nothing to do. B. wants me to catalog company library until something breaks. Probably me. Dinner with Rose. She has a new patient!

Oct. 24. Dreamed about Myrna last night. A good dream: together on honeymoon in Bahamas. Found another hole in

FREEDOM BEACH

my memory. Myrna loved to swim. I remember a trophy: 100 meter freestyle champion of Nassau county. '68 or '69, I think.

Been thinking about sphinx: can't figure it. That's a joke, son. Rose says it was an auditory hallucination. Yeah, sure.

Questions: If the dreamers really want me to join, where's my secret decoder ring? What's the password? Who will make the rest of my trio? Akira and Jihan? Joyce Carol Oates and Larry Bird?

Do I want to join?

Questions: 6. Answers: 0. Same old story.

Oct. 25. Found old story ms. in pages of art book. "'Awful,' he ejaculated forcefully, eyes dropping to the floor in hot shame." That kind of stuff. Still, an idea there. Sat down & tried restart of new story. Wrote four pages in an hour—a record. What am I doing to myself?

Oct. 26. Sunday. Took most of the day to do the *Times*, must have weighed at least ten pounds. Lots of want ads. Business section in ecstasy. U.S. leading indicators up. Predicts most Third World countries will achieve balance of trade in fourth quarter. Crossword was a killer.

Met Rose at her apt. for dinner, then play: Marlowe's *Faust* off-off-Broadway; they updated it, set in 40s, Faust as atomic scientist. Ho-hum. Faust didn't look like Groucho, but a few laughs when Mephisto says "This is hell, nor am I out of it," while wearing a zoot suit. Wanted to stay with Rose afterward—think she wanted me to—but decided no. Still, only a matter of time.

Oct. 27. Headline in Times: STUDENT PRANKSTERS X-RAY DREAMERS AT M.I.T.—Results Indicate Dreamers Are Human. Apparently a bunch of electronics jocks jury-rigged an airport fluoroscopic X-ray machine in a hall of the administration building and caught a trio of dreamers on a goodwill tour of American colleges. Hallelujah, them dreamers gots bones! But the real question is, why do they always travel in threes?

Another two pages on my story.

Oct. 29. Headline: DREAMERS SUE STUDENTS, M.I.T. Fourteen million dollars worth. I don't get it. If they're mad, why don't they just change M.I.T. into a miniature golf course?
Sent $50 to students' defense fund.

Oct. 31. Akira called. We met for Halloween drinks. A man in bar dressed like Sam Spade, drunk, pulls out squirt gun & shouts, "Some of you bastards are dreamers—come clean! Stick 'em up!" Everyone in bar raises hands. Me & Akira, too.

Nov. 3. B. says the *Dreamers' Anthology of English Lit.* is dead. Orders from front office, but who's behind it? Scuttlebutt says Geneva. B. says poor sales. Vappi says nobody.
Assigned to edit new AmHist high school text. They come up with a different slant every ten years. Flashed on Winston Smith rewriting history—throws the past down the memory hole.
Dead end on the story—what the hell happens next?

Nov. 4. Election day. Got up early to vote. Hard to get excited but would feel funny if I didn't.

Nov. 5. *Times* p. 1: Dems in big upset. Reagan vows to stay the course. p. 10. Baravelli in small upset.

Nov. 6. Went to park today to see sphinx. Blustery, cold, bitch of a day. Park deserted except for crazy joggers. Felt like a fool, waiting for it to talk. Froze my ass off, thought about how hot it was at F.B. and L.A., how cold in Wittenberg, Yorkshire. No comment from God's front men.
The whole thing seems to be receding. Freedom Beach, Myrna, the dreams. Like trying to remember what you got for Christmas two years ago. Down the memory hole. Is this good or bad? All I know is that it doesn't hurt as much.
Much later. Tossing and turning in bed—but great idea for the story. *Switch point of view from third to first person!!* That

way increases irony over what J. doesn't know about himself. Maybe now I can sleep . . . clock says 2:17 A.M.

Nov. 7. Called Rose, last-minute date: went to Knicks-Celts game. Celts won going away. Dreamers should look into Knicks management

Nov. 9. Stayed up to 1:30 last night with the story. Worth it. Beginning to worry: Is writing what the dreamers want or what I want?

Nov. 10. Vappi quits. Says he's going to teach h.s.! Always wanted to, he says.
On p. 23. Feels good.

Nov. 11. Rose says she can't be my therapist anymore. Too involved: unethical. Then we made love. Afterward I realized that if we stay together, she'll be analyzing me for the rest of my life. Endless therapy, just what I need! We talked for a long time. Asked her, if Myrna was dead, who wrote her poem? "You did," she said.

Nov. 12. Dreamers revise Knicks management, trade for power forward. Score tonight: Knicks 111, L.A. 96.

Nov. 14. Last night, Akira & Jihan, Rose & me went to dinner after work. Akira was in fine form, asking what she sees in me. Rose said: "constancy." Later, back at her apt., I told her I didn't think I was so constant. She said I was.
The sphinx said I could change things if I didn't like them. Maybe I should start small.
Finished first draft of the story. God help me.

THE PASTEL CITY
M. John Harrison

In his melancholy sea-tower, moody reclusive tegeus-Cromis, hero of the Methven, puts away his nameless sword, thinking he had finished with soldiering forever. Then, on the road from Viriconium, came the massive mercenary, Birkin Grif, roaring out a filthy brothel song, bringing news of the war between two queens. In the Great Brown Waste lives Tomb the Dwarf, as nasty a midget as ever hacked the hands off a priest. They must join forces to fight for Queen Jane and Viriconium, for Canna Moidart and the Wolves of the North have awoken the *geteit chemosit*, alien automata from an ancient science, which will destroy everything in their path, and now they march upon the Pastel City ...

'Harrison is the best writer of heroic fantasy working today.' *Daily Express*

'If you like elegantly crafted, elegantly written sword-and-sorcery, this book is all you could ask for.'
Michael Bishop — Fantasy & Science Fiction Review

A STORM OF WINGS
M. John Harrison

Eighty years have passed since Lord tegeus-Cromis broke the yoke of Canna Moidart, since the horror of the *geteit chemosit*. The Reborn Men, awoken from their long sleep, have inherited the Evening Cultures. In the wastelands, to the north and west of Viriconium, a city is being built — but not by men.

In the Time of the Locust a paralysing menace threatens to turn the inhabitants of the Pastel City into hideous, mindless insects ...

'the best writer of heroic fantasy working today ... Through the spoiled wastelands of our ancient planet travel a resurrected man, an assassin, a magician, a madwoman, a dwarf ... A superior read.' *Daily Express*

'Harrison has made a wondrous thing of this tale of the Evening of the Earth.'
Isaac Asimov's Science Fiction magazine

Also available from Unwin Paperbacks

The Armies of Daylight (The Darwath Trilogy: 3) *Barbara Hambly*	£2.95 ☐
The Darkest Road (The Fionavar Tapestry: 3) *Guy Kay*	£2.95 ☐
The Deep *John Crowley*	£2.95 ☐
Dragonsbane *Barbara Hambly*	£2.95 ☐
The Initiate (The Time Master Trilogy: 1) *Louise Cooper*	£2.95 ☐
In Viriconium *M John Harrison*	£2.95 ☐
The Ladies of Mandrigyn *Barbara Hambly*	£2.95 ☐
The Master (The Time Master Trilogy: 3) *Louise Cooper*	£2.95 ☐
Mirage *Louise Cooper*	£2.95 ☐
The Outcast (The Time Master Trilogy: 2) *Louise Cooper*	£2.95 ☐
The Pastel City *M John Harrison*	£2.50 ☐
The Silent Tower *Barbara Hambly*	£2.95 ☐
A Storm of Wings *M John Harrison*	£2.95 ☐
The Summer Tree (The Fionavar Tapestry: 1) *Guy Kay*	£2.95 ☐
The Time of the Dark (The Darwath Trilogy: 1) *Barbara Hambly*	£2.95 ☐
Viriconium Nights *M John Harrison*	£2.95 ☐
Walls of Air (The Darwath Trilogy: 2) *Barbara Hambly*	£2.95 ☐
The Wandering Fire (The Fionavar Tapestry: 2) *Guy Kay*	£2.95 ☐
The Witches of Wenshar *Barbara Hambly*	£2.95 ☐

All these books are available at your local bookshop or newsagent, or can be ordered direct by post. Just tick the titles you want and fill in the form below.

Name ....

Address ....

....

....

Write to Unwin Cash Sales, PO Box 11, Falmouth, Cornwall TR10 9EN.

Please enclose remittance to the value of the cover price plus:

UK: 60p for the first book plus 25p for the second book, thereafter 15p for each additional book ordered to a maximum charge of £1.90.

BFPO and EIRE: 60p for the first book plus 25p for the second book and 15p for the next 7 books and thereafter 9p per book.

OVERSEAS INCLUDING EIRE: £1.25 for the first book plus 75p for the second book and 28p for each additional book.

Unwin Paperbacks reserve the right to show new retail prices on covers, which may differ from those previously advertised in the text or elsewhere. Postage rates are also subject to revision.

interzone

SCIENCE FICTION AND FANTASY

Quarterly £1.95

- *Interzone* is the only British magazine specializing in SF and new fantastic writing. We have published:

BRIAN ALDISS	GARRY KILWORTH
J.G. BALLARD	DAVID LANGFORD
BARRINGTON BAYLEY	MICHAEL MOORCOCK
GREGORY BENFORD	RACHEL POLLACK
MICHAEL BISHOP	KEITH ROBERTS
RAMSEY CAMPBELL	GEOFF RYMAN
ANGELA CARTER	JOSEPHINE SAXTON
RICHARD COWPER	JOHN SHIRLEY
JOHN CROWLEY	JOHN SLADEK
PHILIP K. DICK	BRIAN STABLEFORD
THOMAS M. DISCH	BRUCE STERLING
MARY GENTLE	IAN WATSON
WILLIAM GIBSON	CHERRY WILDER
M. JOHN HARRISON	GENE WOLFE

- *Interzone* has also published many excellent new writers; graphics by **JIM BURNS, ROGER DEAN, IAN MILLER** and others; book reviews, news, etc.

- *Interzone* is available from specialist SF shops, or by subscription. For four issues, send £7.50 (outside UK, £8.50) to : **124 Osborne Road, Brighton BN1 6LU, UK**. Single copies: £1.95 inc p&p.

- American subscribers may send $13 ($16 if you want delivery by air mail) to our British address, above. All cheques should be made payable to *Interzone*.

- "No other magazine in Britain is publishing science fiction at all, let alone fiction of this quality." *Times Literary Supplement*

To: **interzone** 124 Osborne Road, Brighton, BN1 6LU, UK.

Please send me four issues of *Interzone,* beginning with the current issue. I enclose a cheque/p.o. for £7.50 (outside UK, £8.50; US subscribers, $13 or $16 air), made payable to *Interzone*.

Name _____

Address _____

_____